The Last Good Day

Robert Kugler

DEDICATION

This book is dedicated to my wife, in appreciation of her constant support and love. Also, I dedicate this to my children, in hopes they will always remember that anything is possible.

This is also offered in memory of my parents, who loved the shore.

OUR STORY IN THREE DAYS

ACKNOWLEDGMENTS

Thank you to my amazing Beta Readers. It's a job whose only perk is getting to read the unpolished versions. They've been positive, helpful, critical, and the book would simply not exist without them. Well, it might, but it would really stink. So, to Amy Groetsch, Steve Young, Jen Ehmann, Ginny Kochis (NotSoFormulaic.com), Alison Johansen (MotherNova.com), and Judy Baltas, I say thanks.
Drinks are on me.

I want to thank my children. Their belief and encouragement kept me going when I felt like every word was utter garbage. They gave me the confidence to silence my inner critic. I like thinking that I've modeled something positive for them, but in truth, their honest and thoughtful support has been a model for me more than they probably know.

Both of my parents are gone now, but I think they would have liked this story in particular. Wildwood is where they met and it's been a vital part of my family's life ever since. It is not merely as a setting in this story, but a supporting character. My parents would have liked that.

Without the support of my wife, Heidi, none of this would exist. For over twenty years she's been my biggest supporter and loved me unconditionally, which could not have been easy. She's supported every dream and always brought me back from the brink of my often crippling self-doubt. She never gave up on me and never let me give up on this story.

So, as Gram would have said, I'll "just say thank you."

All the people mentioned above have made this a better book which I hope you enjoy. They also made me a better person, and, as someone once said: "that's not nothing…"

Robert Kugler

And you know what? It really isn't.

The Day Itself

CHAPTER ONE

Angie has been my best friend since the first day of ninth grade. We met in third period Phys Ed. I'd been nervous all day since I was coming over from private school and I really didn't know anybody. She sat right down next to me in the bleachers and started talking like we were old pals. I found her forwardness and quirkiness immediately appealing. That, and her plan to keep us from having to start the year in health class. I hadn't been paying attention, but since our last names both started with "Y," and the PE department inexplicably starting signups with the "A's," we were almost out of choices.

"Come with me if you want to avoid health class…" she'd intoned in her best Terminator voice, which it turned out was not very good at all. I followed her, though, and we were soon enthusiastically signing up for badminton. We made a good team then and have been pretty much inseparable ever since.

Then we graduated and I barely saw her all summer. I

knew she was traveling and stuff, and I was supposed to spend a good chunk of the summer staying with Nana and playing whatever shows my guitar and I could book in Philly. Plus, I had that scholarship audition in New York to prepare for, but I had no idea how we got to the end of August and found ourselves planning our last day together before I left for Boston and she went across town to Princeton, having barely seen each other since the week after graduation.

We'd talked pretty much every day. But I'd be lying if I said I hadn't really missed her. What bugged me the most is once I kinda looked at the calendar of the summer, I still didn't totally understand where she'd been and what she'd been doing for parts of it. It was a mystery I hoped to solve during our last day together before we had to be apart. I mean, I had really hoped we'd goof around all summer like we had in the past, especially since college was looming. But she'd been really hard to pin down, except for that last day.

So, let's talk about that.

We drove mom's car down to Wildwood. I'm still surprised her silly little Mercury Tracer made it there and back. I picked Angie up at six in the morning. She was sitting on the porch when I pulled up. We hugged and she climbed in and promptly dozed off before I got on 539 South towards the Parkway. I almost got caught in that dumb speed trap in Allentown by the bridge, but I remembered to slow down in time. I was amazed they had a guy out there so early, but I think that speed trap might be the town's only revenue stream. Pretty sure the officer was asleep, but whatever. He certainly couldn't have been snoring like Angie, though. I'm used to it by now, and she looked really cute and peaceful with her feet curled up on the seat and her hood over her head.

Like I said, this was the first time I'd seen her in weeks and now that we were together I realized how much I'd missed her. The drive was quiet until she woke up, suddenly full of energy and pulled out her phone and cued up the "Soundtrack for Wildwood" playlist as she called it.

"This playlist has been meticulously researched and prepared for our journey," she commented all perky and stuff, making jazz hands or spirit fingers at me as she hit play. I always get those two confused. Mom's stereo only had a cassette deck adapter so I plugged that in and we were on our way.

I rolled my eyes a bit when The Indigo Girls "Closer to Fine" came on first, but I know it's one of her favorites. Her mom was a huge fan of them and Cowboy Junkies and 10,000 Maniacs and that sorta stuff, and it stuck with her. Angie sang along too loudly as she always does. She still makes me play it for her sometimes, but I don't really mind. I pretend I mind, but I really don't.

So, we drove south, and we listened to music and we talked and she wanted to hear about my classes that started next week and all that stuff even though I'd told her it all over the phone. I remember looking over to her as I was telling her about my music theory class and noticing that the sun kind of set off the slight reddish highlights in her hair. She'd added those for Prom, and while they'd faded, the rising sun accentuated them in a way that made her look pretty.

After we'd driven a while longer I asked her why she wanted to go all the way down South to Wildwood when we could have gone somewhere closer like Seaside or

Manasquan or Spring Lake.

"Dear Avery, you know Seaside is an armpit."

"Yeah, there's that, but the other two…"

"Manasquan and Spring Lake are fine. But they are not Wildwood. Wildwood is, in fact, the only shore for a day such as this…"

I expected as much, but I really had no idea what our plan was besides going there. I'd been a few times with Angie and her family before and it was definitely her people's beach. Her Aunt Jenny and Uncle Bob lived there and they always let them stay in one of their houses. The beach itself was huge and nice I guess, but Mom and I were never much for the shore. My vacations growing up were mostly going to Nana's. I remember one week in the summer when I was maybe eleven and we drove out to Long Island, NY in mom's old Sentra. I was certain that rust bucket was about to explode. We went to visit Uncle Ted and whoever he was shacking up with/scamming then. Pretty sure it was the Yoga lady who lived over the Walgreens. I remember she smelled like Vicks Vapo-Rub, and the beach we went to was all loaded with rocks and cigarettes. Pretty sure I saw a few hypodermics before Mom had seen enough and took us to dinner at "The Ground Round" since they had free popcorn. Outside of that epic journey, we mostly kept to Nana's.

"So, what exactly are we doing once we get there, Ange?" I asked, since I didn't know.

She laughed. "You'll see, sweetie. Though, it may in the end be simpler to discuss what we aren't going to do…"

"So, you're quoting Ferris Bueller to me now?"

She smiled, "About time you actually got a movie

reference…"

It was a fair point. They aren't my specialty. So, I asked, "Ok, so what aren't we going to do today?"

She made of show of thinking intently, squinting her eyes and furrowing her brow before waving her finger at me. "Let's not rule anything out just yet. We're going to have a really, really, good day. I promise." The last time Angie said, "we're going to have a really, really, good day" to me, was Prom. She was right then, as she usually is. I didn't have any clue what her plan was, on either day now that I think of it, but I simply believed her. It felt really good to be with her again, so I let it go at that. I think beyond just missing my best friend over the summer, I'd been a lot more on my own than I was used to. I'd hung out with Will and Brian once or twice, and a lot of my free time was either trying to get booked to play shows or working on stuff to get ready to play shows. Now that we were together, I was pretty much up for anything. At least I felt like I was.

CHAPTER TWO

The miles to Wildwood seemed to move quicker after we turned South onto the Garden State Parkway. I don't know my way around Wildwood, so she had to guide me from exit 4a to Rio Grande Avenue and around a few other places I don't remember until she had me pull into the parking lot outside the convention center right on the boardwalk. It was early so we didn't have to look for a spot. As we stepped out of Mom's antiquated Tracer, Angie took a deep breath and exhaled, and gave me an impish look. Man, had I missed my friend!

"Ahh…it's magic time my friend." Angie walked up the steps onto the boardwalk and turned right past the huge stone beach balls and the iconic Wildwood sign and made a beeline for the water.

"Come on!"

It was windy and I felt cold and damp walking up the ramp towards the giant sign. When she took off I started to chase her and almost got hit by a couple on an old tandem bike. They swore at me, in tandem, but I staggered to the rail of the boardwalk and saw Angie smiling and waiting for me at the bottom of the steps down to the sand.

"Come on, sweetie, there are scallop shells to find…" She held out her hand to me, and I took it. We walked down towards the water together. I had expected her to be halfway to the shoreline already but she waited for me.

"Out of breath already there, girly?" I called as I caught up. That earned me the first of the day's punches in the arm. "Ow! What was that for?"

"I'll show you out of breath," she said as she took off, leaving me fumbling with my sandals. By the time I caught up to her she was already ankle deep in the rising tide of the morning. I remembered how she gets around the ocean, so I knew better than to interrupt her moment. I caught my breath and then walked over to her. She leaned her head on my shoulder. I think I heard her sigh a little, but I didn't say anything. Her hair felt warm on my shoulder as it was kinda cool down by the water and I felt that warmth even through my sweatshirt. We stood there a while before she patted my arm and moved off down the shore, towards the big pier with the giant Ferris Wheel that's on all the postcards. It looked sad without its lights on or anyone around it.

"You did good there," she chuckled.

"What do you mean?" I asked, catching up with her.

"Just being quiet with me for a few minutes. I know how hard that is for you."

She was not wrong. She wasn't being obnoxious either. I have a tough time with silence and usually babble on just to fill any awkward silences. Angie thinks it's because I grew up an only child in the house with Mom, who was dealing with her own stuff for a long time. There was no one to talk to. Well, at least until Angie came along, and she hasn't let me get in a word since. I

7

learned a while back how to tell when she needs me to be still. Haven't figured that out about anyone else, but I suppose I'll get there.

Melissa Carpenter once told one of her cadre that she first started making out with me because I wouldn't stop talking and kiss her. I didn't complain at the time, but I guess I've got some work to do understanding girls. Guys tend to be easier, though I don't really think I'm likely to stay tight with Brian and Pat, or even Will, who I've gone to school with since first grade. Brian is off to Stanford to play golf and Pat joined the Navy. Will and I haven't talked in months since our attempt at a summertime band blew up in our faces at Robyn Kurtz's eighteenth birthday party. She wanted live music and Will wanted to get with her so bad he agreed we'd play her party in eight days. The fact that we didn't have a band or hadn't rehearsed did not deter him. It was an epic failure on every level.

I really don't know that I'll stay in close touch with any of my friends from high school at this point. If I don't get a scholarship for next year or start making a living playing gigs, I may be right back home looking for a job. Maybe I should make an effort with the guys after all. I don't know, outside of Angie, there's really no one from home I'm likely to miss all that much. Especially now. It's not like I didn't like the people I hung out with at school. I still can't even think about Seaside Heights without laughing out loud about some of the crazy nights I had with Will and Brian. The night that Will tried to pick up that Emo girl with the nose ring by spending $42 winning a Pikachu doll still makes me laugh. He was around for some of the darker times, too, but he never really asked a whole lot about any of it, even though it must have been pretty obvious I was dealing with a lot at home. And the three of us survived Boychoir school together and that's something. There's times I feel like they don't know really anything about me. I guess that's partly my fault as I've never really opened up about things with them. Angie's always been there, which has made the time we've been apart this summer harder.

"Don't get used to it, Angie. I plan to blather on the remainder of the day," I said when I felt I'd given her a decent amount of reflective silence. She was quiet a moment longer and I started to feel a little awkward before she spoke again. "I think that would be ok if you do," she said as she stepped away into the water a bit, picking up a shell. She rinsed it off and looked back to me, smiling.

"It's almost unblemished," she called back to me, holding up a scallop shell with a small chip broken off the left side.

"It's nice," I said, never really understanding her affinity for shells, scallop shells in particular. She scoffed at my lack of enthusiasm.

"It is way more than nice…you've got to consider the millions of years of development it took Mr. Scallop here to come up with this design--perfect only for this particular creature. You can count the ridges to see how many years it took to bring about this one shell. Then, there's whatever this one little guy went through to lose his shell--his life ended somehow, who knows when? And, then," her eyes flashed excitedly, "then, its wandering path led it to wash up at my feet in this exact moment, here with you." Her eyes fairly gleamed with the depth of it all and the wind blew her hair away from her face. "I want you to have this one" she said as she walked towards me. She took my hand and placed the shell inside, then closing my fingers around it. "Maybe if you're nice, Aunt Jenny will make it into a necklace for you."

I groaned. "Oh, come on Ange: you know I don't do jewelry"

"I know you say that now, but you're going to have to try new things. You might love it." She was teasing me, but then she seemed inspired. "It could be your fresh look for Fall. The other artsy kids in Boston will love it…it's a nautical town I hear, right?"

I tucked it into my pocket and must have groaned again or something, I don't recall, but next thing I knew she was bopping me in the arm again and pushing me back towards the boardwalk and the convention center causeway.

"Come along grumpypants. We don't have to talk about the exciting adventure in higher musical education that awaits you. Instead we will discuss what you are buying me for breakfast."

I know I groaned this time, "Why do I have to buy you breakfast?"

She batted her eyelids sweetly, "Because you're a nice boy, don't you remember?"

"You keep telling me that, but I could be a jerk and I think I'd still be buying breakfast."

She nodded. "Well, let's not find out." She punched my arm yet again, though not too bad that time, or maybe it had gone numb by this point.

There were people on bikes all over the place. The boardwalk itself is about two miles long and even though I'd come with Angie a few times over the years, I never really felt like I had my bearings or knew my way around. That and it seemed like every other year some old-school restaurant or arcade turned into a stupid Dunkin Donuts or a Chipotle or something. Always seemed sad when that happened.

"So, what is this nice boy buying you for breakfast?"

"Oh sweetie, we are at the Jersey Shore, what do you think we are having?"

"Please don't say Scrapple."

"Oh no, no, just eww. Only your Nana still eats that slop, God love her. We, my fine feathered friend, we will be dining on Pork Roll and Egg sandwiches from the Wawa."

We continued North, passing the piers, the carneys, the water parks, mini golf and casinos and arcades, and five versions of "Mister B's Pizza Palace" that I thought was good last time we'd been there. I was impressed at the gumption of the carneys, some of them already out trying to get people to try to pop the balloons and win a Sixers Jersey from a guy who left the team five seasons ago or a stuffed Minion. We stopped for a second to look out at the big playing surface where they hold the National Marble Tournament every summer. I laughed at it every time as it always seemed such a dumb game but Angie loved it since she was a kid and her older cousin placed fifth in the tournament. We moved on, passing a haggard-looking fortune teller who was sitting outside her shop, already looking as though the day had gotten the better of her.

"Must have been a late night for Madame Marie," Angie remarked after we'd passed her.

"I can't believe that people actually give her money," I laughed.

"Oh, hush now, she's like a part of the furniture down here. People love her and she seems like a nice lady."

I scoffed at that. "Yeah, we should probably turn around and go have our palms read, huh?" I cracked myself up until I noticed that I was walking along the boardwalk completely by myself. I turned around to find Angie staring at me with a mischievous grin.

"I'm game if you are, rock star."

I knew I was in trouble then. She had that look on her face where it was immediately clear I'd fallen right into her trap. I made a mental note to remind myself to shut up for the rest of the day, but I think we can guess how that went. I sighed and walked back towards her as she clapped triumphantly.

"You're paying though, princess."

"Wouldn't have it any other way, sweetie," she replied, taking my arm like in one of those old black and white movies.

"Have you ever done this before?"

"Once, a long time ago."

"What did she say?"

"Oh, I can't tell you that…"

"Why not? It's not like this stuff is real."

She put her finger to her lips and shushed me. "No spoilers." She cracked herself up. She can be very silly, especially when she's getting her way.

I'd never met anyone who could manage to smell like mothballs in a full ocean breeze, but there she was in living color, more or less.

"Good morning, Madame Marie!" Angie began, louder than I thought was necessary, but when she promptly bolted up from what appeared to be a deep open-mouthed and open-eyed sleep, I figured she knew what she was doing.

"Ah, yes," she coughed somewhat phlegmily. "Yes, ah, good morning dears, Madam Marie was expecting you of course, I, ah, was just now meditating on the mysteries of future…"

I was about to say something snarfy but Angie shot

me a look that suggested I choose not to, which I did.

"We would be ever so grateful if you would give us a reading today, Madame."

"Yes, yes, Madame Marie knows you have many questions, many worries and uncertainties…many questions, indeed. Follow me young ones."

As she turned and moved through the curtain that led into her small room, I'm certain I saw sand and dust fly all over. Under my breath, in my best Yoda voice, I said, "Away with your weapon, I mean you no harm…" which made Angie giggle for a second before punching me in the arm, again.

"Knock it off," she said, "this is serious business."

Keeping my Yoda voice as low as possible, I continued, "yes, yes, for the Jedi it is serious too." I cracked myself up, but Angie was not having it. We followed Madame Marie though the curtain to a small waiting area with chairs and an old Cloth-tassel lamp. Madame Marie turned around suddenly in front of another thick curtain, smiling with her palm outstretched.

"Who will be financing our journeys, then? All fees are due prior to our psychic excursion."

"I will, Madam," Angie called, moving past me. I remember I got a face full of her hair as she kinda pushed past me in the cramped space.

Madam Marie counted out Angie's cash, twenty dollars for the two readings, paid in five-dollar bills. She looked us both over through dark and narrowed eyes for a way-too-long-and-uncomfortable silent moment. I was about to say that maybe we should just go when she pointed at Angie saying, "You wait here. I read him first." She flung open the curtain dramatically, revealing what looked like a card table covered with a dusty tablecloth that reminded me of Nana's friend Bea, who always smelled of patchouli. Before I could say anything, I was pushed into a velvety chair and Madam Marie made a big show of closing the curtain, humming to herself as she slid the cash into a small box that she then tucked under her chair. When she finally stopped puttering, I got a look at her face up close and was surprised; she was old, at least sixty something, but her eyes were a striking blue, and if not for the wrinkles and weird costume and weirder actions, she'd probably be kinda pretty for an older lady. That said, I was kinda creeped out but figured I should just be polite to her like I would be to one of Nana's friends.

"Um, so, I'm not really sure how this works, but…"

She raised her palms toward me and shushed me quickly. "Of course, you are not. If you had the gift of sight, I would have seen it in you from the start."

"Um, OK. So, what do I do then?"

She finally sat down in an ornate chair full of pillows, and on settling herself into just the right position, she replied, "You sit quietly and give me your hands, child…" and she placed her hands flat on the table.

So, even though I felt pretty silly, I did so, thinking of Angie waiting in the next room as Madam Marie grabbed my hands and squeezed them a little too hard until she had my full attention. Her hands were strong and surprisingly smooth. "Ok, let us see what we can see here," and she seemed to be sizing up my palms and fingers the way Nana picks fruit, paying special attention to my left hand. She ran her fingers over my guitar callouses, raising an eyebrow at them before nodding, softly muttering something to herself. My right hand doesn't have as many callouses because I use my left for fingering and use a pick a lot unless I'm playing acoustic. Both hands are pretty strong because I put a lot of time in on the guitar. Melissa used to complain that I should moisturize more but I found it used to make my fingers too soft and didn't like how it affected my playing, so she had to deal with it.

"Hmmm...two strong hands, but different strong. And you are clearly a water hand."

"Yeah, I don't know what that means."

She sighed at my interruption, "It means I'll tell you when I'm done, dearie..." with clear irritation in her tone, so I figured this was a good time to hush again, so I did. After another minute of feeling my hands, she took my wrists and turned them up to examine my wrists and the heel of my palm. Her thumb passed over the lump on my right pinkie where I broke it two summers ago at Saint Ambrose Catholic Church. I must have flinched or something because she commented, "It still hurts sometimes, yes?"

It did, but I wasn't sure how to answer her. "Yeah, I guess."

"It will for a while more. Then, it will stop."

I looked up and noticed she was studying my face. There was a brief moment of sympathy in her eyes and suddenly she looked a lot younger than she had earlier. I thought for a moment she might even be around my Mom's age, but she had that same hardened, "don't mess with me kid, I've seen it all" look that Mom always wears. She held my gaze again, another uncomfortably long moment before returning to examine my right hand again.

"You are right handed, but your left shows you are working hard for something in the future. Your dominant hand shows past and present. Your other hand shows the impending." She began to trace the lines on my palm, which I'd never really paid much attention to. I don't really understand which ones she was looking at, but she said something about a heart-line and a hand-line before humming and kinda tracing the different lines until she said "Interesting…"

"What?" I asked. I'd started zoning out to be honest. It was way too warm and dark back there, and I felt sort of sluggish. She grinned at me, tapping one particularly long line on the top my hand.

"You have been rather superfluous with your affections."

"Huh?"

"Not overly bright though it seems…"

"Well, I understood that." I replied, and I could actually feel the color rising in my face.

She sighed somewhat kindly, "It means you have given your heart away rather often and perhaps occasionally without proper care for it." She traced the line again, where there were many little branches pulling away from it. "But, that could be in the past…perhaps…" and she tapped the line again as though pressing a single key on a piano.

"Perhaps what?" I replied, suddenly interested.

"You'll see, perhaps. You must learn to keep your eyes open and see the things and people in front of you, not so much those behind or ahead. Maybe try to see things from the eyes of another now and then."

I was starting to get frustrated, but then reminded myself that I don't really believe any of this stuff, so I just sat back and let her finish. She moved to another line down the middle of my palm, making a lot of "Hmm, I see" sounds and said something about it all "coming together, perhaps." The "perhaps" were starting to irritate me. Finally, she held my hands together and squeezed them before letting go and leaning back into her chair. She folded her hands in front of her and looked at me and sighed.

"If you can only get out of your own way, there is a clear path to happiness, my dear."

"Yeah, I don't know what that means." I said, since you know, I didn't.

"That is evident. You will. Or you won't. Keep your eyes in front of you."

"What's a water hand?"

"Among other things, it means you are artistic, emotional, idealistic, and occasionally without direction."

"Oh," I said, not really sure where to file all that since it was mostly accurate, so I asked "So, will I have a long life or something?"

She stood up and patted my head as she slid open the curtain to usher me out. "Long or short, is not mine to say…or yours for that matter. Only quality, but that part is up to you. Remember what I told you…"

Not knowing how else to end all this, I simply said, "Yes Ma'am," and stepped into the next room. Angie looked both amused and excited as we switched places. She smiled at me as we passed one another, but she didn't say anything. I settled in on a dusty and overly soft couch that felt like sitting on a stale marshmallow only less comfortable. It was clearly designed for a shorter person and I felt like a giant on it. I studied my hands for a minute and wondered if there was anything to what Madam Marie had said, but I kinda blew it off. It was still really warm and the light was dim, so I closed my eyes for a second and must have dozed off because the next thing I remember was seeing Angie throw the curtain aside and storming out of the room and saying something I didn't understand, clearly upset. As I followed her out I turned back and saw Madam Marie with an amused grin and sort of a mischievous look in her eyes.

She nodded to me, saying, "You don't want to let her get away now, dear." I must have looked lost because she then pointed in the direction in which Angie had stormed off. I took off after her, confused to say the least and now suddenly very worried about my friend.

The sunlight blasted me in the face on leaving her store, and it took me a minute to figure out where Angie had gone. She was sitting on the bench just across the boardwalk with her back to me looking out at the shore. She was smoothing out her skirt on her lap and catching her breath so I could tell she was still upset. I walked up behind her and put my hands on her shoulders.

"That bad, huh?"

That was apparently the wrong thing for me to say to her. She stood up quickly and turned to face me, the bench still between us. She exhaled heavily and had her fierce eyes trained on me at first. I must have made a face or something because her shoulders kind of fell and she shook her head and started off back down the boardwalk.

"Come on," she said. I jogged after her and caught up.

"What happened back there, Angie?"

"I'd prefer not to discuss it."

"But you're still upset, Ange. Let's talk about it. What did she do that got you so angry?"

She stopped walking but didn't say anything. "Maybe I can help?" I asked. She could be so closed off sometimes, but I hadn't seen her like this ever before. I didn't know what to do. I was normally the one who needed calming down. She looked at me and seemed to be thinking until she put her arm around me and started walking again.

"She said something I didn't want to hear today, and I decided I didn't want to hear anymore. Because I get to do that."

"Angie, in four years I've never seen you react like that

to something...I mean I've never seen you, um..."

"Flip out?"

"Well, that's not what I was gonna say, but, OK, yeah."

"Well, my friend, that doesn't mean I haven't flipped out in the last four years." She hadn't broken her stride or slowed down but her voice seemed calmer as she continued, "You may now buy me breakfast."

I wonder now if I should've pushed her on that but in the moment, I decided to shut up and not say the wrong thing again.

CHAPTER THREE

We made it to Wawa and got sandwiches and ate them sitting on the bench at the very northern end of the famous Wildwood boardwalk. The sandwiches were awesome with fried egg, pork roll and cheese on South Philly style rolls. They tasted like the amazing Amoroso rolls that Pat's King of Steaks in Philly uses. I almost went back for another one but wanted to keep an eye on my cash. All I had on hand was what was left from my birthday money and the meager remains from a couple of spots I played at the Grape Street in Manayunk. I'd been one of the openers for the June Rich reunion show, one of the local Philly bands that inspired me to pick up a guitar years ago. Tommy, the Grape Street manager usually pays openers in beer, but since I'm underage he threw me $100 for the two spots. I laughed when he said he was coming out ahead on the deal. "The last opener drank $200 worth of Yuengling and broke the toilet." The shows were really fun and the band was great. I've known Gary, the bass player, for a while. He runs the board for the open mic nights where I first played live and solo for like the first time ever, after sitting in the back for weeks on end. After the show, he gave me a few t-shirts and a CD and a whole box of picks and strings their old guitarist had left lying around after he left the band, which were way better than anything I could afford. He said I could open for them if they made it to Boston, but he wasn't optimistic. Said those shows might be a one-time thing. "Everyone got along today," he said, "But…" and he left it at that. It's sad, but bands are hard, I guess.

So, I passed on a second sandwich. I knew we were having lunch with her aunt and uncle and they would have way too much food as always.

Angie was pretty quiet as we ate. I tried asking her again about Madam Marie, but she wasn't having it at all.

"Remember how you haven't really wanted to talk about school and your classes and your audition and leaving Jersey every time we've talked this summer?"

"Yeah," I said between bites.

"That's how I feel about the palm reading right now."

"Fair enough."

She looked out at the ocean for a moment before she spoke again. "You never really told me about the audition. What was it like?"

The scholarship was a bit of a scary point for me. My mom already told me that there's no money left for college beyond this year. She's worked hard for years to give me one year of tuition, but after that I'm on my own.

"It was long and boring and really hot in the building. The interview was OK. They had some old composer who won a Pulitzer or something on the committee who was kinda old-school cool, but otherwise it was kinda dull. They liked what I submitted and are asking for video of a new original and live performance in front of an audience and written scores of three new compositions."

"How do you feel about that?" She asked.

"OK. I'll either be able to do it or I won't. I kinda know what I don't know, so hopefully someone will teach me."

"That's a good attitude!" She said, probably with more enthusiasm than was needed in the moment, but I knew she meant it well.

"Thanks."

"OK, this part of the interrogation is over but, you'd better be ready to yap it up with Uncle Bob and Aunt Jenny because they are very excited and haven't seen you since graduation."

I could have protested, but I liked her aunt and uncle. Bob had played in a pretty good cover band for years that used to gig regularly at the Anchor Inn, and even played the Cape May Jazz Festival once, which is a really big deal. He helped me get a gig at the Anchor Inn two summers ago. I got paid in Garlic Crabs and they kept the Phillies game on during my set, but the gig was OK and the crabs were amazing. Big Bobbie only made them when he felt like it and I was glad he was feeling it that day. The Phillies lost, which made the audience grumpy, but it was a good experience to get through. Better than the one I did later that summer in Moorestown at the Java Bean, where I forgot the words to "American Pie." That was embarrassing and reinforced my disdain of playing the typical bar cover songs. I kept trying to get the audience to sing along so I could figure out which lyrics came next, but in the end, they didn't know them all either. Too many words in that song anyway.

Uncle Bob and Aunt Jenny usually felt more like family to me than Uncle Ted was, and because Bob was always into music I knew he'd want to hear about my classes and what I'd been writing and listening to.

"They aren't going to make me play for them this time, are they?"

"They might. Would that be so awful?"

I sighed again, "I don't know, it always feels weird and Uncle Bob always wants to harmonize."

"Well, there's that, but they love it when you play, and so do I."

I figured we'd see how it all went. It was still morning at that point and I didn't yet know what the rest of the day would hold. Angie had only eaten about half of her sandwich and held it out to me.

"Want the rest?" I did.

"You sure?"

"Yes, I know what you're like if you're hungry, which I am no longer."

"Thanks" I replied, tearing into it.

Angie stood up and walked down towards the water and continued north. I followed her again, catching up to her near the dunes.

"Getting tired already?" she asked, noting my rush to catch up to her.

"Nah, just didn't figure we'd be walking so much."

"Get used to it city boy, you're not going to have your mom's dope ride to tool around Boston in."

"They have trains."

"Ah yes…and you'll have to walk to them, won't you?"

"Well, yeah, I guess."

It was starting to get warm and the sun had burned off the dampness of the morning. The beach up in North Wildwood is way narrower and smaller than in Wildwood or in the Crest, so we found ourselves along the water rather quickly. We both took off our shoes and walked through the wake, Angie scanning the ground for shells. The sand is a bit coarser as you move north and they don't have the same number of natural dunes as the other Wildwood beaches. Angie's Aunt Jenny tried to explain those to me because she works for one of the Coastal Conservation groups, but I didn't follow most of it. Science was never my strong suit.

Eventually the shoreline up north starts to turn west toward the bay and there are huge stones there. We ended up that way and sat on the stones, with the old Anglesea Lighthouse behind us. I remember Angie looking very pensive like she was debating something in her internal dialog and not liking the direction it was going. She'd been quiet for a while, which as I said, I've always had trouble with, so I said something like, "So, what's happening?"

She turned and smiled at me but then looked away towards the lighthouse. Whatever was on her mind right then she wasn't sharing, and I wasn't pushing. I absently rubbed my hand where I'd broken it and she noticed, like she always notices every little thing.

"Does it still hurt?" she asked, turning back to me and taking my hand and examining it.

"Not really. Sometimes when I think about it." I almost mentioned that Madam Marie had talked about it during the reading, but stopped myself, thinking better of it.

"Would you please tell me the story about how you broke it?"

That kinda surprised me. I never thought it was that great a story. "Really?" I asked. "That one? Wouldn't you rather hear about the time I…"

"No, sweetie. This lady has requested that story." And she looked kind of giddy about it, like she was excited to hear it again. I didn't really know why but I didn't see any harm in it. There weren't any secrets between us anyway. I figured I'd ham it up a bit for fun.

"Well, 'Lady,' and I'm using the term loosely here..." which earned me a punch on the arm. "Ouch, thank you, you may recall that I'd finally gleaned, from my Nana, and through deep investigative research in my mom's closet while she was at work that my actual father, provider of half the genetic material that became the specimen you see before you here, had some kind of connection to Saint Ambrose Catholic Church, where Nana and Mom used to go in South Philly. He'd been a visiting priest from the Ukraine, apparently. Once I found the pictures my seventeen-year-old mom had saved from the summer work camp with him, and a few letters, I knew I had to try and find out more."

Angie was still holding my hand, which I'd only noticed when she let go as I laid back on the giant rock we were sitting on and she did the same.

"I know this part. I was with you when you found the pictures."

"I know, but you said you wanted the story."

"Tell me about going to the church," she said as the wind blew the hair back off her face and made her long skirt flap slightly around her ankles. "You didn't want me to come with you."

I sat up and took a long breath. "I had always wondered why Nana, who is so churchy, had only been going to Trinity Church since I was baptized. She seemed like someone who would have gone to the same place since she was born. She's old school that way. I mean, she's been going to Prudencio's Butcher and Market for seventy years even though there's a Safeway on her block now. Mom and Nana, well, they'd never talk about it, but it turns out she left Saint Ambrose the summer after I was born. Once I saw the pictures of Mom with this priest, and he's got my hair and eyes, I felt like I had a right to some answers."

"You still do."

That was a nice thing to say, but I feel like I'm over it now, whether I am or not. I told her again about how I'd pretty much barged into Monsignor Hughes office and demanded answers as to who this guy in the picture was. Hughes turned out to be a pretty mousy guy and he kind of cowered behind his desk almost before I'd said anything. While I was never going to hit him, being 6'3" and pretty fit kinda served the threatening vibe I'd been going for. I mean, I've only ever been in one actual fight and that was after Robbie Olsen ripped the pocket off my Academy Jacket in grade six.

Robbie Olsen. Jeez, that dope still irks me! I'd spent all day the previous Sunday visiting all five Burlington Coat Factories on Route 130 as far South as Salem County trying to find a bargain blazer that would fit me. Robbie was an eighth grader who got picked on by his own classmates, so he looked for the tallest kids from the younger grades to mess with. Everyone knew I was on scholarship, so I was always trying to stay out of trouble, and he figured I wouldn't fight back or make a stink. He'd been right about that for months. He bothered me relentlessly and it never really got physical until he ripped my jacket. I'd been holding it in for months and after that, I flipped out and beat him up so bad he didn't even tell on me from embarrassment. I heard later he told his teacher that he slipped getting off the bus and hit the giant old Oak tree that stood right along where the busses let off on Nassau Street. I remember kinda blacking out in rage and Will and Brian pulling me off of him as I was apparently about to bash Robbie's head into the wrought Iron fence that surrounded the school a second time. By the time the adults noticed anything it was over, and Robbie Olsen never bothered me again. No one else did either, except for Dave Rivers, Robbie's pal who blindsided me on the blacktop before school about a month later, cracking my head. I stood up and laughed all crazy at him and he ran away. It hurt like hell and I'm pretty sure I had a mild concussion, but I just stood up and laughed maniacally in his face. That story followed me to Windsor High too, mostly through Will and Brian, but as a result, no one ever messed with me like that again. They all figured I was nuts.

Anyway, the Monsignor didn't know any of that. He just knew a loud kid barged into his office waving a photograph. "Could you please tell me where I can find this priest?"

Angie closed her eyes; I suppose to better imagine the situation. "You just barged right in!"

"Yeah, I kinda blew past Sister Jane and barked at him. Turns out he was pretty new to the parish and had no idea who I was talking about, but I just kept yelling at the Monsignor: "It was sixteen years ago! Someone knows something!"

"I felt a hand on my shoulder then and turned abruptly to see the nun from the outer office, Sister Jane, in front of me, her hands raised in a calming posture. 'May I see that picture, son?' She asked. I handed it to her. Turns out she'd been working in that office for twenty-five years, and she remembered the man in the picture. She looked at the picture and then my face a few times before shaking her head sadly. 'Monsignor, this would be another one' as she handed the picture back to me. 'He was very charming, Father Pavla. Very charming.'"

Retelling this to her was a little emotional. I'm not sure why exactly because we both knew all this already, but I remember standing up and walking towards the water. Angie followed. "I remember staring at the Monsignor, waiting for him to say something, but he just remained in his seat, unblinking. I said, 'I want to know who this man is. He's probably my father and I have that right!' but the Monsignor seemed to remember himself and he sat upright in his chair and said, 'I cannot help you, son, please leave now before I call the police.' And he picked up the receiver of his phone and pointed it at the door. It was one of those old school clunky phones with the gray buttons and probably weighed fifteen pounds. I glared at him and asked, 'you can't help me or you won't help me?' to which he said, 'either is sufficient.'"

I took a breath and rubbed my hand. "That was when I punched his phone into pieces, breaking it and my fifth metacarpal."

Angie stood alongside me then and sighed, "You left out my favorite part."

I scoffed. "What, where the Monsignor called out that he'd be expecting a new phone in the offering plate after refusing to help me?"

"No silly, the part where Sister Jane tried to help you find his family in Europe and offered to help you and your mother get counseling to deal with the aftermath. I liked that part."

"Yeah, well none of that ever panned out. It was all dead ends."

She leaned her head on my shoulder. An airplane flew

past advertising the "Amazing Pancake Specials at Aunt Karla's Pancake House!!!" It turned around and headed back south to make another run at the beaches, in case people didn't know that Aunt Karla's had amazing pancake specials.

"Yes, my friend. But she tried. And you should have told your Mom you found that picture and looked into it instead of telling her you broke your hand trying to imitate Jimi Hendrix playing behind his head."

Angie was right and we both knew it, so I just let it sit there. I'd had enough time to think about it and I accepted the fact that it was better to not let on to Mom that I knew. She'd had enough drama with all that I imagine. Nana always says I do a good job "navigating my mother" so I figured I'd just let it be. But the hand still hurts sometimes, among other things. My father, whoever or whatever he is or was is not my family. He is not in my heart and if I ever end up amounting to anything at all it certainly won't be because of him. It will be because of my own work and the support of my real family. Mom and Nana and Angie. And of course, music. I wasn't sure what Angie was driving at with this line of conversation, so I asked her.

"Angie, why'd you ask me to tell you all that again? You've heard it before and were basically there for most of it, right?"

"I like that story," she countered, kneeling down to pick at a few scattered shells near our feet.

"Why?" I wondered, crouching down next to her. She picked at the shells a bit more and pulled out a nice Mussel shell with a deep purple swath on its edge before she answered.

"You really don't see what a lady might find admirable about that story?"

"Well, it's probably not destroying an ancient phone and breaking my hand, threatening a clergyman and frightening a nun, right?"

She swatted my arm at that, "No, of course not. But you stood up for yourself and not in a way that resulted in some dopey kid getting his head stuck in a wrought Iron fence."

"He was never stuck, and I only threw him into it once."

"Because your friends pulled you off him. But that's not really the point, my dear. You saw something that wasn't right and you ran right into it, completely unafraid."

I hadn't thought of it that way before.

"There are people out there, my friend," and then she whispered, "some of them girls, who find that sort of passion attractive or at least admirable. You should look out for them." She stood up quickly and moved a bit towards the water. "There are also others who might see as equally admirable, if not more so, the fact that you walked away and made peace with it as best you could and took care of your mother."

I didn't really know what to do with all that at the time. So, I didn't say anything. It still was weird in the back of my mind that Madame Marie had mentioned my hand hurting sometimes and that someday it wouldn't. Makes me wonder.

CHAPTER FOUR

The breeze picked up a bit and Angie's long hair blew off her shoulders to the right, and her shirt had kinda slumped off her shoulder a bit and it revealed a dark splotch on her left shoulder. As I looked closer it looked like a shell.

"What is that?" I asked as I stared at her bare shoulder seeing what was now, up close, a Scallop shell, tattooed on her back behind her left shoulder. She looked over that shoulder at me, a little shyly it seemed, which was a little weird because she never really acted that way.

"Do you like it?"

I moved closer and looked more closely, transfixed. I think I must have breathed on her shoulder as she got goosebumps and shrugged a little. I realized I'd been staring so I tried to redirect myself.

"Did it hurt?" We had talked about getting tattoos once we turned eighteen a bunch of times but we'd always chickened out. We could never decide what to get done and Angie never handled needles well since she was little.

"It hurt a little at first. I'm used to it now. For a while, I was constantly looking over my shoulder at it though."

It was a nice tattoo; a dark gray scallop shell with orange and red highlights along her shoulder blade, but the cool part was the tiny air bubbles that seemed to emanate from it and blend in with her skin in all directions. The shell was partly open as though it was moving through the water. It was really beautiful and at that moment completely unexpected.

"You surprised me," I offered after gawking at her bare shoulder for probably too long.

"Well, that's good," she replied, adjusting her shirt as she turned back towards me, the wind again tossing her hair the opposite direction now that she'd turned, "But do you like it?" She smiled at me and seemed to be in a silly sort of mood all of a sudden.

"It's really cool!" I blathered, which was not really the extent of what I was really thinking. It was a strange moment, seeing her like that, especially when she smiled at me. It made me feel like she was really and truly seriously cute! I mean, don't get me wrong, she's always been a pretty girl, but it was awkward, and I felt suddenly flushed and kind of anxious, actually. I realized that I was staring again and just continued babbling, "Ah, when did you have it done? Why didn't you tell me?"

Angie seemed to be studying my face a bit as her eyes narrowed a little like she does when she thinks I'm full of it. "Earlier this summer." Her scanning of me made me feel like I hadn't reacted enough, so I blathered on.

"It's really pretty. I love the bubbles! And the colors, wow, I mean the whole thing is really,"

Angie interrupted me, "It's really what?" Her unreadable eyes were suddenly locked on mine. If I had been honest, I'd have told her "it's really kind of hot" as that's exactly what I was thinking in that moment but then I remembered, *this is my best friend! I can't look at her like that, much less say stuff like that to her!* I mean, I never had a problem telling her she was pretty or her hair looked nice or didn't and stuff like that when it came up, but this felt different. I was really confused and flushed, so I tried to cover my awkwardness with talking, which seemed to help.

"It's really artistic and pretty! Did you design it yourself? The colors are awesome! Why don't you tell me all about it?" Pretty sure I talked fast and loud but if she noticed how red I was, she didn't say anything. She narrowed her eyes at me a bit further and let the silence sit between us a little longer than I was comfortable with, but at least I started to feel like I could breathe again.

She finally seemed satisfied with my reaction and she spoke as she picked up her shoes and walked up the sand away from the water taking my arm. "I thought I would surprise you and I had a small scheduling window in which to have it done as I wished. I told the artist what I wanted, and she sketched it out for me before we started."

"Did it hurt?" I asked again, forgetting that I'd already asked.

"Not too bad. Just a bump."

"On the way to here?" I offered, probably a little hammily. I thought she'd laugh at that, but she just squeezed my arm and said,

"Just so."

That "just a bump" thingy is one of Angie's favorite sayings. A while back, I came across a picture of her with no hair but wearing a huge smile and T-Shirt that said it "This is just a bump in the road" with a picture of a turtle stuck next to one of those speedbumps in a road. It was from one of the Christmases she spent in the Juvenile Cancer wing at CHOP in Philly. She never complains about it, which I'm amazed by. She just shrugs and says, "I'm better now. It was only a bump."

As we left the beach we found ourselves heading right towards the old lighthouse. We sat on a bench along the pathway to put our shoes back on. I noticed there was a small stone monument near the bench that honored the sailors and lifeguards and fishermen that had been lost at sea over the years, and even though most of the names were from a long time ago, people still seemed to leave stuff at the memorial. There was an American flag and a few stones and shells and coins that had been placed by someone who had been there and wanted to mark that they had been present and remembered them. Someone, a kid I would imagine, left a small wooden toy ship next to it as well, with a yellow ribbon tied around it. Angie noticed me examining the memorial and asked, "What are you thinking about?"

I gestured at the boat "I think that's cool. I don't know why, but there's something really moving about the whole thing, but the boat in particular."

"Do you want to leave something?"

"I don't know any of those people. Would that be disrespectful?"

"Would you mean for it to be?" Angie sorta patted me on the back as she said this.

"No, of course not. I just don't know if it's my place is all." I was back to being uncertain. Angie stood up and took my hand and walked closer to the memorial.

"In memory of those lost at sea," she said as she pulled out a few of the shells she'd collected during the morning and put one on top of the stone. "The shell just means 'I was here, and I thought about the people who were lost and those who lost them.' I think that's really all you need. I think you bring to and take away what you want to from such a thing. What do you think?"

"I think I like how that sounds."

Angie exhaled and handed me a small clam shell that had this really cool gray color with a deep purple slash through the middle. It was smooth and almost flat.

"Why this shell?" I asked as I placed it on the memorial on the same side as the little boat, in between a few pennies and a Sacagawea Dollar Coin.

"What the ocean gives you is what you get."

Angie grabbed my hand and pulled me along like I was on a wagon calling out, "come along, I want to show you something."

We walked into the gardens that surrounded the lighthouse. They were high and mysterious like something out of "The Secret Garden" and felt really out of place this close to the ocean. I could still hear the waves crashing on the narrow North Wildwood shore. The garden, once we entered it, felt like its own world; like it existed on its own outside of the rest of the world. The sun and its heat were absent from it and it felt like the whole space, with its high trimmed hedges and deep shade, was set apart just for us in that moment. That is until the swarm of butterflies flew past.

"Wow, look at all those Monarchs!" I cried. I had raised monarchs a few years earlier for a Science project that was actually pretty cool and fun to do. Was the only time I ever got an A in Science, that's for sure. "You think Hobbes is in there?" Hobbes was the only one who survived to release and yes, I named him after the comic strip tiger. Calvin and Suzy didn't make it, alas.

Angie laughed at me, "I suppose it could be Hobbes's

35

descendants, Mr. Wizard. That was years ago and their lifespan isn't that long…"

Angie never got anything but an A in Science and pretty much every other class she took either for that matter. She finished third in our class, which she was grateful for because the first and second finishers had to give a speech at graduation. I always thought she tanked a few questions on her Calculus final just to make sure that Hannah Mazak passed her for second or salutatorian or whatever it is they call it. Nobody was going to overtake Gordon Winston-Hom for Valedictorian. Gordon straight A's since pre-kindergarten. His speech was actually pretty funny. He just told stories about silly stuff he and his friends and family had experienced during the years he was at Windsor and said something like, "in the future, it might be kind of nice to remember these things." I liked that line. Hannah's was just brutal, though, because she made it all rhyming and poemy, but tried to quote Katy Perry and Beyoncé like eight times. Brutal. Angie was relieved to not have to speak and went out of her way to be kind to Hannah afterwards, which was nice as everyone else was kind of avoiding her afterwards.

"So, maybe it could be his grandkids or something like that?" I asked, still really transfixed by the sight of a bazillion butterflies all hanging around this one giant bush.

"Something like that. Soon enough they will head south, never to return." She sighed dramatically and punched me in the arm again.

"Ow! What was that for?"

"Oh," she moaned melodramatically, "the Monarchs are just like you…off to Boston, leaving all us little people behind to lament about how we once knew you…I could faint!" She swept her skirt dramatically and flopped onto the nearby bench, laying on it with her hand to her forehead. "I feel feverish just thinking about it!" She cried out before falling into a fit of laughter.

I wasn't really in the mood to talk about leaving much less joke about it, but I think she knew that, and I took the bait anyway. "Knock it off, Ange. It's not gonna be like that. I'll be lucky to make it to Christmas up there before they're done with me."

Angie cackled, the way she does when she's having too much fun needling me. "Yep, that's just right! They'll toss you out on your ear before Thanksgiving!" For some reason she seemed to affect a Southern accent out of nowhere, lamenting, "I declare, that boy from Jersey, of all places, thinks his skills are mad enough to play with us up here in the big, and might I add fancy, conservatory? I object!" She giggled.

I knew what she was doing but I really wasn't in the mood. The truth is I was kinda dreading going to Boston for a lot of the reasons Angie was joking about. She'd just dressed down my real fears in a second, while laughing in a Southern accent. I shouldn't have but I kind of got my back up about it, which I knew was what she was going for. She likes to make me talk about things when I don't want to and she's usually right, but I didn't feel like it so I just kind of clammed up and meandered over to the other side of the garden and tried to pretend that a particular plant was interesting. I don't remember what it was since I had bombed the whole "plants" section of the science curriculum. It was green.

She stood up and followed behind me, still cackling, saying "Oh, no you don't get to shut me down on me young man!"

"You're like two months older than me," I mumbled

as she caught up with me from behind and grabbed me around the waist and tried to move me off the spot where I was standing. She grunted like a wrestler trying to move me, but I'm like eight inches taller than her and was able to hold my ground pretty easily. "What are you doing you weirdo?"

She strained with effort through her clenched teeth, "I-am-TRYING-to-geez you're tall-toss-you-out-on-ugh-your-ear!" and she leaned back to strain again, grunting, "like they'll do at school, right?! It-seems-ugh-easy-enough-right?!"

Anyone walking by would have thought we were maniacs or something. It much have looked comical: a 5'7" long-haired brunette in a long skirt trying to suplex a 6'3" blonde dude in a butterfly garden. Fortunately, no one did.

"I'm-gonna-toss-you-yet-rapscallion! Urgh!"

"Ok Ange," I sighed, "that's enough, come on now." But then, she decided to fight dirty. Like I said, she's been my best friend for years and she knows how to get to me better than anyone.

"Are we ticklish today?" she purred as she made it clear she was done trying to tackle me and just tickled the daylights out of me on the one spot on my neck behind my right ear. I have no idea why that spot but the problem was that she knew it and was unrelenting. I'd say I was stupid to tell her about that spot but the truth is, I never really did, she just figured that one out on her own. She was not fighting fair now.

"Angie, stop it. I mean it!" But she didn't stop. I tried catching her arms, but she was too quick and next thing I knew I had fallen on my butt and she was standing over me with her sandaled foot on my chest like a big game hunter that killed a giant wildebeest or something.

"Victory is mine!" she bellowed to the butterflies and to a shocked looking beach-bound family pulling a wagon through the garden. They paused a moment before quickly resuming their walk to the beach. I can only imagine what they thought was going on because once they started moving, Angie continued, in an English accent this time, "Do you yield, young man?!" I looked up and her face was an affected scowl and raised eyebrows, like she was about the break character during a dramatic play and start laughing. "Do ye?!"

"Yeah, yeah, just get your grubby foot off me."

She ground the ball of her foot into me more and narrowed her eyes. "Grubby feet!? I just had a Pedi…I think you need to rephrase that request you, scalawag!" Angie was deep into her "Game of Thrones" accent now which always comes off like a very odd combo of South Jersey affectation meets Cockney, but she has fun with it.

"Scalawag?"

"I already used rapscallion."

"Oh. Now, come on Angie," I pleaded, trying to get up, but her foot stayed put and she pushed back. In my predicament, I did take notice of the fact that her toes looked as though she'd had a recent pedicure and had a nice green polish on them with a tiny hint of glitter. They looked pretty, but I was still grumpy because I'd been put on my butt by her. It was not too different than the way I fell off the bench in the gym the day I met Angie the first day of ninth grade. I'd leaned back trying to look smooth to impress her. It didn't work but we became friends anyway.

"Let me up, please?"

She narrowed her eyes but didn't budge, "I'm afraid that your request, as stated, is not quite going to do it, knave. My toes are still offended."

"OK, OK, I'm sorry I said that they were grubby. They're quite lovely." I meant it, but I said it like I didn't.

She kind of twiddled them around on my shirt, making sure I could see them, "The loveliest in all the realm?"

"Um, yeah, of course, the loveliest ever in all of explored space!"

"They are, aren't they?!" she grinned, removing her foot and leaning down to help me up, or so I thought. I considered pulling her down on the ground with me to see how she liked it but instead of pulling me up, she sat down next to me, laughing but also seeming to catch her breath. I guess trying to pick me up had worn her out a little. "Ah, but that was fun," she chuckled as she exhaled a few times. She was sweating a bit and took a few more breaths to relax before she continued.

"I know you're nervous, but no more talk about you not making it, OK?"

I didn't know what to say, so I kind of grunted and started to stand up. She grabbed my arm before I could stand and held me firm with a strong grip that almost hurt a bit, actually. She asked again, looking for my eyes, "OK?"

I finally looked at her and nodded. She just kept looking at me, like she was searching for more information than I had just given, but eventually she looked away, seemingly satisfied. She looked about the garden.

"Well, my friend, I think we might have spooked away the Monarchs."

There were none to be found at the moment, so I nodded. "So it would seem."

She looked at me again and put out her hands, "Help a lady up, wouldja?"

I stood up and reached a hand down to her and she

extended both to me and she really pulled on me to get up. I guess I pulled her too hard and she got dizzy for a second, leaning into me.

"Whoa, easy there, you alright?" I cried out, concerned.

Angie grabbed my waist tight and held on a moment. "I'm good, just got up too fast."

I led her over to the bench and we sat down as she caught her breath.

"Are you OK? It seemed like you…"

Angie popped up, "I'm fine. Just needed a moment. You know what time it is?"

I looked at the sky and guessed "Um, like 11:30?"

She raised an eyebrow at me. "Is that a question?"

I groaned, "No, Angie, it's not. It's 11:30, I'm certain."

She nodded. "Good. That means that Uncle Bob and Aunt Jenny are expecting us soon. Let's walk through the rest of the garden and head over there. It's only a few blocks," she added, already in motion and putting whatever had just happened behind her. That seemed to happen a lot, now that I think of it.

CHAPTER FIVE

Her aunt and uncle owned a very nice house in North Wildwood that they bought from an old Irish widow back in 1983. Story was the old lady had almost sold the property to a developer who was planning to knock it down and build condos, but at the last minute she decided she wanted a family to live in her home, just as hers had. She even took less money to sell it to them, to have it become what it has for Angie's family, a refuge, a shore house, and a place to build a life. I always admired the old lady in that story.

We walked through the remainder of the garden. Angie's always been a soft touch for plants and flowers and stuff. The lighthouse itself was really more of a large Victorian house, bright yellow with a sort of large tower in the middle. I guess it was a vital lighthouse from the 1870s up to the 1960s, when it was replaced by a new modern thingy. We did the tour when I came with her last summer and it was pretty cool to see how they've restored it and made it part of the community again.

We walked in silence for a while when I realized that I

hadn't asked her about her upcoming 'getting ready' for school stuff, probably because I still really just wasn't ready to talk about my own impending departure. She'd gotten into Princeton and their orientation wasn't for another three weeks, well, because they're Princeton, but I felt like asking as we walked.

"Why does Princeton do their orientation so late?"

Angie raised an eyebrow. "Broaching the subject of higher education, are we?"

"Just yours."

I remember now that she kinda sped up a little as she replied, and I couldn't see her face as she said, "Since you asked, I don't know exactly. I haven't been paying much attention since I'm going to take the fall semester off, actually."

I stopped walking entirely. She kept moving. "What?!" This was totally unexpected. She stopped walking too after a few more measured steps and I noticed that she kinda bit her lower lip a little bit, which I'd never noticed her do before as she turned back to me. She seemed to exhale.

"Yes, it looks like I'm going to take a semester off."

I was confused. "A semester off from what? You haven't even started there yet."

Angie stepped towards me and put her hands on my shoulders like we were dancing the way kids do in seventh grade. "I know I haven't started yet, but I've been running ragged at school for years now and I'm tired. I need a break to do some other things. Maybe I'll start up in the winter term if all goes well, but-"

I totally interrupted her, "If what goes well? This is, Angie, this is major! Why didn't you talk to me about this before today? I haven't seen you all summer but we talked almost every day?! I mean, what the heck?" I remember feeling kinda snarfy about the whole thing, but it just didn't make sense to me and I reacted.

She bit her lip again. I didn't know what this meant and it made me uneasy. I know it sounds weird but when you have spent as much time with someone as I have with Angie, you get to know their idiosyncrasies and gestures and reactions-this one was new and I didn't understand it, and honestly, I was so freaking anxious about leaving myself and was already feeling like I was off my center with things changing. And from the morning we'd already had, I felt the very edges of a panic attack coming on. I hadn't had one in a long time and I wasn't about to here, so I forced myself to take a few deep breaths. I thought I'd gotten away with it, but I don't think I fooled Angie, who grabbed my hands and held them tight, looking right in my eyes. She looked concerned for a second before she continued, "I meant to talk to you about it, but honestly, a lot of it just came together in the last few weeks and I figured we'd get around to it. It was my choice, OK? Does that make sense?"

I was really thrown. Angie loved school and was really good at it, so no, this made no sense to me at all. "But why now?" I asked "You've always wanted to go to Princeton. Why stop now?"

"I never said I didn't want to go to Princeton. I do. But I need a break and it looks like they will hold my spot," and she smiled here, "which is very kind of them, so I think I will let them be kind to me and take the break."

I guess that aspect of it all made sense. I would have liked a break too, but I knew that this was my one year to try and make college work. I had some "forward momentum" going with school and with my playing and the scholarship committee considering me for next year. I knew if I was going to get a "break" it would really only come after I failed.

"So, what are you going to do?" I asked.

She slid her arm through mine and started us walking again like we were "off to see the Wizard."

"That, my friend, is indeed a good and salient question! Quite pertinent!"

I knew how this would end. "And the answer would be?"

"Salient and pertinent question there, young man! Well struck indeed!" she replied, way too loudly, her voice bordering on yet another poor approximation of a European accent of some sort. Almost a Cockney, which signaled to me that she wasn't ready to budge further. We had all day to talk, though, so I figured we'd revisit it when the time was right.

"Have it your way, missy, but I've got my eyes on you..." I answered with narrowed eyes and clenched teeth, accent borrowed from Flo in those Progressive Insurance ads, when she does her dumb 1920s Gangster accent.

We crossed New Jersey Avenue, still arm in arm, and I knew we were only a few blocks from her aunt and uncle's place. She was quiet for a bit before she said, almost under her breath, "Your eyes can look at me all you like, sweetie...not that the pair you have will learn ya much."

I didn't understand that at all, so I asked her "What was that?"

"Oh, nothing. Look, here we are!" She had a weird look on her face like she was overly glad to have found herself at our destination in that exact moment.

Angie's Uncle Bob was a force of nature and when he saw us walking up the sidewalk, he left the smoking grill and ran up to us, lifting Angie into the air in a giant hug that twirled her around. "Angela-baby, it's been too long!" he exclaimed as he spun her about laughing, his long hair whipping about behind him. Though he was mostly bald on top, he rocked a long, almost Willie Nelson sized braid off what he had left in the back.

"Bob, go easy there or you'll make her puke before she's even eaten anything!" Aunt Jenny scolded from atop their wraparound porch. Jenny was as petite as Bob was larger than life, but they both seemed to live life at full speed. She is Angie's mom's younger sister and always seemed to find the fun in things where Angie's mom could be very distant and grumpy. She's always so serious and even after all these years Angie and I have been close, her mom still gives me the occasional "stink eye" when she thinks I'm not paying attention. I still don't quite get that. Jenny is pretty; shorter than Angie but with similar features, same dark but colorful eyes. They really could have passed for sisters if they'd wanted to.

Bob finally set Angie down, rather carefully it seemed after all that, where I kinda caught her arm, remembering her head rush earlier, but she seemed fine. Jenny hugged her as well as Bob greeted me with an equally enthusiastic hug.

"So, here's this generation's next great star! The next John Mayer, Ed Sheeran or Lin-Manuel maybe? Here in our midst! How are ya, kid?!"

Boisterous does not cover Uncle Bob. He always called me kid. Like I said, he's been part of the music scene down the shore for years and always been really positive and encouraging about my music.

"I'm good, Uncle Bob," I exhaled after I survived his

embrace. Even though he and Aunt Jenny weren't my blood relatives, they'd always insisted I call them aunt and uncle and have always been immeasurably kind to me. I've been all too happy to accommodate them on that as when your only family beyond Mom and Nana is Uncle Ted, I think you'll take any connection with good people who seem to like you. Plus, they always just went out of their way to make me feel welcome, which I always have a hard time feeling, even at home.

"John Mayer?" I asked as Aunt Jenny came over and gave me a hug. She was always a tight hugger, but I thought I was going to pass out for a minute as she was really squeezing me. "Ack!" I laughed, "Can't breathe…"

"Oh, you hush now you big baby!" she chided, and she let go and looked at me for a long moment. "We are really glad you came today. You look thin," she said, before hugging me again and turning away to take Angie by the arm and lead her inside the house. Angie waved at me over her shoulder as she was whisked away.

"What's wrong with John Mayer?" Uncle Bob asked, walking back towards the grill farther down the driveway.

"Um, well, nothing really. He's had some hits and can actually shred. Playing with the surviving Grateful Dead members now, I think. Did you see his performance at the Hall of Fame induction of Albert King from a few years ago?"

Uncle Bob pointed at me, "See it? I've got it saved on the DVR. That was a hot set. The young man can play, AND he does the singer songwriter thing…"

"He sure can," I replied.

"His playing is great, but you know…" and he pointed his tongs at me as he puttered with the stuff on the grill, "That singer songwriter bit got him in with a few of his generation's finest young ladies…Taylor Swift, Jennifer

Aniston, Katy Perry…"

"None of them stayed around though…" I countered.

He laughed at me, a sound which seemed to echo off the walls of his house and that of his neighbors across the driveway. "Yes, that's true, but Jennifer Love Hewitt's body was apparently a wonderland!" He laughed at his own joke. "I'll bet it was!"

Bob puttered at the grill a moment before he continued. "Angela finally got around to sending us some pictures from the Prom and Graduation. You looked almost decent in a tuxedo!"

"Thanks, I think?"

He laughed, "Did I hear right that you were originally supposed to go with that girl who won Prom Queen?" He was teasing me now, but I knew he wouldn't let up without the story.

"Yeah, well sorta. I was originally going with 'Queen' Melissa Carpenter, but we didn't make it past Spring Break. She was in my English class and we got along great until we started dating. Then it became all about me being with her all the time and hanging out with her other 'couple friends.' Her friends were cool mostly, but they were all FBLA-high-achiever types who I didn't have a ton in common with. She liked watching me perform but never really considered that I might want to make that my thing, when I could get a 'real job' as she liked to say."

Bob scoffed. "Real job? Good riddance to her."

I nodded, "Exactly, plus, as always seemed to happen with all the other girls I've dated, Melissa couldn't get past my friendship with Angie. I remember vividly the whole 'why don't you just date her already?!' screamfest Melissa bombarded me with as we were splitting up after five months and a coordinated Prom outfit session. I told her it wasn't like that and honestly, she was exhausting by that point. I found the breakup kind of a relief. When I asked her why she couldn't accept that Angie and I were just friends, she said, very calmly, 'you are an imbecile. Really and for truly, a genuine idiot.' That was the end of our bid for Prom King and Queen."

Bob puttered further with the meat on the grill but was oddly quiet, for him, so I continued, filling the brief silence.

"Not to be denied though, Melissa did win with my replacement, Frankie Lambert, and she seemed very happy about it. She was in her glory as she and Frankie danced to 'Wonderful Tonight,' which always seems to be everyone's Prom theme for like ever."

"Geez, that was the theme for one of ours like two decades ago!"

"Still going strong it seems. Did Angie tell you what she made me do?"

"Nope. We only got the pictures this week."

I was kinda glad to hear it hadn't just been me she'd been a little distant from. "So, she says to me, 'please go and ask Melissa to dance with you at the next song,' and I'm like 'we haven't talked since we broke up, it'll be weird, I don't want to, why should I do that?'"

Bob rolled his eyes, "and Angela said you should do it because…"

"She said, 'because I think it would be a nice thing for you to do and you're a nice boy.'"

"And then?"

"Well, then she gave me the 'please' eyes that she only pulls out when something is really important to her. Then she made the long kinda boo-boo face and raised her eyebrows at me ever so slightly."

Bob was clearly trying to not laugh at me as I continued, "Hey, you try staring at her face when she's like that and saying no to her. Not that easy to have a contrary opinion then."

"I've seen that look, son. I know the struggle."

"Exactly. I knew I had no choice at that point, so I told her that I'd try, to which she responds, 'No. Do. Or do not. There is no try. Also, tell her she looks pretty. Girls like that.'"

At this point, Bob couldn't restrain himself and he burst out laughing so hard that he woke up a baby who'd been apparently sleeping in the house next door as it started screaming.

He shushed himself, "Oops, I'm going to hear about that from the neighbors," but he continued chuckling. "Then what happened?"

I saw the haggard mom through the window rush to her crying child as I continued. "Well, I went over to her and I felt the eyes of Melissa's girlfriends lock onto me as I entered their radar range. It was creepy as they seemed kind of like bodyguards now that she was wearing a crown. Frankie and Melissa weren't really dating all that seriously, or so I'd heard, so I didn't think it would be a big deal for me to ask her to dance. I didn't want to make a problem, and I was friendly with Frankie from our neighborhood, so I walked over and congratulated him. He was a junior and was clearly enjoying the extra attention. It was just then, as the words were coming out of my mouth, when I realized why Angie wanted me to do it. I said, "Hey man, would it be cool if I asked Melissa to dance? It would be nice to make some peace before we graduate."

"She's a wise child, my Angela."

"Well, Frankie, who was always a goofy, fun kid smiled and tilted his head in this way he did every time he spoke and said, 'Jeez dude, I've known you way longer than I've known her! Your mom used to babysit me when my mom went back to school. Go ahead dude, we're cool.' I thanked him as I moved away towards the royal court. All of Melissa's girlfriends were present and now apparently serving as shield maidens or something. Heather, Ruth, Tammy, and Holly were fawning over Melissa's crown and her hair and her dress and snapping pictures on their phones and posting them to everywhere all at once, I imagine. Anything to avoid actually interacting with the people around them, like usual."

This got a resounding groan from Uncle Bob, who was not the biggest fan of social media.

"So, Melissa stood up as I approached, and I could feel Angie watching me from across the room. Like I said, I was only just then figuring that she knew I'd be better off if Mel and I could at least be civil if not friendly going forward. It had been awkward at times since we split, and we were sure to run into one another at all the dumb graduation events and awards nights and stuff and then there was the entire summer and Windsor is a small town. I kinda blanked on what I was doing for a minute because it was awkward. Finally, I remembered what Angie had just said so I said, 'You look very pretty, Mel,' and she smiled and thanked me. Then, she said, 'Angela looks amazing in that dress. Green suits her.'"

Bob was performing some sort of spice dance above the grill with shakers flying all over the place, but he nodded. "That's an interesting thing for your ex to say about your best friend."

"Yeah, I was kinda thrown at first. I thought she was trying to pick a fight with me, but she was right, Angela did look great in her dress. The gloves were a nice touch, but they seemed unlike her. Angie joked that she was covering up all her recent tattoos. I didn't know how to respond so I think I said something like 'yeah, she does,' but then Melissa beat me to the punch as Bruno Mars' 'Just the Way you Are' started playing. She says, "Would you dance with me, one last time?'"

"And so, we danced, and cleared the air and said sorry about stuff and when the song was over she held my hands for a moment and said 'It was nice of you to come over. I didn't like the nonsense between us. Please, thank Angela for me.'"

"Well, that's Angela for you. She knows people better than they know themselves, more often than not."

I nodded and let it go at that but I'm not sure why I told the whole thing to Uncle Bob. I think it's just part of the way he talks to people. He makes them feel important even if they're telling a pretty silly story. So, without meaning to, I told him that whole thing. He gets people to talk to him.

Bob pulled a few steaks off the grill and placed several ears of corn in their place. My eyes widened when I realized what they were. "Is that corn from Fredericks Market?"

Bob looked mock-offended and placed his hand on his heart, "Would I serve my favorite niece and the next big superstar from Jersey anything less than the best farm-raised corn in South Jersey?"

I was really geeked up at this. It was probably the greatest corn in all of Jersey, if not the world at large. I really, really like corn.

"Wow, I'm honored, Uncle Bob."

"Well, you should be. Old man Fredericks charges twice what he used to back in the day."

"I really appreciate you getting it. Don't think I'll get anything like it up in Boston."

Bob grunted at that, "Nah-nothing like them from those cats. They like to act like they invented seafood and America and everything else good, but whatever. You excited to go? When do you leave?"

I sat down at the picnic table that sits in the back corner of the driveway/backyard area. Not a lot of lawns at the shore so it was all concrete, but my feet were a little sore after plodding around all morning, so sitting down felt good.

"I have a ticket for the first train out of Princeton Junction tomorrow morning." I said, possibly without any general enthusiasm. Bob puttered with the steaks and the corn a bit on the grill. I could see Angie and her Aunt talking through the window behind him. The window was shut so I couldn't hear what they were saying, but it looked kinda like they were arguing. Angie saw me watching her through the window and I gave her possibly the most uncool wave that's ever been recorded in human history. She'd already turned and moved into the next room, her aunt following her.

I realized that Uncle Bob had said something and that I'd missed it. "Sorry, what?"

He smirked and looked over his shoulder. "Something in the kitchen caught your eye there, huh kid?" I think I stammered a bit as I didn't know what else to do before he continued. "I asked if you're excited to go tomorrow? Big city-good music scene, they say. Ah, the college life…" he let the last word linger a bit with a lack of enthusiasm.

"I don't know, I guess?" I replied, half expecting Angie to fly out the door and tell me not to answer with a question, but Bob was undeterred.

"Now, if I were you," Bob it seemed had given this some thought. He performed a dance of rare grace above the grill with shakers galore. Garlic salt and some personal spice things which were starting to smell amazing. Mom didn't cook a ton as it was, but she never cooked steak at all.

Bob continued with the spices on the grill while continuing with his thoughts. "If I were you," he repeated, again using his tongs as a pointer, "I'd skip college altogether and head out to Nashville or Austin or really even think about diving in hard in Philly or New York. One of these cities with a real vibrant scene and just give it a go there, man! Hell, if I were your age now, with all the tech there is now, I mean, Jiminy Christmas, what we could have done back then! We could have been way more than a bar cover band!"

Bob was wistful, but I could tell he was really sincere. I'd heard him share such ideas in the past. He started taking the steaks off the grill but still managed to gesticulate with his tongs while holding a slab of meat as he continued, "Man, you kids today can record a song, master it, put it online, burn a CD, email the MP3, you can do that all in the space of an hour, man! In my day, at best we could put something on a cassette if someone had a decent boom box and maybe make a few copies to sell after a gig, but the sound was crap unless we spent $200 an hour for a studio, which might not even have a four-track recorder, so it was all live to tape, and if we took more than one or two takes we'd run out of money or beer, either of which ended the night back then!"

He was chuckling but I knew he held some angst over the way things had gone in his musical past. He was a lot more serious about the music than his bandmates. Bob was actually an amazing singer and played a bunch of different instruments pretty well, but most of the guys he played with were Shore guys who were content to play for a free night of beers and then get back to work on other things the next day. I think his stories over the years were why I think I never really wanted to be in someone else's band.

It's almost too easy to make music and record it and get it out there these days. I was late to the party in terms of taking advantage of some the tech stuff, partly because we didn't have all the latest at home, although the new phone I got for graduation is pretty sweet. Much better than the flip phone I carried most of high school. I didn't record a lot of what I was doing as I figured pretty much all of what I was doing was crap anyway. I still do most days, but I figured I'd just keep playing and try to get better. But then Angie started recording my sets for me and showed me how to handle the digital editing and stuff. She's amazing with that and since I didn't grow up with a lot of electronics in the house I didn't know anything, but I get it now, thanks to Angie.

"I can do it all on my phone now, I think." I said, kind of to myself.

"Exactly! You have a complete digital studio in your pocket, man alive, what a world we've found here, huh?"

I shrugged, "I guess?"

Bob narrowed his eyes at me and pointed his tongs at me as though he were in the process of deciding whether or not I was messing with him, "You guess? OK, so you guess, but let me ask you this - with all that power in your pocket why not go jump into that world 'full go?'" He looked around a moment as though he was making sure no one was overhearing him. "Why spend money on college? Why not just get out there and see what's real? Go find a scene and blow it up, man?!"

I heard Angie's voice from inside the house in the silence that followed. I started wondering what she was talking about with her aunt, but I had Bob looking at me, awaiting an answer, so I gave him one.

"I thought about it."

"And?" he replied scraping off the now empty grill with a thick wire brush.

"Three things came to mind. First, I'd really have no idea what to do if I went to Nashville, or wherever. I've barely been out of Jersey yet, so I don't know enough to make that work out even a little bit. Second," I stood up now and paced a little, nearly decapitating myself on the clothesline. "I don't know that I'm a good enough musician yet. I just don't know enough about pretty much anything yet, so there's that."

"And third?" Uncle Bob asked, now holding a gigantic platter of delicious-looking meat and corn and headed towards the back door into the kitchen.

I turned to follow him. "Third, Mom doesn't think I know enough either, and wants me to fix that by going to school and, as she says, 'Go learn something so you can at least grow up and not rob me.'"

Bob laughed loudly, one of those laughs that makes me think of the Ghost of Christmas Past in that play version of "A Christmas Carol" that Angie took me to at the McCarter Theater last year. That guy had a belly laugh of pure joy and I've thought about how it would be cool to have a laugh like that or at least a reason to laugh like that.

"You think she means that last part?"

I shrugged again, "I don't know enough about that yet either, but I kinda hope she was kidding."

We walked into the house through the back door, which led into what they called a "mud room" before turning left into the kitchen where Bob puttered around with some kind of steak butter or something. He stifled his laughter, which had continued unabated, when he saw Jenny, who had a pensive look on her face as she walked past us. "She's in the living room," she offered and then kinda shooed me out of the kitchen. "We will dish up in a few so go sit down or something."

I could tell she was bothered by something, so I was all too happy to leave. I passed through the dining room with its dark wood paneling and rather silly nautical themed décor that had come with the house and joined Angie on the couch in the living room, which was probably my favorite room in their house. It was cool and airy and had these giant fluffy couches that felt like you were sitting on a giant bean bag chair made of velvet. Angie was sitting with her eyes closed on the smaller of the two tan monstrosities, so I sat next to her.

She stirred as I sat down and drew in a breath but then shut her eyes again and leaned her head on my left shoulder once she noticed it was me.

"So, what's Aunt Jenny's deal?" I asked, already feeling drowsy myself on the couches and feeling the quiet of the room, though I could still hear her aunt and uncle bickering in hushed tones from the kitchen. Angie just grunted and repositioned herself against my shoulder but acted as though she hadn't heard me. I was getting increasingly uncomfortable with the argument going on in the kitchen as it was starting to feel like I was intruding on some kind of family business going on and I really didn't know what to do about it, so I tapped her on the knee, "Um, Ange?"

She grunted, much like I imagine a congested koala sounds like. "Um, Ange, are you there?" I asked again.

There was a long pause before she answered, "There is no one here by that name at this time. Please try again tomorrow." And then she nestled deeper into the lean of my shoulder.

Sure, she was funny, but I wasn't ready to handle her family on my own. It was hard enough over the years hanging out with her parents, who, while I like them, well, they are really just a pair of genuine weirdos. Her mom is a late generation hippie and her dad could not be more the opposite, being the vice president of the Bristol Corporation, which has built or invented almost everything for like ever. Time spent at Angie's house was generally fine and awkward only when her parents tried to really talk to me. Or her sister-eesh! She's a piece of work.

Celia is five years older than us and had some challenges figuring out what she wanted to do with herself. She'd gone to college to study Chemistry, but then got interested in Law, and then Theater, and then Art Therapy, which she ended up being quite good at. With her penchant for changing both her mind and direction, I once offered that she ought to get together with Uncle Ted, but that suggestion was not met with a great deal of enthusiasm. Celia had stayed at home a bit longer than had been hoped for by all involved but ended up connecting with a medical group that offered occupational therapy to kids on the autism spectrum, among others. She brought her brand of art therapy to the group and really did some cool stuff. Angie and I helped her out a few times when they did Autism Awareness Fairs and stuff and she was really in her element. Angie thought her sister would live at home forever until she met Duncan, an equally awkward guy who raised ducks down in Salem County. They met at one of those fairs where he'd brought his ducks for the kids to interact with and they hit it off and are supposed to get married next summer. They talked about eloping to

Hawaii but who knows with them?

So, with all that in mind, I really didn't want to get lost in family drama. Celia was always nice to me and I only met Duncan a few times, but I figure if they make one another happy, good for them! There are enough miserable people out there so I'm not going to begrudge anyone who's found that someone who makes them happy.

I've never been comfortable with conflict, though outside of some of the girls I'd dated, I didn't face it a ton. Mom and I never really fought. We'd argue, but if we reached an impasse, we'd leave it until morning and pretend it never happened. Angie always gave me a hard time when I tried to do the same with any disagreements we had, which weren't usually huge or dramatic, but we've been friends for four years now so of course there were occasional 'bumps' as she'd say. She really pushed me when I tried to pull away and ignore the conflict. She was right, of course, but it's still something I have trouble with, the whole 'let's air our grievances and fight it out' kind of scenario. I spent probably too many years doing the whole 'let's pretend stuff didn't happen' thing to be fully clear of it.

"Aunt Jenny seems a bit disgruntled," I whispered. Angie again pretended not to hear me. I could tell as she chose that moment to start snoring loudly, like a leaf blower giving birth to a bowling ball. It was way loud, and she was clearly faking. "OK, quit snoring and tell me what's going on?"

Angie sat up as though suddenly refreshed. "Let's just say she's not on board with some of the choices that certain members of the family have recently made."

I heard something crash but not break in the kitchen and a sudden hush fell over what seemed a sizeable and for me, uncomfortable argument. I wondered if Angie was referring to her taking time off school in the fall, but I really had no clue, so I let it go for now. I could tell she wasn't in the mood to elaborate, but I wondered if there was more going on. I wasn't wrong.

Angie was still leaning on my shoulder and exhaled really long, like one of those "deep breaths" they used to encourage us to take in Guidance Counselor classes at school. After those school shootings and other stuff seemed to keep happening all the time they started doing a bunch of anti-bullying and conflict mediation stuff with us. They weren't all that bad, but they seemed to schedule them when I had a class I enjoyed, like music theory with Z or Jazz Workshop with Mr. Lawrence. I started talking about all of that when I noticed that Angie was completely and totally asleep.

She had kind of a goofy smile on her face, not at all dissimilar from the one she wore while she napped on our drive down to the shore from Windsor. She seemed really relaxed and I didn't want to disturb her so, with her aunt and uncle now bickering again in hushed voices in the kitchen I decided to just close my own eyes for a second too. I don't know how long we sat there but the next thing I heard was Uncle Bob's booming and enthusiastic voice calling out, "Whoa! We leave these two kids alone for fifteen minutes and find them sleeping together?"

I was startled and a little embarrassed and I stood up quickly, which left Angie to flump over onto the couch. "Ow?" she groaned.

Aunt Jenny followed her husband into the room muttering something like "…would do for a start…" which earned her a glare from Bob, so I figured they were still not done with whatever they were arguing about, though I didn't really understand what it was. I don't have a ton of experience being around married people, so I didn't pretend that I understood. They were carrying plates of food so I moved to help them when I heard a muffled voice, from deep within the pillows on the couch.

"A little help here?" Angie called. I turned around and saw her lying on her left side exactly as she'd dropped, a look of narrow-eyed menace on her face. "I was comfy…" she growled. I moved back to the couch too quickly and slipped and fell, landing flat on my back with a huge crash. Wind totally got knocked out of me and everything went quiet for a moment. I looked up at Angie and her face was at first a mask of concern but then began to morph into her "I'm really trying not to crack up at your hysterical discomfort and rapidly failing at it" face. I moaned, a little louder than was necessary before laying my head back on the floor.

"I'm OK, Ange, you can let it out."

The sound of restrained giggles sliding into a belly laugh culminating in her trademark cackle made me start to laugh too, despite the circumstances. I don't know how long it went on but I finally sat up and she sat up on the edge of the couch with her face in her hands, tears streaming down her face laughing at me. She started to lose steam a bit after a few minutes, then she looked at something behind me and smiled sheepishly, pointing a single finger over my shoulder. I turned to look, still sprawled out on the floor and saw her aunt and uncle staring at us, Uncle Bob looking amused and Aunt Jenny looking utterly appalled at our shenanigans. Jenny looked like she was about to say something and started wagging her finger at the two of us which, for some reason set Angie off again which got me laughing again. Bob took

Jenny by the shoulders and steered her back towards the table saying something like, "Let it be Jen, they're fine as they are," but I was too busy laughing again. I still don't know what made the moment so funny, but it felt good to laugh and made me forget about school and Angie's earlier meltdown and every other little thing that had been lingering in the air and just have a fun moment with my best friend. It made me remember why we came to the shore in the first place. We needed to have a good-awesome-spectacular day before I had to go.

Once we'd stopped laughing, the smell of corn and spiced grilled meat reminded me about the fact that there was food available. I stood and helped Angie to her feet and made a show of escorting her to her seat, affecting a deep British accent, like "Monty Python" thick.

"Your seat, Mademoiselle…"

"Enchante'," she replied, but she said it EN-chant-EEE like she was going out of her way to upset a Frenchman. She made a duck face with her lips and seemed about to do more before Aunt Jenny glared a bit and passed the corn, which caught my eye since it was my favorite thing on the table. The steak and all would be lovely, and the tabbouleh looked swell, but I am hooked on Jersey corn. I once scarfed down like eleven ears at Nana's one weekend a few summers ago. That was a lesson in gastric distress.

"Give that boy some corn before he drools on my tablecloth," Jenny said, rather dryly. She smiled a little but still seemed irritated. Angie passed me the corn and I happily helped myself to two of the bigger ears before passing the dish to Uncle Bob on my left. Jenny and Bob always sat next to one another, so I found myself at the foot of the table with Angie on my right. Plates made their way around and I ended up with a small steak and some shrimp and the tabbouleh salad. It was all lovely, but I was too busy tearing into the sweet delicious corn from Fredericks Market to notice that not only was I the only one eating but, everyone was presently staring at me.

Aunt Jenny cleared her throat. "Perhaps we might pray first?"

I'd forgotten that Jenny had started going to church recently and was taking it, as she did most things in my experience with her, very seriously. Bob, as he did with all things related to his wife, joined in and supported her without reservation. Everyone was holding hands and Angie and Bob were reaching out toward mine, Bob looking like he wanted to crack up but thought better of it and Angie looking like she felt a combination of irritation that I didn't remember about grace, uncertainty that she'd told me at all, and mild amusement.

I put the corn down and wiped my fingers. "Oh, wow, I'm really very sorry," I spluttered.

"It's fine dear. Bob, would you do the honors?"

Bob and Angie took my hands and bowed their heads. Nana did this sort of grace before meals too, but we never held hands. I noticed Angie's nails, which were the same color as her toes and how soft her fingers felt and then felt weird about it. Thankfully, Bob started praying.

"Dear Lord, please bless this food, in particular the corn, and help us always be mindful of the needs of others. And we pray especially for our guests today and their future travels and travails. Amen."

"Amen," Jenny said, and Angie squeezed my hand before letting go. I waited until everyone else started eating before I started up again, sheepishly I imagine.

Bob liked silence about as much as I did so he went and turned on their Spotify or Pandora or whatever system they had, and it seemed like small speakers all over the house came to life playing some sort of "cool Jazz" shuffle. I recognized a few tunes, but it was all sort of elevatory music. Background stuff, really. Bob noticed me listening and leaned over and half whispered, "It's all she'll let me play during meals. No words I might sing along to and no artists that I would start going on about…" He noticed Jenny narrowing her eyes at us both and he sat up, winking at me before booming into his next conversational topic.

"So, Jenny my love, did you know that our young man here leaves for the grand city of Boston tomorrow?" It seemed very much like Bob was trying to lead the mood of the room in a new direction and away from whatever he and Jenny were stuck on, which was fine, but it put the spotlight right on me and going to school, which didn't exactly thrill me.

Jenny glared at her husband and truly could not have rolled her eyes more dramatically. It almost looked like the effort could have tipped her over backwards in her chair if she weren't careful. She shifted her gaze from Bob to Angie and then to me, considering my eyes in a way that was actually kind of uncomfortable in like every way.

"Yes Bob, I know that he's leaving tomorrow, but does he know everything that's…"

"Aunt Jenny," Angie interrupted, kinda loudly, "Could you please pass the corn this way?" She was still holding Jenny's hand from grace and it was clear there something going on between them as they stared at each other and Angie did that thing where she stares at you and then raises her eyebrows for the "I mean it" emphasis. I didn't know what their deal was, but it was really awkward and I think I coughed as I said;

"You can have one of mine, Ange, if you want."

She held her aunt's gaze a moment more before

whatever was going on between them seemed to dissipate. They let go of one another's hand and Uncle Bob passed Angie the platter with the corn which it seemed she didn't really need since she already had one on her plate, but the awkwardness passed and I figured I'd let it go.

Anyway, I don't like uncomfortable silences so I kinda jumped on the grenade and dove into answering the question about school, which I really didn't want to do, but I wanted to answer it more than I wanted to sit with an awkward silence for any longer.

"Yeah, I leave tomorrow, first train out of Princeton Junction. It's, uh, yeah, that's what's going on for my going to school and stuff…"

There was an overlong pause as they all looked at me as though I had an onion growing out of my head, but Uncle Bob caught that I was both failing and flailing. He winked at me as he launched into a rant about the positives and negatives of Boston. I was grateful and went back working on my corn and steak and stuff until Bob returned his attention to the now.

"So, are you going to see some live music while you're here in Wildwood? My buddy, Shellie and his band are playing at the Anchor Inn later tonight! I told him maybe you'd stop by," his enthusiasm was overwhelming. "You could sit in with him if you want I think, his band has been around forever down here. Angela, you remember Shellie Bennett, don't you? You used to pal around with his daughter Courtney in middle school, before he and Fran split up and they went to live in Rehoboth?"

Angie replied with more enthusiasm than probably needed. "Of course, how is he? Wasn't he a dentist?"

Bob dove in with equal enthusiasm and launched into

a whole thing about how Shellie had lost his job as part of the Apollo Dental Team when the Lambrose family sold the practice and the building and it became a liquor store. Evidently, Shellie has started his own practice, but it was not going well and he was supplementing his income slightly at Wildwood Catholic High School by helping out with their Jazz Band. Angie tapped my foot with hers under the table and when I looked at her she was smiling at me. She seemed very content as I was digging into my second ear of corn. Bob was still going on about Shellie Bennett and his situation when I noticed Aunt Jenny was staring at me intently. I figured maybe I'd done something maniacal about corn again, so I instantly moved to try some of the other things on my plate, all of which were great. When I looked up again she was still looking at me, undeterred by my clever ruse, but now she looked sort of sad. I didn't get to think any more about it at the time as Angie suddenly kicked my foot. Uncle Bob had asked me a question that I'd completely missed.

I was about to apologize for not having heard, but Angie jumped in, tapping the table with her hand in the space between us, "Yes, excellent question Uncle Bob, I too have wondered if we've lined up any shows in Boston yet?"

"Not yet. I've messaged your pal Haywood to let him know I'm coming but haven't heard back from him yet."

Bob made a big show of pushing his empty plate away, "I'll call him now, he doesn't text or email or any of the new stuff." He was halfway out of his seat before he looked to his wife, whose eyes had locked him in position halfway out of his seat. He seemed to be stuck, waiting for permission to go out and play. She finally gave him a curt nod and he exploded into action.

"Thanks, Hun!" Bob kissed his wife as he ran upstairs

to call his pal, I imagined. I never liked talking on the phone much, except with Angie maybe, but Uncle Bob can talk all day about anything.

Aunt Jenny sighed, "Fair warning, Bob was up early this morning tuning up his acoustic guitars. All of them."

"Yay!" Angie said, kind of out of nowhere. Her face was suddenly a wash of happy I hadn't been ready for.

"Oh yes, my dears, I'm rather afraid that my husband is not going to allow you to leave our home without you playing with him."

Honestly, I by this point, I was kinda OK with it. Playing and singing never really scare me, which I guess is a good thing considering what I want to do. I'd been itching to play all morning as I missed my regular morning practice time because we were driving then. I've been putting in between three and four hours a day the last few months to get ready for school and had some cool stuff I'd been working out chord-wise, but they were just sketches then. It's weird, sometimes I can write a whole song in ten minutes and other times its months of plunking along.

"It's cool," I said through an ear of corn.

Aunt Jenny still seemed kind of sad or preoccupied or something. "You're very sweet to him. He's excited to see you spread your wings up in Boston. Been talking about playing with you all week-even broke out his old Ziggy Stardust wig!" She laughed a little, which was nice considering how morose she'd seemed.

"He did?" Angela cried, "Oh, he has to bring it down!"

"Oh, do I now?!" Bob cooed as he came back down from upstairs holding two acoustic guitars and of course, sporting a long, spiky blonde wig and a pair of the thinnest and goofiest sunglasses on Earth. It looked like he was wearing a stripe of electrical tape or a barcode over his eyes.

"All right lad, now is the time here down the shore when we boogie," Bob said in a slight German accent. "Oh hey, did you ever see that video of the astronaut doing Bowie's 'Space Oddity' from the International Space Station?"

I nodded while chewing.

"Well, we are going to show that guy how we do it on Earth-let's go!"

I left my plate, then turned around to clear my plate in the kitchen but Aunt Jenny waved me off, "Shoo-go play, boys!"

I joined him back in the living room, which previously been so dim and cozy that we dozed off but now, Uncle Bob threw open the shades and the windows, instantly bathing the room in light so bright that it looked like we had stepped in Oz.

"Oh, Bob, it's going to take days to cool that room off again," Aunt Jenny complained from the dining room, but she said it sweetly despite it all. "At least turn the fan on."

"Already on it!" Bob handed me an acoustic guitar, a newer Alvarez with an electric pickup, while he held tight to his Gibson, which I'd never been allowed to touch, much less play. It was a beautiful, deep mahogany color and the brass on the works shined like a new penny. He'd had it since he was a kid he said, but he'd never let me close enough to see if it was a real classic model or just a replica and he'll never tell. Regardless, it always played well. I was cool with the Alvarez, but I'd have been willing to give his Gibson a closer look.

"Check this out," Bob said, all a flutter. It was a little hard to take him seriously with the Ziggy wig on, but not so much more than usual. He pulled a small remote out of one of the seventy-eight pockets on his cargo shorts and made a big show of pointing at the ceiling fan, which promptly did nothing at all. He kept pushing the buttons to no avail. "Jen! The dadblamed remote's not working again," he called out to his wife, who was clearing the table with Angie.

"Try turning on the wall switch, Bob," she groaned.

Bob snapped his fingers, "Ah, yeah. Hey, get that switch for me, wouldja?" He was pointing across the room at a light switch with what looked like a hand painted message of 'Turn me on' and a smiling light bulb where its nose was the switch. I hit the switch and the fan immediately started up and rapidly achieved warp status, wobbling like a drunken top.

"Whoa, baby, whoa!" Uncle Bob cooed, frantically pressing buttons on his little remote thing until it slowed down. "That's good, baby, there we go…"

I was kinda used to Uncle Bob's affection for his toys, vintage and new, cool and silly, but I'll admit, this one was a little weird, essentially flirting with the ceiling fan, but whatever.

I sat down on the smaller couch by the window and started tooling around with the guitar. It was mostly in tune, so I fixed it up right and started playing around with a song I'd really been working on. I had all the chords down and a basic tune and progression, but the lyrics had been a problem. I had a sense it was going to be a song for Angie, but I was really having trouble figuring out how I wanted to start it. That first line would set the table for all the other ones. All I had just then was "There's a girl…" but up until then, I had nothing. Musically, it was pretty cool and different than some of the other stuff I'd done this year. It was minor key-ish all throughout except the chorus. It kind of groves along kind of restrained and all until it rises from Dm7 up to a full G chord for just a beat and then levels back down. Rolling rhythm and stuff, and I thought it would even go well with strings if I make any friends at school who could help me with that.

I'd had an idea earlier when Angie and I were walking through that garden near the lighthouse but hadn't had time to do anything about it so, since Bob was still playing with his remote-controlled ceiling fan, I dove into playing it and kind of humming the tune to myself. Some amount of time passed and as I played it through I started hearing some words come together in my head. I was suddenly really starting to feel it and pulled out my phone to start making a note of the words in my head when I noticed there were other people in the room.

Uncle Bob was sitting on his chair now, a brown La-Z-Boy recliner that had seen better days but was well-loved and worn. Angie was leaning on the wall between rooms looking at me with her hands over her mouth and an excited look on her face. Aunt Jenny was sitting at the now cleared table in the dining room where she'd turned her chair to watch as, I guess, I had kinda gone away for a little bit.

Bob held my gaze for a second and reached into a basket on the floor and pulled out a yellow legal pad with a ball point pen attached to it. Handing it to me, he made a "shush" gesture to Angie, who was wearing an expression I didn't recognize. She seemed both excited and perplexed at the same time and all at once. If that much can fit into one gaze, she pulled it off for sure. I was still puzzling the lyrics in my head and realized that I had something, but I didn't need the paper. I was also suddenly feeling slightly exposed with everyone staring at me.

"Hi, um, sorry?" I think that's what I said, and I started to stand up but Bob raised a hand toward me.

"That was hot, kid! You got it? Or do you need to write it down?" His eyes were wild and excited. I heard Angie sit down next to me, which startled me because I hadn't noticed her move.

"I've got it." I said, leaning back on the couch. Angie did the same.

"I really like that," she said. "What is it?"

"I don't know yet. Not quite done yet I think. Sorry, I didn't mean to blank out there," I replied. I was kind of embarrassed. It's one thing to get lost in the moment when it's just me, or even just with Ange or while performing, but in front of her family in their living room I suddenly felt exposed and self-conscious.

Angie leaned her head onto my shoulder again, "You never have to say sorry for that with me. I love it when you get lost in a song and I know you always come back. And you always bring something new with you and you're generally better off for it. It was nice to see it again."

I felt very silly then for feeling self-conscious and kinda irritated with myself that I maybe hadn't been showing her enough attention. If this was really going to be our last day together for a while, I didn't know that I'd shown her enough of a good time and I was a little confused about what she'd just said and Uncle Bob was still staring at us, so I figured I'd just dive in and ask her. "So, what does the lady want to hear?"

Without moving her head from my shoulder, she replied, "the gentleman already knows what the lady wants to hear, as does the Lady's uncle...."

I could almost hear Bob's teeth grind, "Not the Indigo Girls again?!"

Angie started to rise off the couch to fight it out with

her Uncle, who was groaning. I put my hand up to stop her, gently, but it landed directly on her left thigh! "Easy there," I said, "We will play it for you."

She sat back down and made a face at her Uncle but I felt a little weird. Her thigh had tensed for the moment I'd touched her. We'd always been really comfortable being near one another, even holding hands or arm in arm walking around anywhere, but touching her like that felt a little different for some reason. I figured I'd just surprised us both and since she didn't say anything I didn't either, but the whole thing made me feel sorta anxious.

"I'll play it for you on one condition" I offered.

Angie turned to me, "All right, what have you got for me, sweetie?" Her eyes were bright and her face was flushed, I assumed from her almost-battle with her Uncle over the honor of the Indigo Girls. I was all over the place just then, but I didn't respond right away because I seem to recall thinking again about her hair and having just basically groped her thigh. She bopped my arm again, "Hell-oooo" she laughed. "Anyone home?"

"Ah yeah, um, yeah! Uncle Bob and I will play it, but you and Aunt Jenny need to sing it!"

Bob started laughing, which filled the room and took the attention off of me and my dopiness, "Hey Jenny! Guess what the young rock star has you doing?!" he bellowed out to the next room, before Jenny sauntered in, coolly replying, "I'm in, and I'll take the high part, just like when Angela was little!"

That shut up Bob, which was a bit of a big deal in and of itself. Jenny came over to the couch and shooed us both over so she could sit next to Angie. Bob, not wanting to "sully his wig" removed it and placed it reverently on the end of the stairway handrail so that it now appeared a very small David Bowie circa 1973 was standing silent watch over the room. I found it both a tad creepy and oddly comforting.

Angela beamed at Aunt Jenny as she put her arm around her. Whatever their problem with one another was it seemed to have been smoothed over, so I just started playing the opening chords of Indigo Girl's "Closer to Fine."

Aunt Jenny made a show of putting her hair back off her face, like she was getting ready for a movie shoot. "Wait, I'm not ready!"

Bob picked up the chords too. It's a very easy song to play with words that poetically talk about seeking understanding of life and transition and the search for clarity. It's got a lot of words, though not as many as that dumb "American Pie" to be sure. "Well, you'd best get yourself ready Jen, because your cue is in three, two, one…"

Jenny nailed the start of the song and Angela clapped and hugged her Aunt with a level of emotion I hadn't seen from her in a long time, if ever I had. It seemed for a minute like she was tearing up but Angie doesn't cry at all really, much less about stuff like this. I was having fun in the moment so I didn't really think anything more about it when I started the second verse for them.

They joined in, doing their best imitation of the Indigo Girls tight harmonies before amazingly, everyone, including Bob called out the last line before the chorus, after which we were grooving as much as possible, rocking the whole song and Angie, still hugging her Aunt with one arm. She leaned into me while I was playing, and we laughed and sang it all the way through. By the time we got to the final repetition of the title, "Closer to Fine," everyone seemed exhausted. Some kids walked by the open windows and cheered at the end of the song, albeit a little half-kidding I think.

"And the crowd goes wild!" Bob cried out followed by "Drop the mic!" He then ran upstairs. I'm still not sure why. I figured we'd play more but Jenny, still humming the song, followed him upstairs, leaving us alone in their living room. The ceiling fan continued to swomp.

CHAPTER SIX

"Where did they go?" I asked. The whole thing seemed funny and a little weird. It was like they were running offstage to meet the limos after the final encore at Madison Square Garden or something.

Angie laughed until she snorted again, which I always love. I could have her laugh as a ringtone, I think, and be pretty happy.

"Who knows? They are a pair, aren't they?" She scooted over to the part of the couch vacated by Aunt Jenny and leaned back onto the arm of the couch and put her feet up on top of my thigh. I was still holding the guitar.

"What did Aunt Jenny mean about singing it when you were little?"

"They used to come and sing with me in the hospital," she replied as she settled into the couch like one of Nana's cats, stretching and flexing and nestling herself left and right and up and down until she sighed back into just the right position. The ceiling fan was still going but the room felt warmer. The sun really filled the room and it splayed a brightness that would really have shown dust in the sunbeam but I knew from experience that Aunt Jenny would suffer no dust in her home, especially with guests over, unlike Angie's mom. Angie's house often felt like a museum or library at an old university that used to be better and the occasional sunbeam often shed light on a level of texture that wouldn't normally be found in the air.

As we sat there, the sunbeam off the street-side window found Angie's hair. Seemed to be doing that all day now that I think of it. For some reason, I remember noticing her eyebrows, maybe because she seemed so relaxed in that moment. They seemed sleeker than usual. Kind of an odd thing to remember.

"I didn't know that, but it sounds like something they'd do," I replied after probably too long a pause.

"Yeah, I didn't understand most of the words back then, but that song always made me feel like at some point, I would be 'fine.' And then, one day I was."

She closed her eyes and shuffled herself deeper in the couch and exhaled mightily.

"Would you play something for me?"

"What do you want me to play for you?" I spoke softly for some reason. Maybe I was worried about disturbing her family upstairs. Angie stretched her feet out against me, kinda pushing me away a little bit as she continued her quest for the perfect spot on the couch.

"Would you play the one you wrote for me sophomore year?"

My initial reaction would normally have been to complain about that idea, but like I said, I realized I really ought to be trying a bit harder. That said, she was asking a lot. It was an old song that I hadn't played in forever with good reason.

"Oh, come on Ange, I barely knew how to play back then," I started fingering the guitar a little trying to both change her mind and also remember the chords to the song she'd asked about. The only time I'd ever played it had been when I shared it with her in her parent's basement on a Sunday afternoon in the fall of our Sophomore year. It was the first song I'd written for her.

"I don't know if I even remember the chords to that one."

She drove her feet into my legs, stretching out further on the couch and exhaling overlong. "You forget nothing, sweetie. I know it's old and we were so little then, but I love it anyway. A girl never forgets the first thing a boy writes for her."

I sighed, defeated. "Even if it stinks?"

"Even then."

"Especially then?" I asked, still not sure if Angie wasn't messing with me just a little. Her eyes, when they weren't elsewhere seemed to be on mine more than usual. I'm not sure why actually, but I just seemed to notice her looking into my eyes as we talked all day.

Angie dug her heel into my leg and narrowed her eyes at me. "Just play something for me then. Something just for me." Uncle Bob and Aunt Jenny were still absent, though Bob's ceiling fan still swomped and swomped about like a carnival ride. "Play me that song you were getting lost in earlier then," she said as she closed her eyes and nestled back into the couch.

I started playing through the same chord progression I had been messing with earlier and running the lyrics I'd come up with earlier through my head. As I played the chords she smiled and seemed to drift away a bit. Her hair was splayed out on the pillow of the couch which had an intricate hand-stitched flower pattern that I felt like I'd seen before in her parents' house. Her eyes were closed for a while and then they weren't, and she was looking at me expectantly.

It's funny, but once I saw her face and her hair and her eyes framed on that pillow, all flowery and stuff, I started finishing the new lyrics in my mind. Between that image and the time we'd spent at the lighthouse gardens earlier, the song kind of kept on writing itself. But, she'd asked about the old song so I moved into playing the tune for that one.

Back when I wrote it, I actually felt pretty good about it. It was the first time I'd started branching into some real thick minor/minor 7th chords. I stole the title from The Smiths "There is a light that never goes out," as I think it's a really good line but oddly enough, while I own a copy of their "The Queen is Dead" album, I never actually listened to the song before I wrote my version. It was in Mom's old LP collection that she finally just gifted to me last Christmas, and I remember it seemed like a cool sentiment. I finally listened to that whole album and it's a great song. I wrote the version for Angie sitting in the backseat of Mom's Tracer since it was really late at night and I didn't want to wake her up after a double shift at Jim's. She actually fell asleep in her bedroom for a change which is next to my room, so I knew she'd hear me if I kept playing inside. Not wanting to wake the neighbors, I sat in the car and played around with the Dm7 and Am chords and then Em leading to a drop to G, all of which I'd been learning from following the diagrams on that poster Nana gave me that showed the basic fingering for every chord in existence. I spent months working on learning them all, one after another until I started to figure out how they went together with the music in my head. This song was one of the first ones

I wrote, and it was old and kind of corny but I actually still kinda liked it. More than I was letting on to Angie at least. I always thought it should be a duet, a boy and girl trading verses. Still think that could work, actually.

Hearing the chords, Angie sat up a little and opened her eyes and drowsily smiled. "I know this one." The room was now warm and bright. We'd never been so on our own in this place before either. Other times we'd been here together it always seemed like a crowd of her family was about.

"I thought you might. And, the lady did ask for it…"

"You've suddenly become very accommodating," she offered with a suspicious look. "Perhaps I should have asked for something poppier?"

"I wouldn't push your luck, lady…" She drove her feet back into my thigh and did another full body cat stretch before settling herself back into the couch. Her skirt moved up a bit off her calf. She clearly noticed me noticing it and her eyes caught mine for a second before I looked away and started playing again to allow us to move forward. It had been a confusing day, but I could always seem to change the subject by playing a song.

"Welcome to my heart-I'm so glad you're here,
Please walk with me, there's nothing to fear.
Are you surprised at all that see? You're knee deep in all my dreams, such a part of me.
You say I'm familiar like a hand in a glove.
Who we are has taught me what it means to be loved."

The chorus kicks in here, and I dared a look over at her. She had sat up and crossed her legs beneath her, leaning back into the couch with a throw pillow on her lap. She was looking directly into my eyes as I started the chorus.

"There is a light that never goes out in me.
Born of hope for a better life, their gift to me.
And there is a love that never will die in us-
A love that I'd never known, until I found you."

The second verse is that one that, in a duet, the girl could sing to the boy.

"Please understand-I'm missing you too.
So many things here make me think of you.
I know now that I have locked up my words,
In my heart knowing what they were but not
Letting them be heard.
My dearest friend, such a part of me,
Remember I am by your side, for always.
And again, please remember all good gifts will
come in time. And while I'm in mind and in
your heart, remember that you're in mine."

And then the chorus repeats again. It's what it is, and when I finished Angie did her polite 'golf clap' thing but smiled really wide saying, "I like that one. It's not every girl who gets a song written for her you know."

"Thanks. I don't exactly remember you being really enthusiastic about it back in tenth grade when I first played it for you."

Faster than I would have thought possible she whipped the pillow at my head, which I ducked. Chagrined, she bopped me on the arm again. "Oh hush-I didn't like myself enough back then to understand why you would do something like that for me, much less how to react to it. We were both so silly and young!"

She suddenly put her finger to her lips as I was about to respond. I managed a "Hrm?"

She leaned in close as her eyes moved toward the stairs. "They are sitting on the top step listening to us," she whispered. I craned my neck and sure enough I could make out a pair of feet just atop the stairs. I heard them shush one another and Jenny started to giggle.

"They are kind of cute," I said, leaning back and looking over to Angie and found her really close to me. Our eyes met for a second. It was a strange moment as we were listening to her aunt and uncle laughing and shushing each other. It seemed like Angie was kinda staring at me a lot like that all day.

After what felt like an eternity but was probably only a few seconds she blinked and flopped back onto the couch, leaning on my arm. "It's OK kids, you can come on down…" she called. There was an odd rumbling and more laughing, but Uncle Bob and Aunt Jenny came back down. Since Bob had lost his Bowie wig, what remained of his hair was disheveled. I still don't know what their dramatic exit was all about, but they were always very silly and fun with each other.

"Show me the chords to that one," Bob said, guitar still in hand. "The lyrics are just precious-Jenny teared up and…"

"Bob, help me in the kitchen please?" Aunt Jenny almost sang as she walked straight through the room. I would never have pegged her as someone who'd be moved by a silly high school kid song, but her face did look flushed. Bob gently placed his guitar on the other couch and gave me an "I'll be right back" gesture before falling into line behind his wife. He was doing some sort of tiptoe walk behind her like she didn't know he was there, which was kinda funny.

Angie sighed before slapping my leg, "Ok my friend, we need to get going." She bounded off the couch, suddenly full of energy. "Thank you for playing that for me again." She looked for a second like she was about to say something more, but stopped. She raised an eyebrow and whispered, "You're going to have to put the guitar down."

I'd stood up but hadn't realized I was still holding the guitar and still fingering the chords for the new song, the one I was still, in that moment actually, writing in my head. That kind of thing doesn't happen all the time but when it does it's both cool and incredibly freaky. What was especially cool was realizing that I was really close to completing it and that maybe I could play it for her before I left for school. I must have made a face or something because she crossed her arms and cocked her head to the left, as if examining a statue or something.

"You're stuck in it again, aren't you?"

It's both comforting and eerie how well she knows me. I mean she always seems to know what's going on with me before I do. I wonder if maybe I've taken that comfort for granted.

I nodded, probably pretty dimly, "could I have five minutes?" I asked, sorta sheepishly. She didn't know the song was for her any more than I had when I started it all, but I felt like a tool asking her to wait for me. She made a show of looking at her watch as she walked into the kitchen, calling "Since you asked ever so nicely, you may."

I quickly sat back down and pulled out my phone, frantically typing in the lyrics to the new song that were swimming around in my head. It always felt better once I'd written it all down. It was all about Angie and a garden and stuff. I wasn't completely sure it didn't stink, but it came on lion-fast and was fresh from being in the lighthouse gardens and all the lighthouse stuff and then my impending departure and having just sang to her, so I guess all that led to this explosion. In a few minutes, I had it done and I kinda liked what I had.

It was a little strange sitting alone in her family's house, writing stuff. Like I said before, pretty much every time I had been here before there were loads of people around. It had been way too crowded at times and I remember we usually tried to get outside or walk around the neighborhood. I'd never noticed the pictures on the wall near the stairs before. Since I felt like I'd done what I needed to with the song, I found myself drawn to them. I couldn't look away, really. The pictures started at almost the bottom where the stairs met the floor and continued all the way to the right where the wall got larger with the height of the stairs. It was completely filled with photographs, some of them really old and black and white and whatever that ancient brown color is called. I stood up, gently placing Uncle Bob's guitar on the couch behind me and went over to more closely look.

It seemed like the oldest ones were on the far left and they got progressively more recent as one moved to the right. I was surprised to notice almost immediately a picture of Angie and me at the Prom all the way to the right about at my eye level and another one of us from Sophomore year sitting on the grass in front of the Mercer Oak at the Princeton Memorial Battlefield Park. It had been a class trip I'd actually liked. Angie was wearing her hoodie and making a weird face and I won't even describe what I was doing with my hair that year. It was just two years ago, but if Angie hadn't been next to me, I don't think I'd have recognized that I was even in the picture. As I looked through them all I saw more of Angie as a kid and her family and then the pictures began to get all Kodachrome and then black and white and some of the older ones almost looked like they were small paintings. It was strange seeing so much family in one space at one time, like it was at least 100 years of the same family, or well, Jenny's and Bob's I guess, but we didn't have anything like this in our house.

That thought put me back into song mode and I pulled out my phone and adjusted a few lines talking about time passing and how stuff grows or something, but I didn't muck with it too much as I felt like I had at least a draft version I could play her sometime soon. I figured I'd play around with it because I liked the music and I knew I needed to work something up special for that scholarship anyway.

I was still studying the faces of the people in the pictures when Angie came back into the room. She didn't say anything for a few minutes, seemingly looking at the pictures along with me before she noticed the one of us from Sophomore year.

"Look how young we were all those years ago," she sighed, leaning in to look more closely.

I agreed with her but balked anyway, "Ange, that was like two years ago. Not all that long ago really."

"But your hair is so, what's the word for it?"

"It was not my best look."

She bopped me in the arm again. I knew I was going to have a bruise. "You were cute despite the poofy hair phase." I was about to object but she seemed reflective, so I wisely shut that down. "A lot has changed in those two years."

A minute or so passed and then she said, "Speaking of which…" at the exact same moment I said, "Who's this dude?" while pointing a black and white photo of a man with a gigantic beard the hipsters would go silly over.

We then fell into a "What? No, you? Sorry-go ahead, huh? No, I'm good, you go." Yeah, it was like one of those dopey movie scenes in the RomComs that I've been dragged to over the years by Angie and every other girl in my life. It was really awkward, and I wouldn't have mentioned it at all except that that sort of thing had never, ever happened to us before, like ever. Angie and I always seemed like we were in sync when we talked and all of a sudden, we were stumbling over each other like, um, well, I don't know what like. Like people just meeting maybe.

"That was weird," I said, my hand for some reason still stupidly pointing at the picture like I was in one of those TV shows from the '80s or '90s that ended and caught the actors in mid-laugh or something as the credits rolled and they just seemed to stand there frozen.

"Yeah, a little bit," she offered sorta quietly before continuing, "Um, yeah, but who's that?" and she looked closer at the picture I was still inexplicably pointing at. "Oh, he's some great Uncle or something. Aunt Jenny? Who's the guy with the huge beard again?"

Jenny seemed to sidle into the room silently like she'd been waiting for her cue the whole time. "Which one now?" she asked, putting on her glasses. They were tortoise-shell and they aged her, but only a little.

"Ah, that is your Great, Great Uncle Claude, remember?" Jenny continued, removing her glasses and kneeling down in front of the photo. "He came over on the boat after escaping Austria. He somehow talked his way onto a ship leaving Liverpool for Philadelphia. After the war, he married your twice Great Aunt Jean!" She was clearly excited to be sharing it all. She pointed to the photo next to the one of Claude. "She was a dancer. Got a screen test from MGM and danced on Broadway with

Ray Bolger!"

"The scarecrow from the Wizard of Oz?" I asked with probably more excitement than was needed. I always liked his song. I feel like the Scarecrow a lot, I think, and it always seems to come down to the song for me.

"The very same. She was really talented" Aunt Jenny sighed. "She turned into a nice old lady, God love her. I remember her mostly from pictures though."

"She was so beautiful," Angie said in a soft voice, thoughtfully as she almost reverently touched the frame. Of course, with the way today was going, she made that comment at the same moment I remarked, "You look a little like her, Angie," which led to another awkward silence and my face getting flushed, again!

Angie pretended she hadn't heard me say that she looked like her beautiful yet dead great, great aunt, but I think she did. Aunt Jenny patted my shoulder as she walked back into the kitchen, shaking her head ever so slightly.

It was definitely time to go before I could say anything else embarrassing. Bob and Jenny almost immediately came back into the room. "Well kids, off to church," Bob exclaimed. Angie had mentioned they had some function at their church and had to head out and honestly, I was starting to feel like I was constantly tripping over myself and still wasn't sure why Jenny had seemed so snarfy with Angie earlier, but I figured it wasn't my business regardless of how awkward it had been.

Before I knew it, Uncle Bob had gripped me up in one of his bone-crushing hugs. "Now, you tell Shellie and the band that I sent ya when you get to the Anchor later. Don't be surprised if they ask you to sit in. Oh, and hey!" Bob exclaimed, an expert at interrupting himself. "I talked to Haywood up in Boston too. He tends bar at

"The Plough and Stars," over by Harvard. Ferlinghetti used to hang out there, you know, right?"

I didn't know what he was talking about. "Thanks-oof!" I grunted.

"You're gonna do great up there, kid!" he continued, suddenly side-eyeing his wife and growing quiet. "Listen, for real, whatever happens, stay true to you and keep in touch, you hear me?"

Angie's Uncle Bob could be a pretty intense guy most of the time, but I felt like I saw something different in him just then. He seemed nervous I guess like he was suddenly worried about saying the wrong thing, which never seemed like something he concerned himself with.

"Thanks Uncle Bob, for everything." I was really touched because he'd always been supportive and positive. His connection in Boston could even be helpful too as it's a huge city where I know exactly no one. His enthusiasm was always so infectious that I actually felt like I'd be OK.

Aunt Jenny traded places with Bob and soon he was twirling Angie around all over the sidewalk as we moved outside. Jenny's hug was tighter than I was used to. "Good luck, hon, really. I hope and pray for the absolute best for you, whatever comes, understand?" She looked at me kind of intensely as she moved away. "Whatever comes, we will be here for you, OK?" She looked like she was tearing up which surprised me.

"Thanks Aunt Jenny, I appreciate it, really" I offered, though honestly, I was kinda confused.

"Whatever comes, we are here." She let me go and walked back inside. Bob finished twirling Angie and I heard him say something about seeing her "next week" and then he too went inside, leaving Angie and me alone on the sidewalk. She ran her hands through her hair and seemed to be fixing it after all the twirling. It still had a windy look to it, but she stopped fussing with it when she looked at me.

"That was rather more emotional than I'd expected," I said as she walked over and took my arm and we headed back towards the boardwalk.

"Yes, I imagine it was," she replied, choosing of course to let it go at that, which is where it was left. She was initially on my right arm, closest to the street, but I switched places with her completely automatically.

Angie chuckled, "Do you actually know why you always do that?"

"Do what?"

"Always have to be on the street side when we walk together anywhere?"

"Because Nana told me to." She elbowed my side at that, but it was honestly the truth.

"Well, that is a satisfactory answer, but do you know why it's a thing?"

"Not really," I replied, which was true. I never argued with Nana and honestly, the stuff she was always telling me seemed to go over well with the girls I'd dated and others I'd just been friendly with, so I just did what she told me, opening doors, walking them to the door after we'd gone out somewhere, waiting until they got inside safely to depart, and the sidewalk thing. I never really thought about it.

"Well," Angie began, in full 'I-know-something-you-don't-know' mode. "The story goes that the gentleman, using the term loosely here, should always position himself towards the curb to shield the lady," she gestured grandly at herself here, "from any harm, foreign objects, or runaway carriages."

"I didn't know that."

"Well, now you do. I have always felt safe from runaway horses and their carriages when strolling with you."

That was actually kinda sweet. I sorta wish that I'd responded differently.

"What about out of control trolleys?" I asked. "Am I responsible for them too?"

Angie laughed a second but I could tell she hadn't wanted to. "Well, I don't see any trolleys currently installed pretty much anywhere but San Francisco, but yes, I imagine they would fall under the umbrella of 'all harm.'"

"What about rabid dogs?"

"Yep. You've gotta shield me."

"Mormons?"

"Rabid Mormons?"

"No, just Mormons. They are really polite but they knock on our door at least once a month."

"Well, if they meant us harm, which I doubt, then yes, you'd again have to shield me from said harm, of course. And I also should be able to reasonably expect protection from zombies, vampires, Sith, Golems, and of course any and all biting insects."

We'd covered a few blocks already and I could see the Ferris Wheel off in the distance. "Where are we headed?" The band that Uncle Bob wanted us to see wasn't playing for a few hours and again, we hadn't really spelled out an itinerary for the day beyond what we'd already done.

We were waiting on traffic to ease so we could cross the street towards Aunt Karla's Pancake House when the wind took her hair again. "Is it safe to assume you would like to go see Shellie's band later?"

"Well, you know, if you want to," I stammered, again distracted by her suddenly visible tattoo. "It's cool if you don't, you know, whatever is good."

"Relax," she assured me, "I think that would be fine, but…" and this is where she peppered in the 'I want something' tone of voice that I was all too familiar with.

"Uh, ok…"

"But," she continued as we made the crossing, narrowly avoiding being crushed by a Wildwood Linen Company truck, "I have someplace I'd like to go as well, and it's a bit of a walk and I'll need a nice young man to accompany me." She was smiling and while I already knew that I was going to go pretty much wherever she wanted, I've always loved our banter.

"Well, I don't know…my feet are pretty tired…"

Angie was not deterred in the slightest. "Did Uncle Bob mention that Dr. Bennett sometimes brings his 1980 Rosewood Ovation twelve string to gigs?"

Yeah, she had me at Rosewood, and she knew it. "So, where are we headed, my dear?" I asked, eliciting a satisfied grim from Angie.

"I would like to go to the Christmas Store."

This really wasn't a big deal to me either way. Like I said, I was pretty much down for anything that she wanted to do, especially if it kept me from thinking about leaving. But, I couldn't make it that easy for Angie.

"Why?"

"Because Christmas is awesome and so is the Winterwood store. I've loved it since I was a kid."

Angie's dad was a lapsed Jew and her mom was an Episcopalian, but regardless they only really celebrated the holidays her mom liked. They weren't overly active with any church or Synagogue, but they did both Hanukkah and Christmas to a degree. Far more than I was used to in my house for sure. I'd spent the last few Christmas Days with Angie and her family and they threw a fun party on special occasions. She never really seemed overly interested in the holiday though, so this was kinda new.

"Is the store even open? It's August."

"Oh, ye of little faith. Stay close to me and I'll not let you get led astray."

"Huh?"

"It's open year-round, sweetie. And watch the tramcar."

With that all apparently decided we crossed Pacific Avenue and I could see the big convention center in the distance. The boardwalk seemed a lot more crowded than it had earlier. The tramcars were rolling back and forth blasting their robotic "WATCH THE TRAMCAR PLEASE" and carting tired beachgoers from one end to the other. It really had turned into a gorgeous day-sunny but not blazing hot. I like it warm but really can't stand it when its super-hot and the air feels like you're trying to breathe Nana's Split Pea soup. Angie reveled in the heat, completely wilted in the cold. I'd tried to pin down when she'd come visit me in Boston and she'd bemoaned the cold weather, even though I'm pretty sure they have almost the same weather as Jersey most of the time. She said we'd try to plan something once I'd settled into life there. She didn't want to "barge in" and get in the way of me getting to know my suitemates and what not. Maybe she's right. She's generally more thoughtful than I am and considers things from a long-term perspective way better than I do. I'm working on it. I was still kinda shocked that she was taking time off from school herself, but she'd said her piece about that and it wasn't worth revisiting. I still felt like I didn't fully understand, though.

CHAPTER SEVEN

As we climbed the steps up to the boardwalk the noise was rich and enveloping between the arcades, the rides, the carneys barking to come win a prize, the speakers blaring a loop of Bobby Rydell's "Wildwood Days" song while advertising a number of things, including Shellie's gig at the Anchor Inn later, and of course, the Tramcars. My favorite part was when the driver pressed the warning button over and over to get someone's attention and the affect was something like scratching. Wa-wa-wa-watch-the-watch-the-wa-wa-wa-watch the tramcar p-p-p-p-lease…" I'm amazed no one has made that into a hip-hop song yet.

The carneys were relentless. The one at the balloon dart table practically tackled us as we walked past. I'd always stunk at those games and the prizes were dopey, though Angie claims to have seen people actually win stuff at them. I watched a thing on YouTube a while back where they explained how each of them are rigged-the basketball hoop is like 15% smaller than a regulation hoop. The baskets are angled in such a way that the balls won't land without a certain degree of spin, that sort of thing. Struck me as kind of sad and like I said, I'd never seen anyone win anything, but Angie clearly spent a lot more time here than I did. She kept a jar of Wildwood sand in her room back home. I asked her about it once early on in our friendship and she displayed it proudly like she was holding the Holy Grail or something.

"This is the sand that I played in as a child."

At the time, I really didn't understand it at all, but I'm starting to.

We were headed north again so we of course passed Madam Marie, for what would be the second of three times all day and she was busy ushering a young couple into her parlor, much like she had with us earlier. I'm convinced that she raised an eyebrow at us as we passed. Angie exhaled in a manner that made me think she was about to run out of air. She emitted a low, almost guttural sound at the end of her breath.

I knew better than to ask again. She seemed to pat my arm ever so slightly in silent appreciation, but maybe I just imagined it.

We passed by the Boardwalk Chapel not long after Madam Marie's and they were open and a guy with a guitar was singing about Jesus while several senior citizens played tambourines, a middle schooler apparently was playing drums, not badly actually. A few teen girls gave their best effort at singing harmony to a song that had to be called "Jesus is Real" since that's what they were singing over and over.

I shouldn't have, but I stopped to listen for a minute. I just can't resist live music. I once got in trouble with Mom because I missed curfew because I was talking to a street performer in Philly after doing an open mic at the Tin Angel. Maybe I should have let it go this time, but I was compelled.

The chapel itself was covered with sun-faded bible verses and inspirational quotes, but I focused on the singers. They were very, very earnest as they sang about how they felt, all over their bodies that "Jesus is real!" The guy playing the guitar could play ok and they were all clearly having a blast performing together. Now that I think of it, maybe that was as much what drew me to listen as anything else. I always felt like I wanted to make music with others and so if nothing else, I admired how much this group was enjoying being together.

I could feel Angie gently leading me back towards the boardwalk. I probably should have followed her because the next thing I know, since we'd been standing there for half a song, one of the young, spotless church talkers came up assuming we were interested in the church. He had pamphlets. I don't like pamphlets.

"God bless you both this fine day! I'm Andrew. Would you like to come in and join us for worship?"

He was so clean that he glowed. His teeth probably took AAA batteries at the very least to reach their full level of radiance. He wore a T-shirt that featured a pair of praying hands and the words "KING OF KINGS" emblazoned on it. Angie was actually pulling my arm now, subtly still but insistently as she affected a smile toward our new friend. "No, I think we're good for now, thanks, Andrew."

Maybe I should have let her lead me away. Honestly, it wasn't that big of a deal but what happened next was a bit of awkwardness that maybe the day didn't need. Maybe it did, though.

"So," I started, way louder than was needed. Maybe all the talk with Angie earlier about Father Pavla and the way that church treated my family had put me back in mind of all that negativity, but I found myself ready to argue, just a little. "That song they just finished, I'm assuming it's called 'Jesus is real?'"

Andrew smiled, which nearly blinded the boardwalk and half the beach, and raised his right hand like he was swearing in to testify at a trial. "Amen-Jesus is real, indeed! I'm so glad that it seemed to touch your heart." He seemed to exude positivity from every angle. Angie had now put her arm around my waist and tried to direct me away, to no avail.

"Um, dear…we'll be late for the thing…you know…"

"Oh, yeah, but I have a question for my new friend Andrew…"

Angie dug her nails into my side but I didn't budge. "Please let it go?" she sighed, and I should've maybe, but I didn't. Andrew, for his part was a picture of helpful politeness, even when I asked him and my inner snark made a sudden outward appearance.

"So, Jesus is real?"

He absolutely beamed, both hands up in praise formation, like a touchdown. "He is! Praise God!" He was so excited and looked like he wanted to hug me until I continued.

"So, how about you prove it to me?"

Angie rather quietly removed her arm from my waist and seemed to float a few steps away from me. Actually, I think what she said was "Oh, Jesus," as she moved away, which is kind of funny.

The band and singers had moved into a different song now with one of the teenage girls singing. Andrew had taken a slight step back at my reply, which I hadn't offered in a particularly kind and inviting voice. He remained engaged with me and showed no sense of unease. "Prove what?" he asked, losing none of his charm and effervescence.

The girl on stage singing was younger than us but had a very nice voice and the song distracted me. She was singing, "Your river runs with love for me" and something about a "healer set me free."

"Um, prove that Jesus is real?"

Andrew took a breath. He wasn't that much older than me, but I imagine arguing theology on the Wildwood boardwalk could be taxing to people of all ages.

The older folks with the tambourines seemed to have found a new gear and they were really hammering away. Most of them had their eyes closed and were swaying mostly in unison. People in the audience, though congregation is the better word, were swaying too and raising their hands. Some of them were holding hands in the air and I found that at least a full minute had gone by where the music, or something, seemed to be getting in the way of whatever battle I'd been looking for there. I realized that I hadn't been listening to Andrew's response, so I looked around for him and found that he hadn't moved at all. Angie was still behind me but apparently, I'd moved forward toward the stage and into the chapel, closer to the music and whatever it was that was happening there. He smiled. Angie looked uncertain. I know she was thinking I was about to flip out or something, but everyone was singing the chorus now, "I could sing of your love forever! I could sing of your love for-ev-eeer…" and they were smiling and holding onto one another and they just seemed happy and, well, kinda at peace.

Honestly, it was a very strong power chord song and they played it well. The congregation seemed to know it and liked singing it, so they sang enthusiastically. It was a communal moment of music that came off huge in that little chapel and it got louder the further in I walked. It felt like it was bigger on the inside and I was inexplicably enveloped by the sound. It felt like I was at a stadium and not at a storefront boardwalk chapel.

In truth, it seemed almost like every person present was having their own concert within themselves but at the same time they were sharing it with everyone else. The girl who was singing lead on the song was suddenly joined by two of her friends who were bouncing around like it was an old school mosh pit and they sang together like they'd waited all night to do so. They were good together and spiritedly sang the lines, "Oh I feel like dancing, it's foolishness I know, but when the world has seen the light they will dance with joy like they're dancing now!" And then they went back into the chorus of "I could sing of your love forever…" which they repeated a number of times.

When the song ended with a simple extended D chord, the tambourine corps got out of their seats and shook their stuff with all their might and the girls singing seemed to be having fun and the people in the seats were out of their seats and they were all one big group together through music and something else and in that moment, I wanted to be something like them all. I don't know if they drew anyone else in from the throngs on the boardwalk but when they were done, I clapped, loudly and while I was clearly out of my element, their music had grabbed me, and I had just let it.

"That right there is all the proof I need," I heard Andrew say as he appeared next to me. "Each and every second of the last five minutes is all the proof I need to know that Jesus is real and God is working though us all. And if I may say," and he put his hand on my shoulder and looked me straight in the eyes, "God clearly has something to say both to and through you."

I know that I started the conversation with him looking for an argument, but I didn't find one. I really didn't know what to say. I'd felt something but didn't have any idea what to do with it. I'd spent eight years singing church music at the Academy and it had done nothing for me inside. "That's a damn good song," I offered and gratefully, I felt Angie return to my side and take my arm.

Andrew smiled benevolently at us as he replied. "It really is a lovely song and they know at least two others. Well, three if you count 'I Just Wanna be a Sheep,' but that's really just for the children. Would you like to visit with us a while longer? I could show you around?"

That song had clearly been their closer as the band and singers all came off stage. The girls who had just been singing ran out onto the boardwalk and down to the beach. The tambourine brigade stayed where they were but they all seemed on break. One of them had dozed off and dropped their instrument, causing quite a stir and once the music stopped, whatever it was that had gripped me seemed to ease, but didn't fade altogether.

Angie moved her hand onto my shoulder and patted it as she asked, "Would you like to stay?"

I couldn't tell what was in Angie's eyes when she asked me that. Was she just grateful I didn't make a scene? Was she confused that I'd reacted unpredictably? I don't know, but I felt like there was something else besides the music drawing me into that moment, but, I need to be careful after what happened with Mom and the church.

"I think I'm good for now, but…" I reached my hand out to Andrew. "Thanks for…well just thanks, I guess."

Andrew clasped my hand and pulled me in for a "bro-hug" which is not my favorite thing in the world. He even pulled Angie into it as well. "No, no-thank you! Thank you both for opening your hearts and minds today. You're both always very, VERY welcome!" With that he let us go and smiled, again nearly blinding us in the process and walked over to chat with the tambourines.

It was a few minutes after we had meandered out of the Wildwood Chapel before Angie spoke.

"Hey," she said, her eyes squinting as they adjusted to the bright sunshine.

"Hey," I replied.

She waited another few minutes before responding. "You OK?" She was still holding my arm. It felt like we'd been connected all day.

"Yeah, I think so," I said as we kept walking for a little while. Eventually I just kinda blurted out, all at once: "OK, I don't really know what to make of what just happened there, Ange. I don't know, what that was about? What does it mean?" My voice raised a bit, but it was so crowded that no one really seemed to notice.

Angie steered us towards a bench and sat down facing the ocean. We were just past the first pier and the "shoot a bucket of tennis balls" attraction was in full force making repeated "thunk" sounds as people shot the balls at targets and a group of floating things. She tucked her legs underneath her on the seat and turned her body toward me with her head resting on her hand along the back of the bench. "Would you like my advice?"

"Clearly," I said coolly. She groaned. She hates it when I answer her like that.

"Honestly, my advice is not to make anything of it at all just now. It happened. You had a moment there so, take it as such and reflect on it and see where you end up with it later on." I listened, nodding. It made sense and was good advice, but I could sense more coming as I turned back to her after staring out at the ocean. She was smiling, like almost giddy but holding it inside.

"And?" I asked.

She made that face she does when she shrugs her shoulders and scrunches up her eyes as if to say, "OK. Ya got me..."

"Well, I am really glad that there was no, um, well, ah..."

"Unpleasantness at the chapel?"

"Yeah, that," she said, patting me on the back. "You impressed me sweetie, and I don't really know what to make of it either, but: you know the best part?"

I shook my head as she continued.

"It's OK to not know."

She was right, and I felt like I was ready to let it go too. I reminded myself that we were supposed to be having fun on our last day before I left for Boston, so I stood up quickly and held out my hand to her.

"You're right. But you know what's not OK?"

She tilted her head and narrowed her eyes at me. "What's not OK?"

"The fact that I have no idea where this Christmas store is! I'll need your help finding it..."

She took my hand and we started back towards the north end of the boardwalk. All of a sudden, she slowed down and said, "Hold on, I need a minute."

I turned and noticed that her face looked a little flushed. "Are you ok?"

"Oh, I'm fine, but we are doing this walking thing all wrong!"

"Angie, what are you talking about?" I was starting to wonder if she was getting dehydrated or something, but then I saw her grin.

"I think we need to walk like this," she said, and began to walk with an exaggerated leg kick every third step. So that's what we did, laughing the whole time. We've always done silly very, very well.

CHAPTER EIGHT

The next thing I knew we were standing in front of a pair of giant toy soldiers with "Rocking around the Christmas Tree" emanating from tiny speakers in between the soldiers' feet.

"Winterwood! We've made it at last!" Angie cried dramatically.

"Um, Ange-we walked for like five minutes. It's a lot closer than you made it seem."

"Yes, but we've finally arrived!" She swooned and leaned up against the toy soldier on the left.

"I think I can see the car from here, actually."

She bopped me on the arm again, "OK, enough of that, let's go!" She dragged me by the hand through the door and that was where the assault on my senses began.

"Merry Christmas!"

What looked like an actual elf almost yelled those words with a level of enthusiasm I don't think I'd seen since kindergarten share time. As it turned out, it was really just an enthusiastic teenager in an elf suit, but Angie was all up in the spirit.

"Oh, yes! Merry Christmas to you!"

It was weird, they had adjusted the shades inside to make it look as though it was still sort of dark and snowy outside, but of course we knew it was still August in New Jersey out there. I was curious.

"So, how'd you all do that?" I asked, pointing to the windows.

Both Angie and the elf guy, who's nametag identified him as "Eddie the Elf" gasped and looked at me in horror. Eddie spoke first.

"My good Sir, it is the magic of Christmas itself that lights the festive fires of not only our hearts, but also the fire of the festive décor here within!" He said it like "daaaaay-cor" almost like that Day-o song.

Angie took my hand, more gently than she had all day. Her fingers intertwined with mine, which was different. We didn't usually do that, but I didn't get to think of it much as, our new best friend Eddie chimed in:

"Shouldn't we all embrace the spirit of the season, if not," and he paused dramatically, "the magic as well?!" Eddie the Elf finagled his extremities in what I can only describe as "Jazz hands" and "spirit fingers" had a baby.

I could tell by the way she was squeezing my hand that this mattered to her a lot so of course, I agreed. Eddie became our personal shopper as he escorted us throughout the store, which was way more extensive than I would have thought from the outside. He made a show of picking out just the right green shopping cart. "It brings out the diamonds in the lady's eyes..." he said, tossing his scarf back over his shoulder. Angie was eating it up.

"Well, back home, in the North Pole, we have real icicles all year round, but here, down the shore, tinsel is all the rage!"

"Tinsel?" I groaned I didn't mean to, it just kinda came out. Nana had bought one giant package of tinsel in 1967 and it was still around her house every year at the holidays. Every now and then I'd find a piece on a winter coat or a sweater. It got everywhere but I'm not so sure it bothered me at all, really. That did not stop Angie from bopping me in the arm again.

"Hush, troglodyte."

Eddie was aghast. "Well said, Miss…um…"

"Angela," she said, demurely, and then snorted a little. She was clearly all up in her glory and walked off with Eddie the Elf to look at different varieties of tinsel, which I didn't know existed.

I felt a little jealous, not that she went off with the elf guy but that he'd made her laugh to the point of snorting. That was my thing, but since Angie was having fun I shook it off. By the time I caught up with them I found the cart full of ornaments, tinsel and a few Santa hats, traditional and one that was Philadelphia Eagles green, and a pair of tall twin elves holding lanterns.

"Angie, what is all this?" I asked. It was way more than I had thought she was thinking about when we came in here.

"I told you, Christmas is great, and I've decided to make this Christmas a most especially splendiferously good one. I want to enjoy my time away from school and I'm looking forward to this!" Her voice didn't get louder, but she was clearly taking this seriously. While it seemed sort of impulsive to me, I could tell it wasn't to her. I didn't understand it, which bothered me, but I figured this was one of those times where it was a better idea to listen. Angie was holding the cart a little tight as we continued meandering through the store. I only noticed this because I offered to take it over for her as I heard

Nana in my mind, saying "Why should the young lady have to push that when there is a young gentleman there to offer help?" She wasn't letting go though.

"I've got it, sweetie, but, as I was saying, I just want to focus on my own life and family and I feel like it's time to really, really overdo Christmas this year. So many years I was too wrapped up in midterms or the SAT's or whatever, and so much is changing for us as it is already, so many things are in flux. At least I know that the holidays will be epic because I plan to make them so."

This was Angela in a way I'd never really seen her in our four years together, and it threw me.

"Angie, what are you talking about? I don't understand." She paused in thought as we came around a bend in the aisle that opened up into a large display area. Her entire face lit up and she started tapping my arm rapidly.

"Oh, my God, look at that!" she gasped.

Eddie the ever-so-helpful elf, appearing as if from thin air, gasped right along. "It is goooorgeous, isn't it?" he agreed in his kinda nasally drone. I'm convinced he had a deep bass voice that didn't match his rather waifish appearance in real life, though he never shared it with us. "It took us days to put it together. I oversaw the reindeer." He grinned and looked at us eagerly, expecting us to shower him with compliments, which in this moment were not forthcoming as Angie was completely transfixed.

Spread out on table before us was what looked like an old Victorian home in miniature completely decked out for the Christmas holidays. The level of detail was staggering! Every room in the interior of the house was complete with furniture, people, Christmas trees and garlands, presents, even Santa on the roof with his sleigh.

It was four feet high and even had a small terrier eyeing the cookies left out on the mantle.

"This is amazing," Angie finally said after gaping at the house for a long while, circling the table and looking at every detail. "My Gram told stories about a house like this! She had one as a little girl. I can't imagine it was as grand as this, but I remember she used to tell me every year about how her Papa would help her decorate the 'Christmas house.' Every year he would bring something new home to add to the house. How each year he saved up to buy one more thing to make the house 'more like a home' she said. It was my favorite story of hers. She used to spend all year wondering which room would be upgraded! She'd give hints to her Papa about where she'd like things to improve, but she said he always had a different idea and that she loved it every time."

Angie's eyes were welled up a minute, until she started to laugh, pressing her fingers to her eyes in that way that people do when they are trying hard not to get caught getting emotional. I didn't call her on it.

"I haven't thought about the Christmas House in years!" She'd abandoned the cart and continued circling the table several more times before 'ol Eddie piped in.

"Well, you know, my friends, it is available for purchase, both as you see it here, completely decorated…" he offered with great enthusiasm before continuing, "Or, as a basic house set too," with far less gusto and a half frowny face.

Angie didn't take her eyes off the house but did lean her hand back on the cart as she asked, "How much?" My head began to swim a little. Angie is the most responsible person I know, and while she can be prone to moments of silly impulsivity, she's never been frivolous with money. I didn't know what it cost but it looked way out of my league, anyway.

Eddie was clearly excited as his hands started doing something that looked like a wave. I don't know if they work on commission at that store, but it was clear he was motivated.

"Well, since you asked, what you're actually seeing displayed here is the 'Basic Victorian Home' project set combined with several accessory packages both traditional and holiday-oriented. Plus, this set has the labor already included, plus, Winterwood will bring it all to your home and set it up for you for a one-time low price of $900. Financing is also available through our central office at a very reasonable…"

Angie was shaking her head and her finger about halfway through his pitch, but she allowed him to finish. "Ah, yeah, it's lovely, but that's simply too much. Plus, I want to build it myself." Her voice remained as plucky as it had been, but I could sense a little deflation in her demeanor. She grabbed my arm, "We could build it together, when you come home for Christmas! How much for the basic house?"

"Well," Eddie began, looking a little deflated, "the basic house set is $115 and we recommend at least one accessory starter pack for new builders and they range from $25 for the Kutz brand sets to $50 to $75 for the much nicer Parker line."

Angie looked over her cart, which was already full of stuff and I could see her mathematical brain doing its thing. I couldn't help myself as I did some money math myself. What things cost and tip percentage are about the only math I could manage.

"Ange-that's a decent amount of money in the cart already, maybe you should think about this?"

But she'd already decided what she was going to do

and pulled out her silly purple old-lady change purse. I'd given it to her for her sixteenth birthday after seeing it at the flea market in Englishtown. I'd meant it as kind of a gag gift because it looked just like the one Nana used, but Angie loved it.

"Eddie my friend," Angie started, "Let's make you elf of the month! Ring up that house for me!"

Eddie clapped his hands and hugged Angie quickly, before heading towards the register after placing the Victorian house set and a random accessory kit in the cart. As he walked away I heard him mutter under his breath, "Take that, Tommy Frangione with your perfect hair and dimples," while subtly pumping his fist. I was about to say something, but she swung the cart around to follow Eddie and was virtually skipping to the register while humming along to "Christmastime is Here" from that Snoopy movie.

"So," Angie bemoaned over-dramatically, "Now I have to wait for you to come home at Christmas and we can do this together?"

I stammered something like, "Um, yeah, unless I..." but she interrupted me, laughing.

"Relax, sweetie. It'll be worth waiting for. All good gifts are, they say."

She got a little quiet after that and it wasn't until we arrived at the counter that I understood why Eddie was so excited. Resplendent in his holiday cheer, I caught him gazing adoringly at the "Elf of the month" display on the wall behind the registers. I had thought Angie was being funny earlier as I didn't know that the "Elf of the month" was an actual thing.

"Now Eddie, we're going to do this as two transactions if you please," Angie offered as she rearranged the items in her cart. Eventually, everything besides the house thing was on the belt. She'd found the "accessory" set that Eddie had tossed in, which was the Santa one with the Reindeer and placed it aside without commentary. Angie misses nothing. "I'll be paying cash for all the small stuff," which still amounted to over $73, "and then I'd like to put the rest on the card if that's acceptable?"

"Not a problem, young lady, it's all good!" His "elf" persona seemed to wane a bit in the moment of sale. Once the cash sale was all done, he rang up the house, which came to $120.42 with tax.

"Yikes," I said. To me, that was a lot of money, but Angie took out her MasterCard, which her parents gave her for emergencies, but she'd occasionally used it for other things and hadn't gotten in trouble over it. Knowing her, she would be able to justify anything as an emergency and they'd buy it. She's just smarter than all of us and always has been. It's comforting, actually.

"This is all very exciting," Angie blurted out as she leaned her head on my shoulder. "My mom is going to flip when I show her this in December."

"Well sure, every girl needs a doll house, right? Especially at Christmas?" I was trying to be encouraging but the amount of money being exchanged was a little outside what I was used to. I knew that this meant something to Angie but honestly, I really didn't get why at the time.

Eddie completed the cash sale and was gleefully running the credit card for the house when he suddenly made what can only be described as the dopiest frowny-face ever. "Miss, I'm sorry but the card was declined," he whispered as he placed the card on the little check-signing table.

Angie's face turned red. "Really? It's the end of the

month but, um, hey-could you try it again, please?"

Eddie didn't roll his eyes, but I could tell he wanted too. "Of course," he said, but after a minute he shook his head and handed the card back to her. "I'm sorry, miss. Perhaps your young gentleman would care to help out here?"

Before I could reply that I couldn't, Angie sprang into action. "No. It's OK. I'll be fine," she said really tersely as she gathered the bags of stuff that she paid for and began moving towards the exit.

"Angie, wait!" I called. "Maybe call the card people or your folks or something?" She was mad and I knew it. She stopped short of the exit and I could see her shoulders sag a bit.

"No, it's really fine."

To which I asked, "How do you figure?"

"Sometimes, my friend," she began, "things don't happen the way you want them too because they just aren't supposed to." Her voice seemed suddenly so sad and it had been such a sudden turnaround from her goofy excitement earlier. She'd been all over the map today for sure. "This is just the universe telling me 'not now.' Who am I to argue with the universe?"

I had to let that sink in for a moment. There was a lot of kinda heavy things being left unsaid so far: leaving for school, Angie taking time off, entering a world without high school people in it. There was a lot in our heads. I didn't even know the whole of it then either.

"I didn't know that you and the universe talked." I teased, trying to make her laugh or at least smile a little. I don't think it worked.

"Well, I've had a lot to say to it lately and I suppose this is how it's getting back to me."

I was flummoxed and starting to think that the whole

day might be going down the tubes, so I reached for the first thing that popped into my head. "Would it help if I told you that you're pretty?"

"What?"

I think I cleared my throat and I'm sure my face turned red, but I figured that I had to do something, so I pressed on. "You said that girls like it when you tell them they're pretty."

She looked both confused and amused at the same time as she asked, "When did I say that?"

"Prom?"

"Ah, yes. Well, you were listening, so that's good. It's not exactly germane to the topic just now, but I suppose we could try."

Angie leaned her hand back on a display case with a whole collection of Santa mugs within. She looked at me like she was studying my face or something like Madam Marie had earlier. "Well? Let's have it then."

I'd kinda thought that I'd already actually done it, but then it became clear that I was now expected to do a thing about it. So, I did. I made a scene of looking at her from different angles, like I was examining someone and making a grand realization.

"Hey," I said way too loud after I'd taken way too long, "know what?"

"What?!" she snapped, irritated. I may have miscalculated my efforts to be funny and she was peeved. So, I stopped clowning and looked her in the eyes and said, "Angie, you're really very pretty." I couldn't quite read her reaction but eventually, she looked away.

"Well, I guess that does actually help a little."

We were right near the exit and I noticed that they had a crane machine with small stuffed Santas in it, and that gave me an idea of how to move forward. I could still feel

111

Eddie the Elf glaring at us from a distance, his dreams of Elf of the Month dashed by Angie's card malfunction, but he was keeping his distance. Periodically though we'd hear another elf greet a new arrival to the store, and the enthusiasm would be overwhelming until they either bought something or did a lap and walked out.

I reached into my pocket and pulled out a single dollar bill, which wasn't hard to do as I didn't have an abundance of them left. "I might not have 115 of them in here but I'll bet you I can turn this single dollar bill into Christmas magic."

Angie still looked like she wanted to leave and looked over at the door as another couple entered the store and were set upon by two aggressive elves who I suppose didn't know who's turn it was. "Is that so?" she asked.

"Yeppers-one bit of magic coming right up!" I replied, "No elves required." I walked over to the crane machine, which was one of the older ones that actually worked on occasion.

I knew all this not through some Santa-induced revelation, but because I became an expert on them a few years ago. There was this old bowling alley near Nana's called "Llewellyn's" that had an arcade. That summer I didn't have a lot to do when I wasn't doing projects for her, so I took to hanging out there in the afternoons I had free. They had this crane machine loaded with stuffed pink elephants and I spent a few weeks trying to win one for Shannon Brotman, who I was crushing on that summer. It was weird as I liked her, but really just from afar and never even asked her out or thought about it. It was one of those things where I just kinda liked her and liked thinking about her but never really did anything about it when we got back to school. Anyway, the guy who owned the place was named Jimmy, and he came over one afternoon when I'd been languishing at the machine for a long time.

"Listen, kid, I appreciate you blowing your allowance here every day the last few weeks but your continued failure at grasping the mechanics of grabbing that elephant is beginning to have a negative impact on the morale of my regulars." He was a slight man who always wore a bowling shirt and had a voice like a cat's tongue. His old, weathered hands gestured at the bar area where sat a bunch of older people I didn't know, and they were all watching me with interest. "So, please allow me to educate you?"

I nodded, as I was completely frustrated by the darned thing. Every time I thought I had the thing the stupid little grabber wouldn't hold onto the elephant. So, he went on to discuss how not every claw grab is going to have the torque to grasp an item and hold it through the process of dropping it down the chute. So, unless the item is already out and not stuck in the pile, it's never going to pull it out of a tight spot. As that had been what I'd been doing all along, I was frustrated.

"So, what do I do?

Jimmy put his arm on my shoulder and leaned us closer to the glass of the machine. "Well, kid, you have to wait for other people to fail and then swoop in once they've loosened things up for you. Don't play right after someone wins something. Be patient and wait until the thing you want is loose on the top, then you swoop in and spend your quarters." He mussed up my hair and smiled as he walked back behind the bar. He smelled a bit like mom used to when she smoked but he had an air of honesty about him, so I listened and watched and as a result, I got pretty good at the old-school crane machine.

I did eventually get an elephant for Shannon, but I just included it as part of a basket a group of us put together for her Sweet Sixteen. I think I liked liking her enough that when that ran its course we were just friends and it was cool.

Of course, there at Winterwood, with a machine I'd never seen before I was kinda going out on a limb, but I felt like I had to try something, and luckily, as I looked at the machine, there was a cute little Santa sitting right on top of all the "tucked in" prizes.

I slid my dollar into the machine and studied the positioning a bit before leaping into action. Angie sidled up next to me and watched me, curious and I was hoping I looked awesome, just a little. "All right, I got you now, Santa," I whispered as I maneuvered the crane to where I was pretty certain I had a good shot.

"You're talking to machines now?" Angie asked, clearly not understanding how these things work.

"You can talk to the universe, but I can't talk to inanimate objects?"

"Fair enough."

I stepped back from the machine, almost bumping into a nearby table with bobblehead Santa's and Elves and Rudolph's and all the gang. The heads all started shaking as I touched the table with my hand.

"Would the lady care to press the button?" I asked as I'd settled myself and double-checked the crane position.

"Sure, why not?" She still had a little snarfy tone but she seemed intrigued by whatever nonsense I was attempting. She pressed, rather lackadaisically I might add, the button atop the joystick that I'd painstakingly positioned, which then sent the claw diving down into the fray to where it, just as I'd planned, snatched up the smiling 'lil Santa Claus stuffy and raised him up. The mechanism predictably slammed against the glass at the top but we were lucky and the claw managed to maintain its grip and then safely maneuver him to the drop chute. I reached down into the metallic "victory door" and then handed Santa to Angie. She wore a look of amazement and seemed deeply impressed.

"OK, how did you do that?" she asked, staring at Santa like he was made of star stuff.

"I promised a pretty girl some Christmas magic. Thought I was kinda clear on that…" I smiled like a game show host and I might have done some 'spirit fingers' as well. To be honest, I wasn't sure it wasn't going to take me a few tries to pull it off, but wow, it could not have gone better.

The next thing I knew, Angie was hugging me around the waist, very suddenly and tightly. "That was very sweet of you! I love him. Thank you!"

I almost thought that she was tearing up for a second as she buried her face in my shoulder and held onto me to the point of discomfort.

"You're-oof-welcome-but-I-can't-breathe…"

"Aw hush up you, you're ruining the moment."

"I certainly don't--ouch--wanna do that," I grunted. She held on a bit longer before she released me and looked at the machine and the Santa again.

"I've been coming to the boardwalk since I was born, and I've never seen anyone win something on the crane machine, like ever!"

She seemed genuinely impressed. I liked that. "It must have been the magic of Christmas." I saw no reason to tell her about my training at Llewellyn's.

"Wow, must be." She eventually stopped hugging me and put her arm into escort position and moved us toward the door. "This is going to be the best Christmas, ever!"

"Um, it's still August, Angie…"

She doubled down on her enthusiasm, "Yep, loads of time to make it the bestest one ever!"

"Bestest?"

"Yep, but for now, it is time to move on," she kinda sing-songed as we exited out onto the boardwalk. We walked for a minute before I felt like I had to say something about Winterwood.

"That was some kind of store there. I'm sorry about the house thing though, maybe you could…"

"Mooooving on, my friend," she boomed, making a truck horn noise as she did so. "Let us away to the car to drop off our hard-earned treasures and collect this lady's sweatshirt, as she feels a chill."

It was still pretty warm out, but I knew it would get cool when the sun went down and with that we were off like a shot once again. She seemed to be catching her third wind. My feet were kinda getting sore and I'd thought she was getting tired but here we were trekking down the boards once again. I don't even want to speculate how many miles we'd walked during the day. It was still crowded being the last weekend of the season and all. There were loads of kids running around. I was a little surprised that we didn't run into anyone from school, but we were pretty much keeping to ourselves and we'd only really stopped at the fortune teller, the chapel and the Christmas store, not typically the hangout for recent high school graduates.

There were cars frantically circling in the parking lot as we approached the Tracer. Two different drivers swore at us when we just dropped off stuff and left the car parked.

Angie retrieved her old green and gray hoodie, which she affectionately referred to as her "armor" and wrapped herself in it immediately.

"Ah, much better."

I got mine too but like I said, it was still pretty warm to me so I just threw it over my shoulder for the moment. We walked back up the steps to the boardwalk and sat on a bench near the giant Wildwood sign. The crowds sitting on the beach had thinned considerably as the day moved into evening. I knew we'd have to head to the Anchor Inn soon, but I tried to just sit with her for a minute. I was starting to realize that the day was really winding down and that in 24 hours I'd be almost in Boston if not there already. I'd put off thinking about it all summer and refocused on not thinking about it all day, but as we sat there it kinda started eating at me. I must have sighed or something because the next thing I knew Angie was patting my shoulder.

"It's going to be alright," she said, almost in a whisper. I looked over and she was still staring out at the ocean. The wind took her hair off her face again and she pulled up the hood from her sweatshirt and hunched forward a bit trying to avoid the chill.

"How do you know?" I asked. I'm certain in my worst teenage whine.

"A little bird told me."

I groaned. "A bird? What bird?"

Angie looked around and pointed at a seagull that was in the process of trying to secure half of a Tastykake Butterscotch Krimpet in its mouth. "That's the one."

"Him? What did he have to say?"

"It's a 'she' actually, and she told me that you were going to do great at school and learn amazing things and create ever more amazing music, all before Christmas."

Robert Kugler

"She said all that?"

"Yeppers!" Angie was clearly enjoying herself to the point that I had to smile a little despite my unease. "Aaaaand she said that you'd figure out how to use that fancy new phone of yours to actually talk to me over video, aaaaand you'll make lots of new friends and that I shouldn't worry about you."

That last line made me squirm just a little. I was clearly worried for myself, but I felt awful because I didn't want her to be worrying about me. She'd always said I would be a mess if I were alone and she's not wrong. I hadn't had to make new friends in a long time. Plus, I'd never been away from home on my own before. I was nervous about being on my own and meeting my suitemates.

"That's one chatty bird," I said after a minute. I was getting better at letting there be quiet moments not filled with my yammering.

"Oh, she totally can be. It's all those Tastykakes she eats. Way too much sugar."

"And murder on the waistline, too."

For some reason this cracked her up, including a snort, which cracked me up and it was a few minutes before we stopped laughing and she caught her breath again.

"Oh, sweetie, that was funny! Thanks for that!"

I didn't really get it but a laugh from her is always worth it, so I stood and took several bows. "That's it for me, I'm here all week with two shows on Sunday Please remember to tip your servers!"

"I'll be at them all," she replied, her voice lowering a little.

I didn't want to wade into the melancholy stuff, so I switched gears, "Speaking of shows…"

"That's right! Shellie's band is playing. We should get

118

moving." She grabbed my hand and started pulling me away from the bench. I played around like I couldn't move at first but eventually she cried out, "Onward!" and I fell in line next to her in the direction of the Anchor Inn.

CHAPTER NINE

The Anchor Inn is really just kind of an older hangout for locals from what Uncle Bob had told me about it. "Big Bobby" owned the place for years but he'd allowed "Young Bobby," his son to manage it for the last few. He'd started bringing in more music all year round, not just in the summer season. He wanted to compete with the North Wildwood and Cape May bars that were hot for live and local music. I'd seen a few acts with Angie and her family - they were usually just bar bands that played old Eagles tunes and stuff like that so I didn't expect much different with Shellie's band. I was a little surprised, though, as we finished the five-block walk. There were people milling around outside and the doors were wide open along with all the windows. I was intrigued to see what was going on inside as in the past the Anchor Inn always seemed dark and wooden and kinda foreboding. It still had all those features but with the doors flung open and music pouring out into the street the vibe was welcoming and there was definitely a cool groove. As we approached the door, Angie squeezed my arm, which she'd been holding for the last several blocks.

"Richie is on the door! Yay!"

I looked where she was now pointing. He wasn't someone I'd ever seen or heard of before, and I'm sure I would have remembered this guy. It's not often one encounters a nine-foot-tall African American gentleman from the mean streets of Dayton, Ohio.

OK, maybe he wasn't nine feet tall, but he was quite simply the largest human being I'd ever seen, except for maybe that time Uncle Ted was in his "Pro Wrestling for Life!" phase and we went to an event in Philly. There was some giant guy at that show whose name I forget who wrestled a man smaller than Nana. It was actually one of the more fun things Uncle Ted brought me too. Way more fun than the "conventions" he dragged me to during his "Bounty Hunter" phase. The little guy in the match, Sabu or something like that, was fun to watch flipping around, but the big dude didn't look like he could hurt anyone unless he sat on them.

Richie, on the other hand looked like he could hurt people. He zeroed in on Angie as we approached. If a look can cause physical discomfort his totally did as he scanned me through narrowed, meticulous eyes. I immediately felt I'd done something wrong and was about to start apologizing when Angie, practically screaming in giddiness blurted out, "Hi Mr. Richie!"

I could have sworn she was about to hug him, but instead she leaned down on one knee, like genuflecting and she raised up a closed fist toward this gargantuan man, awaiting a response. I didn't think it was possible, but he narrowed his eyes even further, making his brows look like they might split his head open. He held his position stoically for several long moments but finally, he almost thought about grinning and put his fist out to her, which she enthusiastically bumped and then did a whole "blow it up flippy-do" thing.

Angie stood up, still positively glowing as he greeted her.

"Miss Angela," he nodded, his voice a deep ocean of "don't even try." He looked at me again and I felt like a barcode. "Person I do not know who is with Miss Angela…"

Angie seemed completely star struck by this enormous man guarding the door, who had not in fact moved a hair to allow us entry to the club, and somehow seemed to have thought that his last statement had contained a question. After yet another awkward silence, she recovered, blushing. "Oh, him. Right, sorry, Mr. Richie, he's with me."

His eyes moved slowly back and forth from her to me and back again several times. This was really taking a long time, I mean, we weren't trying to storm the state house or something. Finally, he spoke, and his voice seemed to come from all around at once. "You may proceed. Your uncle called earlier. I believe Dr. Bennett is expecting you both presently within." With that he seemed to slide to the left on thin air, moving just enough of his considerable form to allow us entry. Once he moved, we could hear the noise from within much louder. Yep, he was so large that he was a barrier to the sound from inside the Anchor Inn. He can't have been real!

It was a little much, but we thanked him and walked inside. There was a young band on stage, probably our age or younger, finishing up what sounded like a reggae version of "Twist and Shout." There were a few girls dancing oddly in front of the stage, though there really wasn't room for them there. The bar was full and the tables were all taken as well.

"Thank you, beach people! We are 'Skipping Detention!' Check us out on Instagram!"

The drummer then triumphantly tossed his sticks into the crowd, which did not in fact go wild in a scramble to collect them, but rather failed to notice and allowed them to land unmolested on the floor. The plinkity-plink sound was both cacophonous and highly awkward. One of the dancing girls picked them up and handed them back to the drummer, who was clearly embarrassed. After that, people moved around a bit as some left and others came in, and we were able to secure a small table in the second row from the stage, to the right, where it seemed that the parents and brother of someone in the last band had just been sitting, all decked out in their homemade t-shirts. They were really just white shirts with sharpie writing on it, but I thought it was sweet that the parents and family were supporting their kids by coming to the show.

It made me a little sad actually. I mean, it's not like Mom didn't support me. She pretty much let me do whatever I wanted when it came to shows and going to gigs and stuff, and she'd bought me my first guitar and always encouraged me to play and was obviously financing this year at school in Boston. It's just she was always so tired after work and had never really seen me play live, at least not recently. She went to a coffeehouse thing I did sophomore year at school and she came to one of the Jazz band things I did last year when I played with them, but the stuff that was really important - the real work I was doing and the real heart of what I felt I was building toward happened during shows at places like the Anchor Inn for now anyway. She'd never seen me play those kinds of places. Even Nana brought her Ladies Club to see me open for The Knee Jerk Reactions at the

Tin Angel in the city last spring. She got to meet her favorite Philly sports writer and music wonk Reuben Frank who was at the show, mostly to catch the middle act, The Empty Stairs, who are this awesome twin sister act from Lancaster. They were really cool - they both played bass and had a drummer and that was it! Wickedly weird and awesome and they were both really pretty too. Nana took her first ever selfie with Reuben, who couldn't have been cooler. I like sports and stuff, but I didn't know him as a big-time writer until Nana said something. To me he was just this guy who I saw around the clubs a lot when there was something cool happening. Honestly, there are times I'm not sure that Mom really understands what it is I'm trying to do. She supports me and leaves me to it, but I guess sometimes I'd rather she didn't leave me to it so much on my own all the time.

After we sat down, a slight girl with blonde hair asked, "Hey, are you kids staying for the next band?" She couldn't have been much older than us. She had some kind of accent that reminded me of Jimmy Laughran, my guru of crane machines.

"Yes, we're friends of Shellie'" Angie replied.

Our new friend tilted her head, "Shellie? You mean the old head who looks like a dentist?"

"Yep, that'd be him there." Angie pointed toward the stage, where Shellie was checking the levels on the in-house amps as they were plugging in. It saved a ton of time when places wired up to plug and go as opposed to having each band bring their own sound systems.

"Well, that's grand. I'm Betsy if you need anything, dears." She was about to head off when Angie waved and asked, "Is Big Bobby here doing his Garlic Crabs today?"

Betsy grinned knowingly, as if Angie had just asked

some sort of secret question that allowed her access to the inner workings of the Matrix. She tucked her hair behind her ear and winked, "I'll ask the big heaper if he can trouble himself...," and she moved off toward the kitchen.

Being in between bands for a few minutes allowed the natural noise of the Inn, which was really just a bar with an open space that used to have pool tables in it, bubbled and flowed. I always like the sound of a place in between sets. It always seems so full of possibility, like the calm before the potential storm. Every band is the greatest band in the world during sound check.

Shellie Bennett obviously didn't just look like a dentist, but every other time of his life he is a band guy and he, according to Uncle Bob has been doing it in some capacity or another for over twenty years. As we were the only ones already sitting at a table, he noticed us immediately and came over.

"Angela! It's so wonderful to see you!" His voice was so full of Brooklyn that it almost sounded like a put on. Angie stood up and gave him a half hug. "Nice to see you Dr. Bennett, this is..." she replied, gesturing to me.

"Oh, your Uncle Bob told me all about this young man," Shellie crowed. "So, you're hoping to sit in with 'The Cozy Morleys' tonight, 'College boy?'"

Now, I'm always up to play but I don't know that I would have categorized it as something I'd been "hoping" for. To be honest, Bob had kind of given me the impression that I was doing him/them a favor. Angie gave me her "play along" eyes, so I did.

"Well, yes sir, if you'd like I could maybe help out some."

Shellie shook my hand longer than seemed particularly necessary but eventually let go. He sat down at our table after pulling a chair from a nearby table, which got a silent scowl from Betsy. "So, Bob said you can play lead or rhythm and sing too? Triple threat, college boy?" His tone seemed really dismissive and kinda guarded like he really didn't want me to answer at all and I found myself getting annoyed. It felt like he was jerking me around which was honestly part of the reason I didn't stay in a lot of bands. Maybe I was overthinking it but he seemed really passive aggressive, which is my least favorite type of aggression.

I leaned forward in my seat as his band was tuning up beginning to get louder. "Listen Dr. Bennett…"

"Please, call me Shellie," he offered with just a twinge of 'used car salesman.'

"OK, Shellie, Angie and I are just here to listen to your band. Please don't feel like you have to include me if you don't want to. I'm good either way."

Shellie smiled broadly, and I made a mental note to send Gary from June Rich a message to say thanks for his crash course in talking to, or stroking the ego of, bandleaders earlier in the summer. They never wanted to give away the spotlight, "no matter how well or poorly they inhabit it," Gary had said, but they might share it if you make it seem like their idea and as though it could help the overall show. "If they see you as a threat, you won't gig. If they see you as a fool that can benefit them in the moment, you might gig. Once you're behind the mic, you go do your thang, kid," he'd said in his wine-soaked drawl before taking a sip of his ever-present chardonnay.

"My thang," I'd echoed, nodding. I liked the word.

"Yeah, man! You don't have a thang to do, you gonna have some trouble out there," he'd said, shaking his head and tossing his dreadlocks off his face. He was always doing that. It seemed like his head was constantly in motion.

"Trouble with what?"

"Doin' your thang…"

"My thang."

"Right on young man, your thang," he exclaimed, poking his finger right on my heart several times. "Your thang! You dig?!"

And I did. I dug.

Shellie clapped my shoulder and grinned, a little less smarmy now, like a shield had been lowered. "Son, if half of what Bob had to say is true, you'll help me get booked through winter if we don't screw it up. We've got a basic set we'll do for about eight songs, then maybe I bring you up for," with this he took a sheet of paper out of the pocket of his neon yellow Hawaiian shirt and scanned it.

"Um, lemme see…do you know Into the Mystic?"

"Van Morrison, sure. I know it. I sometimes do the Warren Haynes version."

Shellie looked impressed, I think. "On a twelve string? Bob said you'd play a twelve."

I grinned and cocked an eye at him. "If it's in tune and plugged in, I can play it." I felt pretty badass until I noticed Angie roll her eyes at me. It was like falling on my butt in PE class back in freshman year. Thankfully Betsy returned in that moment with waters and then started talking to Angie. I shifted my chair to look at Shellie's set list while downing the full glass of water.

"How about Green Day - do you know 'Good Riddance?' You know, that 'Time of your Life' song?"

I nodded that I knew it while drinking Angie's water, which she'd passed over to me. He rattled off a few more songs and I then realized that they were really planning on having me sit in for over half of their set! That was way more involved than I had planned as I'd figured they'd have me pop on and do "Sweet Caroline" or some Beach Boys song or something like that. I must have made a face or something and Shellie leaned in like he was passing me a note in Math class and spoke softly, looking over his shoulder at his band, still setting up. "Listen kid, I need all the help I can get right now. I'm trying to get booked for Irish Weekend next month and beyond. These guys are my pals and they are OK players, but a little extra sizzle could help me get over a bit of a rut we are in and Bob said you've got sizzle." His eyes were wide as the pint glass in front of me and he seemed really intense.

I felt Angie's hand on my arm and I looked back to see her smiling at me, having finished whatever she was talking to the waitress about. Her eyes looked tired, but they brightened when I turned to her. "So, what's the final song, Doctor B?" she asked.

He immediately discarded the "help me out" persona he'd just been sitting in and returned to the salesman without missing a beat as he answered. "Well, lately we've been doing Springsteen's "Mary's Place" from the "Rising" album. He turned to me suddenly, "You know that one?"

"You mean Bruce's version of Sam Cooke's 'Meet me at Mary's Place' released 1964?" I was definitely showing off, but he'd irritated me and I just blurted it out. That, and I had just listened to that Sam Cooke album at Nana's. He didn't need to know that though. The stunned look on his face was priceless and I made a mental note to thank Nana as we'd listened to all of her Sam Cooke records on her Silvertone turntable and talked about the liner notes and stuff. I kinda liked showing that off to the good doctor as petulant as I know I must have sounded.

Shellie finally blinked after a few seconds. "Uh, yeah, OK kid, you'll do fine. Come check the instruments and tuning and let's play a few licks, but I think we're square. Why don't we have you chime in on vocals too?" He rose, wagging his finger and sauntered back towards the stage where I saw him setting up another vocal mic.

Angie was still holding my arm. I turned my chair back towards her. "I don't have to play with him if you want to just hang or…"

"Hush. I would never deny you the chance to sit in with Shellie Bennett and THE Cozy Morley's on our last day together. You think you'll be able to play nice with the other kids in the band?" She said it like she was kidding but her raised left eyebrow made it clear she was actually asking.

"I'll try. He's not asking a lot musically, so I think I'll be fine. He's a little different, but I think we understand one another."

I felt weird all of a sudden, like I'd hijacked our day. Between the stuff at the chapel and the awkwardness after we'd gone to see Madam Marie, not to mention the weird vibe when we were at Bob and Jenny's, I figured I should ask her if she was sure she wanted us to be here doing this right now.

"Are you sure this is where you want us to be right now?"

She narrowed her eyes at me almost to the point of ridiculousness, like when Mr. Richie scanned me earlier. "Who wouldn't want to be here for your last show in Jersey? I'll be able to tell all my friends and family that I was there!"

I knew she was tweaking me a little but I reacted anyway. "Come on, I'm not going away forever, Angie"

"Relax 'College Boy,' she smirked, echoing Shellie's earlier nickname. I wasn't a fan, but she was clearly having fun teasing me, so I let her. "Why don't you just go do sound check with the guys and then come sit with me until they need you. They are bringing us some of Big Bobby's Garlic Crabs"

The prospect of garlic crabs nearly derailed me, but I continued, "Are you sure? I don't want to make this about me and -"

She interrupted me. "I know. Go, make you ready." She pushed my arm away and shooed me thoroughly. I knew I'd heard that line before so I paused as I stood up and must have scrunched up my face in thought trying to place it before she helped me out.

"It's from Hamlet sweetie, now stop stalling and go get ready to rock, College Boy."

I grumbled, but did as she requested, but honestly, I was starting to feel almost like I was following a script at times. Anyway, I went over and checked the equipment they wanted me to use and chatted with Shellie and his band. The drummer was a cop in Wildwood Crest and the bassist was the associate pastor at the local Methodist Church. Shellie played guitar and there was a keyboardist whose name I never got. They checked sound levels and I checked the tuning on the guitars that were strewn about. The twelve string Ovation hardback they wanted me to play was really tight, like it hadn't been played much. Once I'd tuned it up and goofed around with it a little it sounded fine. I was excited to play it actually. I'd only ever really played a twelve string at school or when hanging out at Farrington's Music Shop in Princeton. I spent a lot of time just playing around with stuff I couldn't afford there. It was nice to play something other than my own guitar.

Once we got everything set, I was about to head back to Angie when Shellie pulled me aside.

"Listen 'College,' thanks for helping us out. Bob says you're headed to Boston and I don't blame you, but just watching you warm up, I think you'll add something tonight for sure. We're going to record it and hope to get a spotlight at the Irish Fest or even the Cape May Jazz fest if we kill. Is that cool with you?"

Recording never bothered me, especially since Angie had started doing it for me and taught me how. I said it wasn't a problem. I then had a thought as Shellie nodded and turned away. "Hey, if it goes well, could you send me the recording?" I remembered that I might need some stuff to build on at school and maybe a good recording would help me get work at the clubs up there.

"No problem, College Boy, if it comes out well I'll dropbox it over to you."

I figured I could ask Angie how a dropbox worked and nodded. Shellie smiled as he walked off to finagle some other stuff. I put the twelve string back on its stand and walked down from the stage to rejoin Angie. There was a giant bucket and two piles of napkins and another empty bucket on the table. The only thing that I loved food-wise down the shore as much as Fredericks corn was the Anchor Inn's Garlic Crabs. You could only get them if Big Bobby felt like making them and apparently as he'd aged, he only felt like doing it for people he knew and/or liked. I'd had them twice before and they were simply ridiculous, an oily garlicy symphony of crab fabulousness. The first time I'd eaten them I felt like I walked away forever changed.

"Oh, heck yeah!" I said as I sat back down at our table and put my hands on the bucket. It was warm and smelled like Nana's next-door neighbor's house. Every

Sunday Mrs. Donatucci made her "gravy" and would invite anyone within 100 yards of her house to have lunch with her and take buckets of her sauce home. Mom always called it just "spaghetti sauce" but to me there was so much more going on it was unreal. The flavors were amazing and, well, Mom was never known for her cooking.

The buckets were untouched, and I looked at Angie before I ate anything. She did a "royal highness" wave and pushed the bucket towards me.

"I waited for you. Go ahead."

I pulled out one crab for me and another for her and set them on the small plates that Betsy had brought. It didn't seem right to start without Angie since she'd waited for me. Again, I heard Nana's manners lessons burning in my ears. That said, I ate the daylights out of those crabs which were, of course, transcendent. Amazingly fantastically awesome.

Anyway, I think I was on my third crab when I noticed Angie was picking at her crab but really only eating the bread that Betsy had dropped off while I was knee-deep in a claw. I was about to ask her about it when the band started playing. She was watching me eat, wearing a look that made me think that if we weren't best friends she'd have laughed at me and changed tables. I looked at her and shrugged, asking in my own way "OK, what?" and she calmly pointed at the stage where the band was deep into their first number, a serviceable cover of AC/DC's "You Shook Me All Night Long."

I quietly shifted my chair to be next to Angie instead of opposite her, so I could see the stage and talk to her. I took a pile of the napkins and wiped off my hands and mouth and drank some more water, realizing that at some point Shellie was going to call me up, but more so realizing that I'd kind of made a mess eating the crabs. Not very "future rock star" of me to show up with a greasy face and crab hanging out of my teeth.

As they played their set, I started thinking that I didn't really understand why they wanted me along. They were pretty tight for a bar band and seemed to get over well with the crowd. They played some other rocker songs, after the AC/DC song. They did "I Get Around" and "Mustang Sally" and a few others before they slowed it down and moved into a sort of acoustic/punky version of Justin Bieber's "Love Yourself," which I really kinda dug and got a serious pop from the crowd. Angie, who had a closet affection for the Beebs enjoyed that one in particular, and it actually drew in some noise from the people outside, who were now standing at the windows, subject to Mr. Richie and his control of the door.

Shellie followed up his Beebs moment with a cover of Rick Springfield's "Jessie's Girl," which is a hot song but seemed to split the crowd a little age wise. An older woman got up and started dancing around in front of the bandstand, but it was one of those times that it seemed really out of place. I looked over to Angie and she seemed distracted. I immediately started thinking it was a mistake that we'd come but then she caught my gaze and smiled. I leaned over towards her, and mouthed "are you alright?" She leaned her head on my shoulder and spoke into my ear, her breath warm all about.

"I'm good," she mouthed and I found myself nodding and putting my arm over her chair for some reason.

Shellie and the Cozy Morley's kicked into a stomping version of Flogging Molly's "What's left of the Flag," which popped a whole corner of the room and reminded me that he'd mentioned trying to get a gig at the Irish fest next month. The crowd went nuts for that song with everyone, including Angie and I singing along with it, as it's a great singalong. Angie was still leaning into me as the song ended.

I thought she looked tired, but suddenly she was tapping my arm and pointing at the stage. Shellie had apparently been introducing me as the "College boy who's gracing us with his presence before he begins his world tour of Boston," which got a few chuckles and a few more jeers. Angie pushed me out of my seat towards the stage. I tripped a little, which, regrettably did not go unnoticed by the now growing crowd.

"Careful there!" someone called out.

"Hey, Shellie, cut that kid off!" said another.

I ignored it all and tried to lock in on the twelve string I was supposed to be rocking. I'd never drank anything in my life but here I was getting catcalls for walking up drunk. That seriously irritated me, but I moved on when I noticed the kid filming the performance. He was at the table directly behind Angie and looked repeatedly at Shellie, giving him a thumbs up.

Shellie pulled me aside by the arm, gripping me tighter than might have been needed. "You ready, College?"

"Sure thing, Doc," I said. I had my hands on a guitar I could never afford about to play for a decent sized crowd down the shore. None of that sucked at all but honestly, I think I was really just getting ready to play for Angie. I wanted to do something special for her and once I had that in my mind, the rest was easy.

Shellie nodded at me and the drummer counted off the one through four and he and the bass guy started the familiar "bah-dum-pum" of Van Morrison's "Into the Mystic." I popped in on rhythm guitar and was pleased to realize that they'd slowed it down like Warren Haynes and even the Allman Brothers have played it live in the past. Van always seems in a rush when he's done this song and pretty much any other song he's sung live. I went long strum on the twelve string chords so that might have slowed them down too, but everyone seemed cool with where we were when Shellie came in on the vocals.

There was actually some applause once the song started from the now pretty much full room. The band kicked in and once Shellie heard that I was carrying the guitar part, he turned and put his axe on the stand behind him and he focused on singing, but gave me a look that seemed to say, 'handle this, OK? His voice was fine but, in the moment, I set myself on trying to stay in time with the bass and the drummer and was hoping for the best as we were clearly winging it all. I focused on just playing that first song, especially as I had just found myself playing lead guitar for Shellie and The Cozy Morley's when I had really only expected to be a background player or rhythm or something other than what seemed to be playing out. That said, it's an easy song and the band knew it well and we made it through fine. We did that Green Day "Time of your Life" song and then "We're Having a Party" which everyone in Jersey gives to Southside Johnny but it's really another Sam Cooke song, as Nana taught me. I sang a bit of harmony here and there where it seemed appropriate but mostly focused on playing with these guys. While I knew the songs, I'd never really played them with other people before. I flubbed a few chords here and there since I wasn't used to the double strings on the Ovation. It was a great, rich sound, but I wasn't used to it. Kinda hurt my fingers after a while.

We finished that song and the crowd was definitely enjoying us, but I was feeling guilty a little as Angie was sitting at our table alone. I realized it was getting later, and it was our last day together and I started feeling the weight of that pretty hard. I had avoided thinking about it all day, but it hit me as I was on the stage. As I looked out at the crowd I saw Angie leaning back in her seat and she was clapping like the rest of the crowd, but she was the only one looking directly at me. I didn't like the way it looked with her sitting alone at that dinky little table.

I put down the twelve string guitar after that song because while it was fun to play it was becoming a bit cumbersome and increasingly difficult to keep in tune. I gave Angie an "are you OK" gesture or at least what I thought conveyed that message to her. She waved at me like she was fine, and then Betsy was next to her refilling our waters and chatting her up. I noticed that Betsy looked at me for a moment while Angie was talking to her, but I couldn't hear anything outside of Shellie's banter on the mic setting up the next song, which I'd figured was going to be "Mary's Place" based on our conversation earlier. I tuned up another guitar, a Red Fender Telecaster that Shellie had put on a stand earlier.

But, that was the moment all heck broke loose on stage. We were all set to go on with the set when a beautiful redhead dramatically stormed into the room through the kitchen. The door made a loud thud as it blasted against the wall and everyone turned to look as she came in. She seemed to move in slow motion as the door swung closed and then marched across the room and sat at the table with the kid who was recording the show, on the table behind Angie.

The drummer, I think his name was Kelly, the cop, immediately stood up and swatted Shellie in the arm with his sticks repeatedly and pointed at the woman who'd just walked in and they started having an animated conversation. I figured I should stay out of it, but I heard, as I imagine everyone within earshot heard the drummer holler, "Hey, she came!" and then, "We have to play it!" and then, with a pair of drumsticks poised precariously beneath the chin of Shellie Bennett, "You promised, Shel! You promised!"

After a few minutes of Shellie waffling, saying something like "Let's stick to the plan…" Kelly the drummer dropped his sticks and the Pastor bass player guy and the mystery keyboardist all took a step backward from Shellie.

Kelly the drummer pleaded, grasping Shellie around the shoulders. "Shellie, please! It might be my last shot with Shannon! Help me, man! She came here to hear me play our song!" And Kelly gestured to the redhead, who for her part nodded along with what Kelly was saying. Shellie's shoulders slumped and he walked away from his band with a sort of "give me a second" gesture. The crowd was murmuring, both restless and curious. The redhead, Shannon I assumed, had her arms crossed and was staring at Kelly with daggers flying out of her eyes. Shellie pulled me aside and away from the mics. He seemed deeply bothered and almost in a panic.

"Yeah, here's the thing, kid. Kelly there needs us to play 'Everlong' by the Foo Fighters for his lady there. It's a long, long story, but I may have promised him and never learned the song as I never thought she'd actually come, and well, yeah," he was flustered. "It's a long story with them, years in the making, but now he needs me to deliver and well, I can't play it so, please tell me you can?"

The crowd was starting to get loud as I guess they were in on the drama between Kelly and Shannon that I'd found myself dropped into. It was weird having so many people in the know about someone else's needs and desires. I wondered what it was like to share like that.

"Electric or acoustic?" I replied. Shellie then swore under his breath and went back over to his drummer. There was an animated conversation between them both and when Shellie came back he pointed at the Fender electric I was already holding, which I'd kinda already started to have a crush on.

Shellie looked like he'd aged twenty years in the last few minutes and the crowd was starting to get antsy, some of them catcalling. "It's gotta be electric so Kelly-boy can wail and rock out on the drums for his gal." Shellie had the flop sweats pretty bad and he actually kinda looked like Uncle Ted after a Gaga concert. He seemed every bit the dentist he happened to be in that moment as opposed to the rock star I know he aspired to be. "Honestly kid, I don't know the song, can you play it loud for this lovesick dope?"

I'd played "Everlong" more times than I could count. I'd studied the acoustic versions and the live versions a ton, It was a song I really connected with and totally grooved on. I usually did it solo with my own guitar and the chords were simple enough. I looked up and Kelly and the other guys were all kind of flashing between looking expectantly at me and disappointedly at Shellie.

"So, you want me to play lead on a song I know but you don't know and that I've never played with a band live in front of an audience without rehearsal?"

Shellie didn't flinch in his reply. "Yeah, we're really living the dream here, kid, can you play it?"

I felt like I could and of course I knew I was going to try anyway but I checked in on Angie and she was now deep in conversation with Kelly's "friend" Shannon, who'd now moved up to sit with Angie at our table. The buckets of garlic crab had been removed I noticed, which made me a little sad. They were all still waiting for an answer so I said, "Yeah, let's do it."

Shellie exhaled and looked like he might pass out. Kelly literally vaulted over the drum kit and pointed his sticks out at Shannon, which brought about an increased murmur from the crowd. I still had no idea what was really at play there, but it seemed like it all boiled down to playing a song to a girl. That's something I understood.

I put the strap over my shoulder and tested out the opening chord, not realizing it was already plugged in and hot so the audience heard the opening chord and started to make noise, which sent the rest of the band scrambling back to their instruments. I was amazed at the sound that was coming off this guitar of Shellie's and I slowed down the opening a bit to let the guys get set. Once I started playing the opening for real, Kelly looked like a guy who was ready to chop a mountain in half.

Shellie picked up the Ovation and took the spot to my right, where I'd been before, allowing me the band leader spot at the center of the stage. He didn't actually play it, but he was there sharing the stage. The night had not gone as I'd expected to be sure, as I was now serving as front man for The Cozy Morley's on a song that hadn't been on their set list. I'd be lying if I said I didn't feel anything other than deeply and amazingly alive in that moment.

I played through the opening a second time so everyone could get used to what we were doing. Like I said, they were a tight band and responded to my cues and while I didn't know Kelly at all, how could I not want to help a dude impress his lady, especially through the music of Dave Grohl? I turned towards Kelly and the rest of the band as I finished the opening chord progression the second time and nodded my head at each of them to kind of lock in the rhythm and they were with me, which was really cool. I was deeply in unknown territory, but I remembered something Nana had said to me. She said, "Fake it 'til you make it, dear heart. Do it well and only you and I will know…" So, I figured I'd act like a bandleader and the next thing I knew, I turned back to the mic and started singing.

"Hello…" I said/sang by way of beginning, and the band kicked in like it was the actual Foo Fighters behind me. Overall, I think we rocked the song properly. I had to turn back to the band to cue a few tempo adjustments, but we rocked and Kelly definitely got to shine, playing out of his skull. Shellie chimed in on backup vocals in the later verses once he'd heard them a few times but otherwise stayed in the back for this one. Kelly actually had a mic setup at his drum kit and he screamed his heart out into it, although it seems his mic wasn't turned on. He still came off like a Don Henley-style badass as some of the crowd sang along with us, his sticks blazing as we did the final chorus, but I was so focused on not screwing up that I didn't catch how fired up everyone was.

Shellie impressed me as a bandleader, and I definitely learned something from him. He made the whole thing work for his band, even when he didn't know exactly what to do, he found a way to get the show done, at least mostly as I was about the find out.

When we finally finished "Everlong" to a great response, there was time left on the set but it was clear that The Cozy Morley's were done for the night. Kelly the drummer left the stage after slapping me on the back and determinedly walked up to Shannon and kissed her in front of everyone, to the thunderous and raucous applause of everyone. It was amazing! Everyone was cheering and clapping as Kelly and Shannon eventually stopped making out in front of everyone and left the building. I looked for Angie in the crowd and found her looking directly at me. I was about to walk towards her, figuring we were done, as that was about as close to a "drop the mic" moment as I'd ever been a part of to date. The crowd was happy and knew they'd been a part of something cool, but the next thing I knew, Shellie was pulling me back on stage. The rest of the band had left. Pastor Bass Player Guy was over at the bar and the keyboardist seemed to simply vanish like a phantom. Never got his name. I looked at Shellie, who looked panicked for some reason.

"Not bad. Great closer though," I offered, handing him the Fender. "That's an amazing instrument."

He took it from my hands and put it on a stand but looked pissed.

"What's the problem?" I asked, "They totally dug your band!" And they had. It was a really solid set with a killer ending complete with a love connection. What more could they ask?

"We are like ten minutes short and the band just left!" Shellie was clearly on the verge of a panic attack. "We don't get paid if we are short, even a minute! Bobbie is a tyrant with that stuff!"

The crowd had not dispersed at all and was milling about waiting to see what happened next. Shellie's band, however, was now nowhere to be seen. Big Bobbie, emerged from the kitchen and was currently greeting Angie at our table. He was hard to miss. He was easily six and a half feet tall and almost the same wide. He made Mr. Richie at the door look small as Richie was only big tall, not wide. Angie chatted animatedly with him for a minute and then he offered an almost dainty handshake as they shared a laugh about something. Then, I saw Big Bobby shift his eyes to glare at Shellie and then pointedly at the clock on the wall.

"Oh crap!" Shellie groaned, "I've got nothing! No band, no songs! I'm fried, kid, hey!" he suddenly grabbed both of my arms tight and started almost massaging my shoulders. It was creepy. "C'mon kid, tell me you have something?"

I could have picked any number of songs to fill the last ten minutes of the set. I could also have just left Shellie hanging, which really wasn't an option for me. He'd been nice enough to me in the end and it had been a fun hang playing with them. I couldn't just leave the poor guy when I had the ability to help him. That would have been wrong. Then, I had an idea.

I picked up the twelve string and slung it over my shoulder, checking the tuning again before I plugged in. "Yeah, I've got something. It's new and it might stink, but it'll cover your time issue." Shellie looked like he'd just been saved from execution or something and he half-hugged me before backing off the stage at an almost run.

"Go for it, kid! I'll just, um, sit over here and supervise…"

And so, I found myself on the stage at the Anchor Inn in Wildwood, New Jersey, with an Ovation hardback twelve string acoustic guitar suddenly performing solo in the name of Dr. Shellie Bennett and The Cozy Morley's. It was not where I'd planned to be to be sure but oddly, at that moment I felt like I'd been heading towards that moment all day long.

I think I'd felt like I was swimming upstream most of the day. When I finally took the stage, I sat down on a stool that had previously hosted Pastor Bass Player Guy's beers, a point I learned upon sitting down and finding my pants wet immediately. Seriously, there were hundreds of coasters nearby.

I pulled out my phone and placed it on my knee as I didn't completely trust my command of the new lyrics yet. I mean, I'd just written it a few hours earlier and for that matter I hadn't ever played it through even once anywhere but in my head.

Big Bobbie heard me plug in and sat down next to Angie. Betsy immediately brought him a very small glass with what looked like beer in it. He took a tiny sip and then leaned back in his chair. I looked at Angie and really couldn't read her face. She didn't know what I was doing any more than I did. The room had quieted and everyone was looking at me. The boisterous energy from our version of "Everlong" was long gone and the room was now awaiting whatever came next. I remember thinking to myself that they were all thinking, "We're here! Do something!"

I'd played solo plenty of times. To date, it has generally been my preferred way to play and I'd always prepared and practiced anything and everything I might do or say on stage. I always had a plan, until this time. I'm still not sure why I chose to play this new and untested song except that it was what struck me to do. I don't know what drove me to do it but it's what I did. I had to start playing something. It was getting awkward with the audience staring at me expectantly so I did that thing where I just start talking.

"So, I guess I'm sitting in for the rest of The Cozy Morley's, who've um, well…"

"They've become indisposed, College boy!" called a voice from the bar. Pretty sure it was Pastor Bass Guy, but I'm not sure. Whoever he was, it got a solid laugh from the crowd.

I'm sure I turned red, but I called back, "Yeah, well, that's great. Well done there," which actually got a chuckle too. "I'm going to play something that you've never heard as, um, well, I've never played it before. I hope you like it."

I was looking at Angie as I said it, so I saw her eyes widen in recognition as I started strumming out the first few chords. I liked the guitar, but it felt different than my own. Once I got into it, I remembered that I'd been working on the song for months, and it felt right to me once I got out of my own way. The words seemed to fit and the moment felt right so I just went for it and sang this song, the one whose words had come to me earlier, sitting beneath Uncle Bob's ceiling fan. I don't know if it's any good, but this is how it started.

"There's a girl in the Garden. Quietly she sits, watching the Earth breathe.

Gardener's little helper. Silently taking in everything she sees."

After I finished these first lines I ventured a look at Angie and she sorta had her hands in front of her, folded almost prayer-like. I noticed that Betsy had taken up the seat next to her with Big Bobbie on the other side. Visually it was an odd grouping that almost took me out of what I was doing for a moment.

"Perhaps that's where she learned to love another.

Perhaps that's where she learned the golden rule.

And it all seems so simple, how she lives it.

Is it any wonder why she'd saddened by the things we don't do?

There's a girl who plants a flower.

All that she wants to do is share its bloom with me and you.

Though we take it all for granted, how can we be so frozen when each petal is an open hand?"

Everything up to this point was going back and forth in some variations of a Dm9 chord and something else that escapes me right now and a lot of fingerpicking before moving into a G Major/Am7/Dm7 thingy before resolving back into G major again, kind of dramatically growing warm before settling back into the original Dm stuff. Was cool and mellow before getting big sound-wise.

As the major chords developed, this was the chorus that followed:

"The only reason I can thrive today
Is the garden within me remains in bloom.
All of you who journey through leave a footprint,
Plant a seed. Do not tread on me.
Nature must be nurtured, somehow.
We all walk the garden, but the soil beneath us,
seems to rise to greet her footsteps.
We connect, under a gardener's watchful eye,
 and he knows, and she knows, and we know,
That there is love-out there!"
The pace picks up here and I was grooving!
"Sometimes I walk softly, and sometimes
I make noise.
Sometimes I forget that we were all once
girls and boys
And then we grew. And then we grew and
here we are."
I was out of lyrics at this point, but I was really into the song. I felt like the song wasn't quite done so I vamped for a few bars and looked around. The crowd seemed to be listening and looking at me. Something

came to me as a way to end the song as to be honest, I hadn't quite figured out how to bring it home by this point. I looked at Angie and her hands were still folded, pressed against her face like she was protecting her nose which meant I couldn't read her expression. Out of nowhere a line came to me to end the song so I went with it.

"See yourself, through someone else's eyes tonight."

Angie's eyes went wide as I sang that, but I don't think it registered with me in that moment. I was still trying to figure out how to end this thing. This is what came to me so it's what I sang.

"See yourself and I promise you, I promise you,
I promise you…That this is me…"

I let the last chord fade out on its own. It was minor and kinda dissonant and I'd played it in a long strum up higher on the neck so it was a little tinny it its tone quality. It wasn't quite the triumphant ending we'd had for "Everlong" but there was polite applause.

Shellie came back on stage and leaned into the microphone, "Thank you! We are The Cozy Morley's!" he called out, and got some applause. He muttered "more or less," as he backed away from the mic.

Angie was staring at me and Betsy the waitress was talking in her ear, but Shellie came over and kinda grabbed my head in a manner that I'm sure he thought was affectionate and paternal but really just kinda hurt. "You were great, kid! Totally saved my bacon, especially since my band vanished…" he let the end of that sentence linger as Pastor Bass dude returned to the stage to help break down their gear. He was a decent-looking guy and there were a few ladies from the bar who had followed him over to the stage eager to help.

"Oh, hush now, Sheldon," the Pastor replied with his surprisingly sonorous voice. "We don't get to 'drop the mic,' ever," winking at me and helping the ladies up onto the stage to assist him. "Had to see what that was like and I, for one, think I will enjoy it a great deal." He pulled me aside. Until that moment I had continued to stand there awkwardly. "I imagine Kelly is otherwise occupied at the present moment, but please let me thank you on his behalf. We've been suffering through Kelly and Shannon drama for several seasons now. You play well," he said, extending his hand. "I wish you good fortune wherever you're going."

"Boston" I replied, kind of stupidly.

"Yes, well, there too," he sighed, smelling of vanilla. He then flittered off to help his new lady friends break down his gear.

At that point, the next band started lingering around waiting for the Morley's to vacate so they could set up. They were all young, around my age and they were all wearing the same T-shirt with their band name "One Blue Eye" emblazoned on the back and a giant eye on the front that looked way more professional than the Sharpie shirts of the earlier band. They had a troop of girls with them too, all in the same shirt, each with a pile of shirts clutched in their arms, I assumed for future use.

At this point, I realized we were done. "Sitting in" with Shellie had been way more intense than I had planned, but I'd had fun, and helping out Kelly and Shannon was cool and if any of the video came out, especially the new song I did, I thought that it might be something I could build on going forward. I waved at Shellie, who was now arguing about something with Big

Bobby. I stepped off the stage and headed back towards the table.

Angie was sitting alone as I approached, which I was already in the process of beating myself up over, and moved to sit down. She stood up and had a look on her face like I couldn't believe at all! Her eyes were welling up and her face was red, and in all the time I've known her, I've NEVER, and I mean, EVER seen her really break down. Yeah, she might have teared up at the end of "Lord of the Rings," but I did too, and we were both cool enough to pretend we hadn't noticed. This was way different. She looked like she was about to explode and as I made a move towards her, she pulled away from me, again, her face screwed up in a way I didn't have any idea how to deal with.

I think I tried smiling, thinking she was just moved by the song, which I obviously wrote with her in my mind. After she'd been so encouraging to give me the time to flesh it out earlier, I figured she'd dig it, right? I mean, she was always the one telling me to play live more. Jeez, her "secret" recording of me performing at that hipster place out in New Hope was the reason I got into the Conservatory in the first place!

So, we were standing there near the table, and even though I knew I should probably have just waited and been quiet, my can't-deal-with-it-self blurted out, "So, what did you think?"

She glared at me, eyes searching my face again, and then there were tears pouring out of her eyes, and this wild look on her face. "Damnit! Why do you have to ruin everything?!" She ran out of the Inn, out onto New Jersey Avenue, leaving her sweatshirt on the back of her chair. I grabbed it went to run after her before Mr. Richie at the door rather forcefully reminded me that I hadn't paid for our crabs, so I peeled off most of the remaining cash I had left and handed it to him, running outside and tearing down the street, before I realized that she was sitting in a heap just outside the door, crying. Huge guttural sobs that seemed to come from the same place as her snort when she laughs too hard.

I had no idea what to do. So, I just sat down next to her. She went on for a while before she leaned her head on my shoulder and I put my arm around her. I gave her the sweatshirt and she wiped her eyes on it before burying her whole face in it and crying some more.

It really freaked me out! In the four years that we've been friends, I'm the only one of us that's really cried to the other, and I did it plenty enough for both of us, especially in the early days. I'd like to think I've leveled out a little as I've grown, but I probably haven't. I'd just never seen her lose it like this, I mean, we'd gone to Proms and graduations and I even went with her to her great-aunt's funeral. I'd gone to visit Great Aunt Barbara at the nursing home a few times. She liked the New York Times Crossword puzzles and nonpareils candy. I couldn't help her with either of those interests, but she was a fun lady and liked listening to the cool Sunday morning Jazz show on WPRB out of Princeton, which I liked too. I sat with her and her parents in the family section of her funeral. She was stoic and reserved so I was also, though I really kinda felt their loss myself, to be honest, on her behalf even maybe. I'd never really had anyone to lose.

Anyway, the point is that I was completely and totally lost and befuddled. I figured it was another one of those times where it would be better for me to shut up and let her talk, if and when she wanted to. This was certainly driven by the fact that I really had no idea what to say or do, so we sat together on the sidewalk, leaning up against the Anchor Inn. People stared a bit as they walked by, but they left us alone. I think the fact that I was holding her made most people feel like it was appropriate to walk past a crying girl.

My mind was trying to figure out not only what I'd done wrong, but how to fix it and I was coming up empty. Angie's just always been so stoic! She's the one who's always saying that everything is "just another bump in the road to here" whenever I lost it about my lack of a dad, or some issue with Mom, or one of the girlfriends I obsessed over or getting discouraged with writing and music and whatever. I guess I never conceived the notion that something existed that might make her cry. Maybe I am truly, really, a selfish, selfish person after all.

She seemed to calm down after a while and she leaned her head back on the wall. Mr. Richie, who had been glaring at me, caught Angie's eye and she nodded at him, which sent him back to his post blocking the door and ignoring everyone. I'm quite convinced he was prepared to dismantle me and dump me in the ocean if she'd asked him to. She took a deep breath and then stood up, wiping her face on her hoodie again before putting it on and zipping it up.

"It's cold out," she said, offering me a hand to help me up. I took it and stood.

"Um, yeah," is what I think I said. I was still not sure what to do.

"You have no idea what to do right now, do you?"

"Pretty much, no."

She laughed and punched me in the arm again, not too hard this time, but I was certain I'd have a bruise in the morning. She still looked upset, but I was really afraid to say anything so, I remembered what she'd said at Prom, and by way of rebooting the situation without thinking it through, blurted out:

"You look pretty."

"What?"

"I said, 'you look pretty.' I hear girls like it when boys tell them that."

"You did that one already," she replied, but she almost laughed, and I saw her eyes well up a little bit, but she wiped her eyes with her sleeve and took my hand and started walking. I followed.

"You are simply not helping things, my friend." Her voice did that thing where it goes all over the place.

"Where are we going?"

"Back towards the beach. If we're going to really talk, I want to it be there."

"Why?"

"Because I'm a girl who's upset and it's what I want!"

I saw no reason to argue with her, so I didn't.

CHAPTER TEN

My head was swimming. She held my hand the whole time as we walked up Spencer Avenue towards the boardwalk. It was only four blocks to the boards, but it felt like the walk took forever. When we got there, we were right near one of Morey's piers, the one with the Ferris Wheel, its lights bright and dominating the skyline. The area we were in was crowded and noisy, but Angie was locked in on that giant Ferris Wheel.

"Would you please ride the Ferris Wheel with me?" she asked. She'd stopped crying but there was something really sad about the way she asked. She kept looking me in the eyes, which was a little unsettling as it just seemed like we were having a staring contest after a while. I started to wonder if this was just about me heading off to school the next day, but there was something else behind her eyes. I nodded and we walked over to the ticket booth and got enough tickets for us both and we got in the line to ride. I had to let go of her hand to buy the tickets, and it seemed like she didn't want to let go at first. I kinda didn't either, now that I think of it, and after I paid and put my wallet away, we held on again.

I still wasn't really sure what was wrong or what had made her so upset, but it seemed a little like she'd been waiting until we got onto the ride to start talking.

"I'm sorry that I lost it before. That wasn't supposed to happen."

I was so relieved she was talking to me.

"What was that all about? Was it something I did? Was the song that bad?"

She bopped me again on the arm, "No you idiot. The song was good, really good. It was beautiful and unexpected. You surprised me."

"Are those good things?" I asked.

She grabbed my hand with her other hand and leaned onto my shoulder again, kinda nuzzling into me. It felt good. Natural. "Those are good things, sweetie. They are. It just made things feel more complicated for a minute."

I didn't understand. "I don't understand." I said.

She patted my hand. "I know. I know. I'll explain. Let's just ride the wheel for a while, please."

And so we did. I knew it was a big wheel and all, but I was surprised how high I felt. We were clearly at the highest point in all of Wildwood. It was getting darker now, but looking out at the ocean from that perspective made me appreciate even more the place and the whole concept of the beach. I remember thinking I wanted to spend more time there next summer, after school was done. We rode for a while in silence, Angie nuzzled up next to me, which again, felt nice. She was holding onto me almost completely, and while we'd sat on couches or laid on the beach together before and been as close as we were then, something felt different in her, as it had all day, and I think it felt different in me too. When we were at the very top of the wheel, she finally started talking.

"I really am sorry about before. You didn't ruin anything. I just wanted one last good day with you before you leave tomorrow is all."

I was confused. I turned to look at her and remember her face being shrouded in the blinking neon lights of the ride-first purple, then red, then green. It was hypnotic.

"What do you mean a last day? I'll be home in a few months, if not sooner. And you can come visit me in Boston, it's only a few hours away. What are you talking about? I'll probably come home for Homecoming in a few weeks."

She took my face in her hands and looked into my eyes, her face serious. "No. You won't. You can't. Not now."

I took her hands in mine and pulled them off my face, "What do you mean I can't? I don't understand…" It seemed like we were stuck in that position at the very apex of the wheel for a really long time, the car swaying in the breeze. There was music blasting from the nearby waterpark at the end of the pier. Then the evening fireworks started as she spoke. The sky seemed to split open along with my world.

"Avery, I have cancer, again. I've just started treatment."

Time seemed to stop and everything went quiet. When the Ferris wheel started moving again, I felt a pit in my stomach. We'd been stuck at the top for what felt like forever as they let people off below, but the fireworks continued unabated. I was completely overwhelmed as everything became clear to me at once. All at once: She did look a little paler! She wanted to do so many different things! She asked for that story about my dad, and she had some kind of drama with her aunt at lunch. Everyone we interacted with during the day seemed to treat her gently all day long and she fell asleep at her aunt's house and she dozed off on the way here. She got that head rush in the garden earlier and she didn't seem to eat much and she'd went and gotten a tattoo and maybe this was why she wasn't going to school in the fall! It was too much all at once and the colors of the wheel and the fireworks and the noise of the music and of the people cheering all at the same time might have overloaded my circuits. It was a minute or so at least before I said something. I didn't know what to say, again, like an idiot. I should have said something like, "I'm so sorry" or "Oh God, are you OK?" or something like that, but what did I say?

I said, "Huh?"

I'm a real winner. She looked at me and I thought she was going to laugh at me again, but she saw something in my face that I didn't so she pulled me in and held me. It took a few minutes to realize that I was crying now too, just a good solid openly mellow weeping. We held each other until our car made it to the bottom. It was a little uncomfortable as the operator opened our car and we were both were holding one another and crying. He said, "Oh, come on now young flutterbyes, it couldn't have been that frightening..." in a thick Irish accent. His nametag said "FLORIS" all in caps.

I don't know why that was - everyone else had normal letters. He was around our age even, but something about him seemed old and fatherly all the same.

Angie stood up and dragged me along with her. We left the pier and walked down towards the water. It was dark and getting colder, but I let her lead me. I don't think I really had a choice in the matter. We walked along the beach a bit before she found a spot she liked and sat down, patting the sand beside her.

"Thank you for taking me on the Ferris wheel," she whispered. Angie is not generally known for her subtle whispering. She was so calm. For her to go from the meltdown of earlier to the sudden calm, I was perplexed. I started to wonder if she had practiced this conversation a few times.

"Uh huh" I said. I was reeling. I mean, hell, I didn't know what to do or say at all. I was feeling way too many things at once, so I let her do the talking.

"I've known for a while now, and I know you'll want to be mad at me for not telling you right away, but I hope you won't be, because I need you. I really need you, and I kept it from you out of love."

Honestly, until she said that she thought I'd be mad at her, I don't think it occurred to me to be mad at her. It did then though.

"Why didn't you tell me?! What the hell, Angie?!" I went on like that for a bit, and she took it all, sitting on the beach, her arms wrapped around her knees, letting me vent. I think a few times she said something like, "You're right…I know," but I'm not really sure. I was so upset with her but I think I was feeling scared for her too and it all kind of bubbled over. I paced around the beach and probably looked like a lunatic and after a while I ran out of steam, but not before I'd frightened an older couple walking their dog, who sped up to get further away from us. I could still hear the rides and the carneys and the fireworks in their finale. It was several minutes of silence between us before she tapped the sand next to her and I sat down, out of breath and drained.

"Feel better now?" she asked.

"I don't."

She smirked at me and said, "That was quite a rant, sweetie. Quite impressive, actually. Catch your breath, and then we'll talk, OK?" I nodded and we sat there a few minutes before she started. I remember the moon reflecting in her eyes, which were clear and calm and beautiful.

When she started talking again it felt like I was listening from the end of a long tunnel at first. "Avery, I was starting to feel really tired and was in a decent amount of pain in early June, so we went back to my old doctor, who ran some tests. I found out right before Prom that my blood counts were off. They ran a bunch of other tests and, lucky me, I've got a whole new kind of cancer this time."

Angie cupped a handful of sand in front of her and let it slowly sift through her fingers as she spoke. "They think they've got it early, but since it's a second visit, they don't want to fool around with it. I just started Chemotherapy and we will do that another six weeks, a total of four cycles of chemo, and then we'll see how things are."

It all sounded so matter-of-fact that I had a hard time hearing it at all. She looked out at the water a minute. I asked her how she was feeling, and she smiled and said something like, not too bad yet, but "that was a good question."

"You didn't tell me."

"Sweetie, I didn't tell you because I wanted us both to finish out school and not have it be about me being sick. I just wanted to be a normal girl, going to Prom with my best friend, going to graduation, all that dumb stuff. Whatever happens, I wanted us both to have that, and you can be mad at me if you want, but you should know that I'm at peace with it now."

"At peace with what, exactly?" I asked her. Again, I was so confused.

"All of it. I'm at peace with choosing not to tell you, despite how much I might have wanted to tell you how I was feeling. I really hated keeping this from you these last weeks. It was really hard and I've felt really alone at times. Chemo sucks big time! And I'm at peace with whatever happens with me. I just wanted one good, good day with you before you go off and set the world on fire, I mean, look what you managed to pull off with a half set with Shellie Bennet and his whatever's tonight! I've known for years that you were going somewhere, but I wanted you to myself one last day, one last, good day where it was just you and me doing our thing, you know? I like who I am with you…"

She trailed off on this, and I felt like my head was wallowing in motor oil, but she continued: "And I like who you've always been with me. You're my best friend and your song was great, it's just, I wasn't expecting it! I wasn't ready for it and it kind of got to me is all. You surprised me, and I think I forgot that you could do that. It's selfish of me, I know, but I didn't want to have to share you today."

I heard everything that she'd said, but as I tried to navigate it all, I felt a panic creep into my stomach, even worse than when we were on the Ferris wheel. I kinda lost it again, grasping at the most glaring detail about it all.

"Angie, there's no way I'm letting this be any kind of last day. I can't go to Boston while you're going through this! I'll call the school in the morning and get a deferment or whatever it was you did and then -"

She cut me off, turning toward me and taking my hands again, holding them between us. "Now you listen to me Avery Absalom Young," she started, which completely threw me because she'd never used my middle name before.

"You are getting on that train tomorrow morning and you are going to Boston and you are going to work damned hard to do well and earn that scholarship you need to continue next year. You are not going to stay here and make me soup and hold my hand and watch my hair wither and my skin bruise. You are going to go and do your damnedest to blow the minds of those people up there because that is what I, who loves you with all her heart, need you to do for me. I need you to go and do that and work hard for me, and for your mother who has busted her ass for the last eighteen years as a waitress at Jim's Country Diner to provide you with a year's worth of tuition. That's what I need you to do, love. I need you to do that. You have to do that for me."

I tried to pull my hands away, but she held on tight. Her eyes were tearing again, but they kept scanning my face, looking for something. "Please?"

"Angie...I,"

"Say you'll do this for me."

"I don't want to."

"I know you don't. That's why it's hard, but I've thought about this a long time, longer than I've known I was even sick. You were always going to have to get out of Jersey to see what's out there for you. I have my own talents, sweetie, but they are different from yours. You're going to have to try and do something with the things you have, I mean, look at what you did tonight without even knowing what was coming! You just sat in with those guys and you were amazing! You did that, and you did it without thought of reward or compensation, you simply dove into the music, 'just because!' and that's special! That's a gift - wherever it came from, don't you dare waste it. Avery, I won't let you! And think about what happened at the chapel. You surprised us both there. You need to get out of here and meet the rest of the world. Whatever else happens, I'm asking you to do this out of care for me and out of love for you."

That was the second time she'd used the word "love," and it hadn't yet registered. So, I continued, "I don't want to go now, and I could help you." She shook her head and was like;

"My parents, my sister, and Bob and Jenny are around, and your mom may help out too."

"My mom knows about this?"

"Yeah, she's known a while. I asked her to let me tell you and she agreed."

I felt really angry right then, like I'd been lied to by the two people I was supposed to trust the most. I felt completely played or manipulated or something, I don't know exactly, but I know I was mad. They'd both just decided when and if I should know something about all this. I felt the anger invade my chest and it began looking for a route to explosion. I controlled myself after a minute and regrouped. I was about to tell her how angry and belittled I felt until our eyes met, finally.

Even though we'd been together all day and connecting all day and looking at one another all day, I felt like it wasn't until that moment that we'd really seen each another. The anger I'd nearly been overwhelmed by seemed to dissolve just as suddenly as I really looked at her again and opened my eyes.

I studied her long hair that over the years seemed to be in an argument between blonde, blueish that one time and something else too, but was now her natural brunette;

her deep brown eyes that always seemed to have a glimmer of something, flecks of gold or green, but they were always striking; her skin, which always bordered on the paler side but looked more so in the light of the moon and maybe even the battle her body was going through. She has this dimple in her chin and a really light freckle on her left cheek bone that I couldn't see in the darkness that had settled around us, but I remembered it being there.

Her lips. That's where it started.

I'd never really noticed them before, but I did just then and I couldn't look away. Her lips and face always seemed so strong, like the rest of her, but there was something else there in that moment that drew me in, looking at Angie in that moment I realized that while I'd typically been dim about it, I'd probably been in love with her for pretty much ever. I felt overwhelmed in every manner.

My heart might have figured it out earlier, as it had been telling me all day how I felt being so close to her, but my head has always been behind the curve. Angie had always been the only stable thing in my life, so no wonder I hadn't been able to see her differently, until now.

I reached out and touched her face with my right hand and she leaned into it. She reached out and held mine the same way, like we were mirroring one another in some weird Jersey shore-mime thing. She looked at me again, in the eyes, like she'd been doing all afternoon, and she knew. She exhaled, in relief it seemed as she smiled, running her hand through my hair. She blinked and a single tear fell down her face.

"There are the eyes I've been wanting to look at me…" she said, before I kissed her, holding her face in mine and wiping that tear away before wrapping my arms

161

around her and pulling her close to me. It was amazing! I've never felt anything like it. My body had tingles like when your foot falls asleep but like all over and I felt like no matter how tight we held each other we couldn't get as close as we wanted to be to one another. I don't know how long we kissed but it was a while before she pulled back and looked at me and laughed a girly kind of laugh I'd never heard before.

"Wow," I said.

Angie just kind of exhaled, like she'd just come up from under water before kissing me again quickly and bopping me in the arm at the same time.

"Ow! Why do you keep hitting me?"

"How long did it take you to see me!?" She smiled as she said it and she rubbed my arm where she's been slugging me all day. "That was the last one, I promise. It was either that or give you a hickey, and I wasn't sure you'd come around enough to kiss me." She seemed out of breath. I didn't want to let go. "Took you long enough!"

It's difficult to describe what I was feeling. I felt this warmth in my chest and the pit that was in my stomach earlier seemed to have been filled up with everything that Angie and I had always been to each other, but now it also held all that we might be. All that we were going to be. It was an amazing feeling. It was like we tripled everything we had been. Feeling her close to me I suddenly felt safe and loved and honestly, just home, in a way I'd never felt at home, if that makes sense. I felt like I never wanted to be anywhere else. We kissed more and for a long time and it felt like no matter how hard we held onto each other, we couldn't quite stop reaching for another place to hold.

My heart was full. I was in love and I felt amazing! Then, I remembered I was supposed to leave and that she was sick and I kinda tripped over the moment.

"Angie, I can't leave you now, especially not now. I love you."

That kind of ended the make out, which as I said was beyond anything I'd ever felt. All we did really was kiss and touch but, it was like her touch was electric. There was a ringing in my ears and I felt hot all over in a way I'd never felt before.

Angie stood up and reached out her hand to me, which I took and we walked a bit. We passed some dude with a dog wearing a blinking red light on his collar walking along the water's edge. And after he'd passed, she turned back to me and kissed me again, a quick one, and then wrapped our fingers, both hands one on top of the other, as we walked along the shoreline.

"Sweetie, you've given me the best day of my life today. I have never been happier. In all my hopes about today, I never truly let myself believe that we would be right here, on my favorite beach in all the world with our hearts really open for the first time." She grabbed my face with both hands and kissed me again, long and deep. For the fact that we'd never kissed before you'd have thought we had practiced for years as un-awkward as it felt.

She laid her head on my chest and said, "I still want you to go tomorrow. I still need you to go." I didn't know what to do with that, so I pulled away a bit, but she held on.

"How am I supposed to leave you now? I know I've been an idiot and should have seen it sooner, but, Angie, I love you and want to be with you. What kind of guy am I if I finally realize that I'm in love with you and then leave you to face all of this without me?"

"Say that again,"

"Say what again? That I'm an idiot?"

"No, that is well known. Say the good part, silly."

"What, that I'm in love with you?"

"Yeah, say that part again."

It might have been overkill, but I cupped her chin and said, "Angela Marie Yarrow, I am in love with you."

She held my gaze a few seconds before she snorted. "OK, we're even on the middle name thing, sweetie. But that was nice."

"Understood." I found myself laughing, despite that I was still upset by the fact that we had just professed our love for one another, yet she was asking me to leave her to face a huge medical crisis without me. "I don't want to leave you."

"I understand, but I have something else I want to say to you before we say more about that, OK?"

"I suppose."

"I want you to understand that am hopelessly in love with you and have been for a very, VERY long time. Do you understand that?"

I nodded.

"Good, then let me explain to you why I need you to get on that train in the morning." She took my hand and started walking down the beach again. The moon was way high in the sky now and I wasn't sure what time it was, but I knew it was late. Some of the noise on the boardwalk had eased after the fireworks were done and the crowds had dissipated. "If you stay home to care for me, you would likely do a wonderful job of it. You'd be supportive, you'd be kind, and we'd get to spend all sorts of time exploring all aspects of our newly expressed love. And don't think that's not appealing to me too." She gripped me around the waist to emphasize her point here, which had an effect for sure. "But if you stayed now and gave up this chance to really study and learn something, really create music or whatever you come to glean from this year, which your mother has worked really hard to give you, it would be a genuine waste of an opportunity that I want for you. I need you to try. Even if you don't get to go beyond this year, you have to go away and try. I need you to. You'll be no good to me or to anyone else if you're always wondering about what you might have done."

There are times I feel like not only an open book to Angie, but a forgone conclusion. I long ago dealt with the fact that she's smarter than me, but in that moment, I felt almost like a youngling being taught by an older student. She has a wisdom I can only admire.

"But I understand now, Ange. I can try to get into school here and still be around for you…"

"Understand this, my love," and she giggled in that girly way again. "Sorry, I just kind of liked saying that…" and she kissed my cheek. "Understand that I started loving you the day you fell on your ass in the bleachers at gym class that first day of freshman year and it's grown by bits and pieces every day since. You are my best friend, and I have waited, patiently I might add, for you. I watched you lavish your affection on a whole army of pretenders: cheerleaders, that artsy girl with the pink hair, gothic music geeks, and prom queens, and all the rest. I have waited for you and have loved you the whole time, without reservation, hoping desperately in my heart that you would someday see me for who I am: a pretty amazing girl who also happens to love you."

Angie paused a moment and stopped walking and

turned back towards the ocean, which had been our soundtrack most of the day, always there. A wave lapped up on our feet as she went on. "After all these years I, know this: my love will hold until Christmas, which is when I will see you next. Please let me get through these treatments and tests. Then, you come home to me at Christmas, because I know that my love will hold. Will yours?"

I was just blown away by what Angie said to me right there. I know in my heart that the answer I gave her is true, but as I consider it against the real gravity and power of what she said, I wonder if I came up a little small.

"Yeah, it will," I said.

She didn't seem bothered in the least. In fact, she hugged me and then skipped away towards the water, leaving her shoes in the sand and stepping into the surf, scooping some of it up in her hands and running it through her hair. She looked back at me, grinning and said, "had to get my hair a little wet."

I took off my shoes and walked out and put my arms around her waist as I came up behind her. We stood along the shore and she wrapped her arms around mine and we stood there what felt like only a few minutes but was probably more - time was becoming finite - before she turned her head back toward me and kissed me again, her hand reaching up to run through my hair. Honestly, I'd never felt the swirl of emotions and passion that I felt in that moment. It was a very full day in that regard, but I didn't know what to do next. It was all so new and exciting yeah, but strange and unknown.

Angie turned back to toward me and hugged me around the waist tightly and sighed.

"What?" I asked.

"Oh, nothing. It's just I'm really happy. I just never was sure if you'd ever come around, sweetie."

I suddenly felt like a complete jerk. "I'm sorry," I said. I wasn't really sure what I was apologizing for but it felt like the right thing to say.

"For what are you sorry?"

"I don't know really. Just that, well, it took until now. My timing kinda stinks, huh?"

Angie made a face like she was thinking and then took my right hand in her left and led me closer to the water.

"Well, it's funny now. Before today, I would have given anything for you to finally notice me in all my awesomeness, you know, at some point in the last, oh, I don't know, four years? But now, I'm happy, but it wasn't the way I'd imagined today going."

"What do you mean?" I asked. I watched her scanning the dark and wet shoreline for more shells. None of note appeared as far as I could see.

"Today was a really, really, good, good day for me, in so many ways. But as happy as I am, I want you to know that I didn't plan on things going this way. I always hoped you'd see me, but I didn't plan on all the," she paused, searching again for the right word. She rarely did that.

"All the what?"

"Well, all the moments I couldn't control. Though I tried…"

"Like losing it at the Anchor?"

She elbowed me in the side, but it was pretty weak. "Well, yeah, that! You surprised me with all that, more than you know. I guess everything caught up with me in that moment, as it was really hard for me to keep everything from you. I know it sounds wrong, but I was going to anyway. My plan was to not tell you at all, at least until later. Aunt Jenny has been furious with me for

167

weeks for not telling you."

Now it all made some sense. "I was wondering what that was all about. Why did that matter so much to her?"

"Let's go this way," Angie said, leading us back towards the pier and the Ferris Wheel. "Jenny and Bob really care about you and thought I was being selfish and unfair to you. She's always been big on truth and openness. It's why she and my parents are always at odds. She shares every opinion she has, regardless of whether she's been asked for it or if it's helpful or constructive. She held it in for me though, just barely. She hated it, but when I told her I wasn't ready for you to know yet, she respected it."

I was kind of blown away by her aunt and uncle's feelings about me. I'd always liked them but I never imagined that I was someone they thought about if I wasn't right in front of them. "Something kind of sweet about her thinking of me like that."

"Don't do that."

I had no idea what she was talking about. "Do what?"

"That thing you do where you're amazed that people care about you. Uncle Bob and Aunt Jenny have always liked you. They'll freak when I tell them about all this," and she drew me tight to her for a second before impishly pushing me away. "If today has taught you anything at all, please know that some of us really do think about you when we're not together."

I had taken her playful shove and made it into a slow-motion dramatic fall because it's just the sort of thing we do, but I was blown away by how she'd known pretty much exactly what I had been thinking, again. I wasn't used to that sort of family relationship where you think about people you're not around all the time and they think about you. I was used to living with Mom and honestly, outside of the last few years with Angie as my best friend, I was alone a lot. I grew up by myself a lot because Mom had to work, and Nana was around but she had her own life and it's not like she lived next door. I had friends, sure, but it wasn't like we did stuff regularly and the girls I dated up until now usually brought me into their own circle briefly, before those connections all inevitably ended with the relationship. Once I got into music and performing, that brought more people into my life but they all had that context of music or clubs.

But there was always Angie. My hand was in the sand and I was preparing a dramatic pratfall into the water when I decided to stop clowning. I stood up and brushed the sand off of myself before turning towards her, putting the ocean at my back. The moon was just over her shoulder and a slight breeze seemed to pass suddenly. It was warm and I remember thinking to myself, "how could I not have seen this girl who's been right next to me for so long?" I didn't say it just then, but I thought it.

I think it's simple in its own way. I have always loved Angie, if I'm honest. She's funny and smart and beautiful, even more so now than when we first met, and she not only gets me, she understands me because, for whatever reason, she wants to. She's really been the most important person in my life for years, but I think maybe I'd never, ever in my life felt the real and genuine kind of love that loving her as more than my best friend entails. There was no question that I am feeling it with four years' worth of interest.

I'd had something to say to her after I brushed myself off and started to walk towards her but I honestly got lost in looking at her in the moonlight with the light of the pier behind her. I'm sure it sounds corny, but it was like everything I was seeing was through one of those photo filters that tighten everything up and enhance the colors. It was like the entire world suddenly looked sharper and more in focus, at least as long as I kept looking at Angie. I didn't want to look away.

She coughed as I guess I'd been staring a while without talking.

"Oh, yeah. Um, I forgot what I wanted to say."

"Really? That was a pretty dramatic, dare I say almost 'superhero slow-mo' walkover with a real impressive 'I'm about to say something important' vibe to it."

"Yeah, um, about that, well…"

"I was really looking forward to hearing whatever that was!" She pouted but she had that twinkle in her eye where I knew she was genuinely enjoying messing with me. Our dynamic hadn't seemed to change at all really. But we got to kiss now, which became apparent just then. "Perhaps this will jog your memory?"

Angie put her hand on my chin and pulled my head lower, kissing my forehead followed by my nose and chin before giving me a very soft peck on the lips.

I think I probably stood there stupidly for way too long after she released my chin and stepped away. "Did that help?"

"Ah, no. Not exactly. Now I'm completely distracted. What was I talking about?" I meant it completely! My head was swimming with feelings and the rest of my body was doing something else entirely. I felt like an afterthought to my own physical being as it was doing its own 'thang' and leaving me out of the loop.

"Let's walk. It'll come back to you." She slipped her right arm through my left and we started walking back towards the Ferris Wheel Pier. The dramatic moment had passed but I did think of a question after we'd trudged halfway up the giant Wildwood beach.

"Why did you change your mind and tell me what was going on with you? I'm glad you did now, but you said a few times that you planned different, so, I guess I'm wondering why?"

"Hrmm," she started, slipping into her Yoda voice again, which always makes me laugh. I can't count the number of awful moments we'd gone through together that were smoothed over due to her timely use of that voice.

The very best was this one time that we were out to dinner with my mom at the "Golden Coach Diner," which we always used to call "The Roach" although it was a really classic Jersey diner. Mom, as a server at a rival diner that was literally a mile and a half further down Route 130 South, "AND on the other side of the road" Mom would have said, was being awful to the older lady who was serving us. She was really in a mood that night and all I really wanted was a plate of their gravy cheese fries. She was belittling and nasty, making a real scene. I was about to completely lose it, as I'd grown really sensitive to the way servers get treated because of Mom's work, but I'd also had enough of listening to Mom criticize things all the time. We were in kind of a rough patch then and Angie knew all about it and knew I was about to blow up, which wouldn't have helped things and I remember she made the same, "Hrmm" noise putting herself in character I guess before continuing.

"Fries Gravy Cheese? Hrmm? Or Cheese Fries Gravy? Can't figure out how to this thing say!!!"

She couldn't even get through it without laughing and that set me off, and I suggested in my own Yoda voice,

"Cheesy Grave Frieseys" and then she started snorting and we were both just laughing idiots throughout the rest of the meal which, gratefully gave Mom something else to focus on and she left the poor server alone after that. I still think that's funny.

Anyway, after she'd 'hrmmd' she continued with, "Difficult question you ask." That was the last word on the subject as we kept walking until we reached the stairs that led off the beach and back onto the pier, where we'd come down earlier. A lot had happened and changed since we stepped onto the beach. We sat on the bottom step, feet still in the sand as we talked. I moved to lean back onto the stair behind me when she gasped, "Careful there!"

I sat up quickly, "That was four years ago Ange!"

"Still 'Classic Avery' but if it helps, I liked you from the start there in gym class," she laughed. "Right after you fell on your -"

"You're avoiding the question, Jedi Master Angie..." I rolled my eyes and gingerly leaned back onto the step behind me, you know, just being careful.

She folded her arms over my knee and leaned against me. Her hair draped over my leg and the breeze, still oddly warm, brushed it against my calf which kind of gave me a charge. It was kinda like when I saw her tattoo earlier except now it felt OK. It felt normal and natural even. Love really is an amazing thing. That moment with her leaning against me and her hair reaching at me on the whim of the wind never goes away entirely. It felt so far away from any other time I thought I'd been in love. It makes me wonder what I was really in, before.

"So," Angie began, dropping the Yoda voice. "You want to know why I changed my mind and told you about my cancer?"

I got a pit in my stomach that swallowed whole the butterflies that had been there just a moment before. I must have made a face as she turned her head left towards me, still leaning on my knees. "It has a name. It's called cancer because that's what it is, but it's just a word. We can't be afraid of a word and we are going to have to be able to talk about it. But, I know that right now it's new for you."

That made some sense to me, so I nodded. I was still working to wrap my head around it all. I know that Angie and her family had gone through treatment for her when she was a kid, but I'd never experienced anything like that. Nana and Mom were really my only family and they never even discussed a cold with me. I've never even been to a hospital, except that one time the Jazz Band played a holiday show at Princeton Hospital, and even that was in the lobby as people came in. It's amazing to realize how little you really know about the world, until you're forced to know something new and it becomes everything.

"So, do you really want to know why I told you after all?"

"Yeah, I do."

She swatted my leg and stood up, again all full of energy. "Well, then we must take a short field trip for full dramatic effect," and with that she padded up the steps back onto the pier. I caught up with her as she was passing the Ferris Wheel and I took her hand, just as our old friend "FLORIS" noticed us and waved his arms dramatically.

"Well done, lad, overcome your fear of our giant wheel! Oh, and look at that," he crowed and postured his hands like he was sizing us up for a picture, "Your pretty flutterbye is holding your hand! Good on ya, lad! Come see us again soon for more exquisite thrills!"

Angie's laughter and almost immediate snortage could be heard quite well over the way too loud music the Piers still had playing, even as it was clear things were slowing down on the boardwalk. It sounded so much louder now with fewer people around. We exited the pier and turned left heading back down the boardwalk in the direction of the convention center and the car. Everything was still lit up but some things had closed already as people headed back to their hotels or houses or whatever. I let her laugh it out for a while without saying anything as "FLORIS" had kinda irritated me earlier but honestly, he didn't bug me the second time around. I mean, how could he?

"Where are we headed exactly?" I asked.

"Soon you shall experience the first part of my explanation. Soon…" She'd dropped the Yoda voice, but I think she was doing his word-styling-thing without really meaning to. I let her have her mystery. There were a few Tramcars that passed that were filled mostly with families holding sleeping children who'd had their fill.

After a few blocks, I had an idea where we might be headed, and I was not really surprised to find us once again sitting on the bench across from the storefront of Madame Marie, Fortune Teller. It was one of those cool beach benches that you can move the back part to sit and face the shore or flip it to face the boardwalk. It was currently positioned to gaze directly at Madame Marie who was once again nodding off in her chair, hands folded contentedly in her lap.

"So, as you may recall, our day stared here with my brilliant suggestion that we have our palms read by 'Sleepy' over there," Angie began. "With me so far?"

"Um yeah, Ange, it was like this morning…"

"Indeed, it was. Now, we both went in and one of us came out frustrated and angry."

I felt like I needed to tread lightly here but my mouth couldn't stop itself. "I remember you told me not to talk to you about it." I'd kinda put the whole Madame Marie thing out of mind until just then.

Angie patted my back, kinda dorkily, "And you've done a marvelous job respecting that, so well done."

"Yeah, but what does that have to do with this?"

"I was just getting to that. The truth is, she said something to me that I didn't want to hear. Something irritating and it got stuck in my craw."

"What's a craw? You have a craw?"

Angie rolled her eyes and patted my hand. "Stay with me, sweetie. She said something I didn't like so I stormed out dramatically. It was pretty dramatic, right?"

"Oh yes, very."

She nodded, satisfied. She leaned close to my left ear and kinda whispered, "Would you like to know what she said to me that caused all the ruckus?"

I did, so I nodded.

She leaned in closer, right next to my ear where I could feel her breath on my neck, which made me turn red again, I'm certain. She put her arm around my waist and pulled me towards her as she spoke. "She said, among other things, that 'you,' in this case meaning me, 'have had your eyes set on something for a long time but they may never see the right ones look back.'"

I let that sit for a minute. It was getting cold and the boardwalk continued to empty out. Even now, looking at what Madame Marie said, I have no idea what it means. I mean you expect a palm reader to be cryptic but sheesh, that's a rough one. Fortunately, Angie thought so too.

"I didn't totally understand what she meant so I asked

her what that meant. She sighed and gripped my hands tightly - too tightly maybe, like old lady strength tightly and she added, looking straight into my eyes, 'it is a shame he cannot see himself through your eyes for a moment. Then he would understand.'" Angie leaned away after that and made almost a "ta-da" gesture with her hands and face.

And then all the pieces seemed to fall into place and I suddenly got seriously freaked out. I stood up and took a few steps away from the bench before turning and sitting right back down again.

"But, I…"

"I know, right?"

"No, but, I used a line like that in the song!"

"You sure did," she crowed, wrapping her arms around my left arm.

"No, but, listen!" I kinda yelled, which startled her as I took both of her hands in mine and held them between us. "I hadn't written that line before I sang it! It just came to me on stage at the end!"

"Whoa. Really? OK, now that is really something, huh?"

"Something? Yeah, but what does it mean? Where'd it come from? How did she know? What does she know? Should we go back over there?" I was feeling a little dizzy and I think my hands were shaking. I'm not entirely sure what I was so worked up about. Angie grabbed my hands and intertwined our fingers and squeezed.

"Take a breath. It's alright."

"But what does it mean?" I took a few breaths, but it didn't seem to help. The next thing I know Angie had slid over closer to me and kissed me. That seemed to settle me down and after a few minutes of that she pulled away and held my face in her hands.

"Better?" she asked.

I nodded, though I was still out of breath but for a much different reason. After a minute, she continued. "Honestly, I don't know what it means. I don't know that I care. I'm just glad that we had today, and I am so grateful for how we got here in the end."

I liked the way she summed it all up. "Me too." We sat a while longer before the breeze off the ocean seemed to turn colder.

"I wonder if we should head towards the car, Ange. Won't the cops start kicking us off the boardwalk soon?" I felt anxious as I said it, just the thought that this day was winding down and what that meant for tomorrow, but it was like almost eleven and getting colder.

She snuggled up next to me and held my arm tighter. "Just a few more minutes."

"OK." I didn't want to go either. I was happy right where I was, especially when I thought about how long it had taken to get there and how foolish and dim I'd been when she'd been beside me all along. After a bit, the music that had been blaring from speakers the length of the boardwalk all day suddenly faded away and a ridiculously cheery voice thanked us for spending the day at the Wildwood boardwalk.

The sudden silence was stark and glaring. It seemed to rouse Madame Marie from her nap, and she stretched her long arms and shook them out as though they had fallen asleep on their own accord, separate from the rest of her. She folded up her chair and was about to go back inside her store when she noticed us and stared, narrowing her old eyes before seeming to nod slightly and wag her finger at us before turning back to her door and turning her sign to closed.

"What do you think that was about?" I wondered, standing up and stretching a bit myself. The prospect of a two-hour drive home appeared daunting, but the thought of dropping Angie at home began to feel even more so.

"Oh, I imagine Madame Marie is likely congratulating herself on another successful day of soothsaying. Speaking of which," she began, reaching my hand again to stand up, "what did she have to say to you this morning?"

I had to think for a second to remember and I think she took my pause as an indication I didn't want to say, so she sorta hip-checked me. "Come on now, I shared mine with you…"

"OK, OK, um, she said something like that if I could just get out of my own way I'd have a chance at true happiness, or something like that. Honestly, it kinda went out the window after you came out so upset."

"Well, that just proves she's for real. She had you summed up pretty well." She wasn't wrong. We were heading towards the car but not talking about the fact that we were headed towards the car.

"She also said that I'd been 'superfluous' with my affections in the past."

"Yeah, well there's that too."

I couldn't really argue with any of it. I was kinda embarrassed by how open a book I could seem to everyone else, but in the end, I let that go. It had all worked out pretty well for us both as far as I could figure. I know I was dreading the coming of morning, but in the midst of all that, I was feeling so much else, everything else really and all over. I didn't know what else to do or say so I figured it was absolutely the right time to be silly. I was right.

"Madame Marie failed to mention anything regarding

an end of evening piggyback ride down the boardwalk…"

She stopped walking and turned to me grabbing my chin and pulling my gaze down to hers. "Don't you dare tease me, young man, especially not on our last day…not fair…" but her eyes were wild and excited.

"I'm serious," but before I got anywhere near the end of the sentence, Angie jumped on my back, arms around my shoulders. My arms held onto her legs, which had wrapped completely around my waist. We'd done this sort of thing before loads of times. She used to love doing it at the Quakerbridge Mall around the holidays, but it felt different now with her holding onto me tighter and my hands on her thighs through her skirt, which flapped behind us like a Bat-cape. It felt more intimate, even in its silliness.

I tore off down the boardwalk with her laughter filling the air around us. There were still some people around and I weaved in between them as I ran like one of those ski club kids at Big Boulder Lodge. Despite the looks we got, we stormed through the remainder of the boards, passing the Wildwood Chapel, long since shuttered for the night. I ran several blocks with her on my back, and by the time we arrived outside the convention center we were both laughing like idiots. I fell to my knees so she could climb off in as ladylike a manner as possible, after which I rolled over onto my back making a show of gasping for oxygen. The convention center sign was blinking its nuclear high-beams about a dog show next week and then an upcoming show for "The Ring of Honor Wrestlepalooza," which of course was followed by an ad for the "30th Annual Cheerapalooza" in October. The lights turned Angie's hair all sorts of colors as she leaned over me, loudly and slowly repeating, "Can-you-hear-me? Hellloooo Mister!"

"Well," I gasped as I leaned my head up a little, "isn't that one too many 'Paloozas' on the same sign? How can you have multiple 'paloozas?' That's like two different 'A-thons' at the same time!" I put my head back down on the ground adding, "I feel ever so slightly short of breath." I did actually, but I may have played it up a little.

Angie leaned over me as an older couple changed their route to move closer to us, looking concerned that I was really in distress. She sat down and placed my head in her lap, purring almost "Well, let me see if this helps," and leaned over to kiss me, gently biting my lip ever so slightly. I'm not capable of describing what that did to me, so I won't.

The older lady nudged her husband as they changed their trajectory, saying "Oh, Henry, remember when you used to kiss me like that?"

Henry shrugged. "No, not really Stella."

"Yeah, me neither Henry…"

They both chuckled and moved off, though I thought I saw Stella put her hand in Henry's back pocket, leaving Angie and I in the continuing blinking heaven that seemed to have appeared beneath the lights of the Wildwood convention center's rotating sign. When we finally came up for air, I really did feel like I was out of breath, my heart pounding and my neck sweating like, well I don't know, something that's really sweaty! Uncle Ted used to say, "sweating like a Yak in heat," but I've never seen a Yak.

"Whoa," I said, sitting up after I don't know how long.

"I know, right?" Angie's hair was all messed up now from the wind and from the fact that I'd been running my hands all through it without realizing it. She brushed it off her face. "Making up for lost time…"

When she said, "lost time" it hit me again kinda like it

had been hitting me all day, that I was leaving in a matter of hours. I got quiet immediately. We'd just been basking in one another and having fun and I immediately felt like I might lose my breath again. Like being stuck outside on a cold night with no fire and a blanket that's far too narrow. It had grown cold suddenly and cloudy as I looked up at the sky. I think I was trying to look at anything other than Angie in that moment, who was having none of it because she misses nothing ever whatsoever in perpetuity, though I am not sure I was really trying to hide my nonsense at this point.

She stood up and held her hand out for me this time. "Oh, now, we'll have none of that sad, 'I'm cool with my pensive face' tonight, sweetie. None of that now."

I was about to argue with her for some inane reason when it started raining, hard. Once I was on my feet she pulled up her hood and swatted me in the same arm she'd been swatting all day. "Tag - you're it!"

Her laugh and the rain seemed to get me moving and the next thing I knew we were running to the car. She was cackling and I found myself laughing too despite how sad and nervous I was beginning to feel inside about leaving her. I always knew I would miss her, but I'd thought things would be different. I guess I really didn't know what I thought things would be like. I mean, I'd never actually missed anyone before. I'd never really had to, before this summer and I felt the weight of it, heavily.

CHAPTER ELEVEN

I ran to her side of the car to open the door for her when she pulled me close again. "I've always wanted to do this!" she hollered above the storm as she leaned back against the car and grabbed me around the waist and pulled me tight to her, kissing me deeply as the rain clobbered us. Feeling our bodies that close with the rain penetrating from all sides with its touch and echo off the blacktop was pretty much a sensory overload. There was a flash of lightning and a huge roll of thunder that sent us scrambling into the car which was now shrouded in a foggy mist.

We were both freezing cold as I started the car and fumbled for the heat. The windows were immediately fogged up. I reached into the back seat and grabbed the old wool blanket that we'd always kept in the car and handed it to Angie.

"Thanks," she shivered, wrapping it around herself and curling herself into a small orb on the seat. "That was totally worth it, but we're drenched! Where did that rain come from?"

"Well, it's coming from the sky I think," I suggested. Angie didn't really respond to it as she was clearly cold but I still maintain that it's quite funny. I leaned over and put my arm around her shoulders and noticed she was really shivering. The heat started to kick on in the silly old Tracer so I cranked it up and let it run until it became uncomfortable, which took a several minutes. The windows cleared out and Angie had warmed up to the point that she emerged slightly from the blanket bubble she'd nestled herself into so I could actually see her face again.

She sighed and smiled at me, although all I could see was her face beneath the blanket. Her eyes looked tired but beautiful in a way that both thrilled me and yet bothered me that I hadn't seen them properly before.

I remember that I stared at her a long time in the car trying to memorize every inch of her face. During those few minutes where she was warming up under the blanket, I was storing details about the day for sure, but I spent most of it just looking at her. Memorization was always a gift I'd leaned on, so I put it to work with helping me take it all in: all that had changed and all that hadn't with me and Angie, all day long, but, she was onto me, again.

"You're trying to stockpile all this, aren't you?" She even did air quotes for "stockpile." I leaned back into the seat and grumbled.

"Am I that easy to read?"

"Oh, sweetie, there is nothing easy about you. But, I think you just might be worth the effort."

I looked away from her, out the window toward the now nearly empty parking lot. I focused on the drops of rain still popping off the roof of the car and the blacktop beneath. Great, huge streams of rainfall were channeling away from us into the sewers. It seemed like so much had fallen all at once. While I've always been of the mindset that "hey, sometimes it rains," there was something about the suddenness of everything that happened that seemed to make a lot of sense to me. But of course, being me, I couldn't just leave it there.

"I don't know that I am, Ange."

I kept staring out the window. I heard Angie sigh heavily when I said that. The rain suddenly turned to hail, which banged loudly off the roof and seemed to leap from the pavement as though it knew it didn't belong there. The noise was all there was between us until she spoke.

"No," Angie said, drawing from a voice I'd never heard from her before after a minute of me staring out at the hail. I'd meant what I said but her only response was that "no."

I turned towards her and she was still wrapped in the blanket, but she'd sat up, no longer huddled over. Her eyes were locked in on mine and she looked fiercely at me, more so than she'd maybe ever looked at me.

"No," she repeated. "You won't be doing that thing you've done to every other girl that's ever cared about you. That thing where you let them get close to you and then push them away because of your fears and feelings and your inaccurate sense of self-worth. You don't get to say that you're not worth it! I get to choose! Everyone who's ever cared about you deserved to choose that and you've driven them all away, one way or another."

I was floored. I didn't know how to respond and the hail falling outside seemed to tumble right in line with the pounding of my heart and the shortness of my breath. I started a weak response, "But, what if I…" but I only got that far before she gripped up my face in her hands. They were soft and warm and I wanted them holding me, but as she held me there, she looked me so hard in the eyes that I think I can still feel it.

"Do you trust me?"

I nodded, which was awkward because she was still holding my face.

"Do you believe in me?

"I do," which came out kinda muffled by her grip, which she then loosened as she leaned in and brought her forehead to rest on mine, sitting almost all the way out of her chair to do so, the blanket falling to her lap.

"Do you think I'm a good person?" She looked away from my eyes for a quick second as she asked this. I only remember it at all because it was the only time she did looked away during the whole time we were within this moment.

"Angie, you're the greatest person I know." I meant it.

Her eyes welled up when I said it, but she didn't look away again as she asked, "And do you really, truly love me?"

There was a moment there where I felt like I wanted to stop her and tell her that I knew what she was doing, trying to make me feel better about myself but then I remembered what Madame Marie had said to both of us and I decided to just get out of my own way for once. My doubts about myself have always seemed crippling to me, but they looked very small in light of Angie's question. The answer was always simple, was always there.

"Yeah," I laughed, "I really do." Angie kept staring at me as though my answer needed further detail, so I pressed on. "Do love you that is. I think I always have kinda, but yeah, yeah, definitely. I love you."

A tear rolled down her cheek and I moved my hand

up to wipe it away and she let go of my face and hugged me. "If you really believe all the things you just said, about me and you," she whispered as she held on tight, "then you simply have to believe that if I think you're worth it, I probably know what I'm talking about."

I'd never really thought about it that way before, but it all makes sense. We stayed in that embrace until the hail stopped and morphed into a light rain. I think I probably cried some too, but it was as amazing as I'd ever felt. Fully loved and safe. It was so amazing that I'm pretty sure I might feel it forever. It was the first time in my life that I felt really safe. Secure is maybe a better word, like that everything would be OK, that it all would work out, which was ironic considering the changes that were coming for both of us, together and separately. I suddenly and for the first time in my life really felt like I was loved as myself, whoever that might be. No one knew me better than Angie, that's for sure. She'd seen me in all my dopiness over the years and was witness to all my nonsense so, if she could deal with all that and face her own challenges and still not only find the strength to carry on but could also find a way to be around me and even love me, maybe I'm not the waste of space I've so often felt like. I felt a weight lift that hasn't returned. I don't think it will.

It was the greatest moment in my life. In that moment, I felt so completely at peace and well, complete. It was as though Angie and I had been holding the keys to one another for all these years but had been turning them in the wrong direction. I felt like I'd finally really let her in and allowed myself to let go of the fear and doubt and angst I'd been swallowing all along. All the stress about school and music and mom and who my father is and money and scholarships and leaving home, all of a sudden, none of it mattered at all because I'm in love with my best friend. And because she loves me and she does so knowing exactly how much baggage I come with.

I think I started laughing because of how amazing I felt, my face just tingled.

"Whooo!" I hollered, completely startling Angie after we'd settled back into our seats.

"What was that for?"

I pounded the steering wheel, "This feels awesome! Angie, I've never felt like this before!"

"Oh?" She looked at me quizzically, not sure what I was talking about.

"Yes!" I honked the horn in celebration, which led a few of the other cars who were also waiting out the weather to honk back.

"Now look what you've started…" Angie chuckled.

"Yep, I'm a trendsetter. Hashtag, 'one of the cool kids' right?" I honked it one last time, probably for too long.

"I think that would be your first hashtag," she laughed, "If you actually had an app or two on that thing." She rifled through the bags from Winterwood for a minute before pulling out her new plush Santa and then tucked herself back into the blanket cocoon and smiled sleepily. I knew I'd have to take her home soon but I was so completely charged up that even that thought wasn't enough to make the dread I'd been feeling earlier return.

The rain lightened up even further and a few more cars started pulling out of the lot. The car was beyond warm now and Angie had rolled part of the blanket into a pillow and put it against the window, where her breath fogged it up. She drew a little heart in the fog and then closed her eyes. Her hair had fallen into her face and I reached over and brushed it behind her ear. She opened her eyes for a moment and smiled before closing them again. She looked very pretty. I'd seen her asleep before but never through "these eyes" I suppose.

"Time to head home?" I asked. She grunted and repositioned Santa on her lap but otherwise seemed to have dozed right off. I took another look around the now empty parking lot, the lights of the convention center now off. The giant Wildwood sign was still lit up as I put the Tracer in gear and headed up Rio Grande Avenue, toward home. With Angie asleep I didn't turn the radio on, which was weird for me, but after the crazy day we'd had, it actually felt kinda refreshing to be within that quiet. I had a lot to think about.

As we crossed over the bridge out of Wildwood I could see the Ferris Wheel in the distance with its lights still flashing as a beacon on the otherwise darkened coastline. I started replaying the events of the day in my mind. It was a momentous day which, now as it was ending, was really going to require a lot of time to unpack. I felt happy.

CHAPTER TWELVE

We crossed over the bridge leaving the islands of Wildwood behind. Seeing the Ferris Wheel still lit up in the distance made me think about what Angie had said on the ride about her cancer returning and about her chemo and all the challenges ahead. None of that had sunken in yet. Seeing the wheel also made me think of Floris, or I guess I should say "FLORIS!" I have a feeling that he'll seem funny later on, but as it happened, he made me feel like a dork.

Angie was snoring quietly before we made it to the Garden State Parkway. I felt tired too after everything we'd done all day, but I was still really wired and my head was spinning from it all. I plugged along in silence over an hour before I turned off the Parkway onto the more rural Route 539 and Angie's phone buzzed which roused her. She fumbled inside her little blanket nest and pulled it out.

"Welcome back," I said. I'd been silent over an hour so I was obviously welcoming the conversation.

"Don't know what you're talking about, I was awake

the entire time, resting my eyes," she lied, yawning as she looked at her phone. "It's my mother wondering where we are, out after midnight."

"Am I going to be in trouble with Linda?"

Angie scrolled around her screen for a minute and typed something back to her mom, sighing a few times in the process. "No, I think we'll be fine as long as we don't wake her and I don't let any bugs into the house." I wondered how her parents were handling everything and then thought about how they would react to our changes too and I was about to ask about both when she yelped, "Oh, wow! This is great!"

She sat up quickly sending the blanket flailing as she fumbled around for the cassette adapter to connect her phone to the Tracer's antiquated stereo.

"What are you…" I started to ask but that was as far as I got before I was drowned out by the sound of the set I'd just performed with The Cozy Morley's. As it turned out, Shellie Bennet had sent the recording of the show to Angie who was now watching the video while channeling the audio through the tinny speakers in mom's car. The sound was rough but it did give me an idea how the performance sounded, which didn't seem that bad for people who'd never played together. Angie let the full set play out as it happened and before I knew it there was the long pause and the hushed chatter before we attempted "Everlong." The recorder had been just behind our table so it picked up Angie and Betsy and their conversation while we were figuring out what was going to happen onstage.

I heard Angie say, after the whole drama with Shannon and Kelly was playing out, "Wow, she just threw them for a loop, didn't she?"

Betsy rather dryly replied, "Those two have been

smelling one another for years. I hope your fella can help as the dentist looks cooked, and the lot of us here, we're far past done in waiting them out. It's like being back in school! It's grown tedious, it has!"

There was a sound of feedback from the stage that I remembered causing and then there was the sound of a whole room reacting to it. And then I heard myself play the opening chords and the audience hush and Angie inhale deeply before she said, "Yeah, he's got it…"

We listened to the recording of it and it didn't suck that bad. It was fun hearing it back so soon and I dared a look at her screen when we were stopped at a light in the middle of the Pine Barrens, because that's clearly where a traffic light is urgently needed. It was interesting seeing myself standing at the front of Shellie's band. The audience sitting in the area around the camera was definitely into the moment. They went kinda bananas when the song ended and Kelly and Shannon went off together.

Then, the recording continued into my playing "The Garden" and Angie got real quiet, intently listening. It was weird listening to myself but then it always was. I never liked my voice on recordings and this was no exception. As the song played out I could hear some chairs moving and people murmuring a little which I understood, as I was some stranger playing an original song as an encore to what had been a really cool moment. It could only have been a letdown and to say I'd lost the crowd would be an understatement.

As it got to the end where I did the whole "see yourself through someone else's eyes" thingy I heard Angie audibly react on the recording with something between a gasp and a shriek, but it was very quiet as I hadn't heard it from the stage. We'd passed through the

Pine Barrens and were rapidly approaching the suburban delight that is Windsor Township.

I'd been quiet for far too long, so I asked, "Should I ask about that little noise at the end?" I was teasing her, I guess, but I didn't know where else to start.

"Do you need to now?" The recording ended with Shellie staring into the camera and clearly having trouble figuring out the camera, which he then knocked over as it went to fuzz. Angie ejected the adapter and tucked her phone away but the silence in the car remained. We were passing through Allentown, with its far too many traffic lights, so it seemed like we were constantly stopped and bathed in red and then green lights. Made me think of that light on the dock in The Great Gatsby or maybe even some kind of Christmas light montage that I'm sure we were subjected to at Winterwood.

After we finally cleared Allentown, we were soon headed North on Route 130 where we'd started just this morning. I looked over at Angie and she was rifling through a box of mom's old cassette tapes that had been sitting on the center console for as long as I could remember. I never played with them much but knew she kept a copy of the Eagles Greatest Hits Volume 2, Patti Smith's "Horses" and Springsteen's "Nebraska" and "Born to Run." "Born to Run" is the only one I'd ever popped in when the radio was stuck in commercials or something and it was the one Angie was examining just then.

"It's close to the end of one side," she began, flipping the tape over and over in her hands. "Which song do you think is cued up?"

I put out my hand and she handed me the worn-out tape as we sat at a red light near the old Dairy Queen and new Bowling alley. We were so close to home but I wasn't ready to be done and I don't think she was either, so I stopped at a lot of lights. As I looked at the tape, I knew exactly what song would be cued up as I was certain mom had turned it off right before "Jungleland" again. Ever since Clarence Clemmons died she can't bring herself to listen to it.

"I think it's very likely the perfect song," I replied as I pushed the tape in and the mellow string and piano opening stretched out before us like we were driving home at the end of Kevin Smith movie or something like that. As Bruce started singing about the Magic Rat and his sleek machine I found myself with no red lights left to keep us from her house in Pin Oak Manor. As the song poured forth from the Tracer's truly average speakers, Angie took my hand and leaned up against my arm. I was driving really slow, a point which was punctuated by the fact that I got honked at twice at stop signs. Clarence's epic saxophone was just beginning its solo as we pulled up to the curb in front of her home.

There were a ton of street lights in her part of the manor so the whole area was bright enough to read by. Theirs is the last house on the street so their yard, always impeccably manicured, blends into the woods where Angie and her sister used to build "fairy forts" as kids. The porch light was on, as well as the light that resided in Angie's parents' bedroom. We sat and listened to the end of the song. It seemed fitting to be ending our day with the last song on "Born to Run," which is about a journey not completely unlike the one we'd just been on now that I think of it.

Angie squeezed my hand as Bruce sang, "Beneath the city, two hearts beat…" I think I was holding my breath when he sang the last line of the song, and "they reach for their moment and try to make an honest stand. But they wind up wounded, not even dead, tonight…in… Jun-gle-land," and I really felt like "they" was a little bit "us" as silly as that sounds.

As the tape clicked over, I turned off the car. Beyond that. I think I imagined that maybe if I didn't move at all, maybe if I just could find a way to be still, maybe I could stay just there, hoarding that time with Angie forever. I think I'd have been just fine with that.

After a while though the windows fogged up and I had to roll down a window. Angie let go of my hand which made me sad because I knew it was just the first step on a walk away from one another. She looked very tired. Amazing still, but tired.

"Are you tired?" I asked, my voice cracking for some reason. It was after midnight at this point.

"I am, sweetie. But I have something for you inside. Will you walk a lady home?"

That was another one of those things I'd always done because Nana had taught me to. "Always walk a lady to the door. Always." So, I did, every time I took a girl home. Even if we weren't dating, it was just something I did. I stood up and went around to help her out of the car and collected all of her Winterwood stuff. She caught me checking out her legs as she stepped out of the car and winked at me.

Angie opened the front door to her house and stepped inside with her Christmas store stuff, returning with a leather bag before shutting the door behind her, leaving us outside on the porch. I had thought we might be going inside but now I wonder if that would have made it even harder to leave.

She handed me a very cool shoulder bag, black leather with a long thick strap. She placed the bag over my shoulder and took my hands in hers. I noticed the light in her parents' room flick off after she'd shut the door.

"There's a book and a pen inside that bag. I want you to use them both."

"Use them for what exactly?"

"I want you to write about today, all of it. This wonderful last day."

"Just for a while," I injected.

"That's right, just for a while. Until Christmas."

"I could try to come home for Thanksgiving, maybe…" I offered, already doing the 'number of days' math in my head as I put my arms around her waist. She reached her arms up around my neck, brushing the back of my hair.

"Christmas will be here before we know it. Your mom said you need to stay until then or you won't even think about really committing to being in Boston."

"Oh, yeah, I'd forgotten you and my mom might hang out now."

She flicked my ear, which stung. "Chemotherapy is not exactly a cool hang, my friend. She is really just serving as a backup driver for me, but mostly I think she's planning to bring me Jim's Gravy Cheese Fries, which remain far superior to those at 'The Roach.'"

I immediately felt like a jerk but tried not to dwell on it. "We can talk too, if you want. Like, when you're there and stuff." She rubbed the ear she'd just flicked and rested her head on my chest.

"We will talk. Often. But I don't want you to spend all day worrying about me and not doing your work."

"But -"

"No buts, Avery. Remember what I said earlier: I want you to give this semester everything you can and make some new friends. Learn some new things about all the musicky stuff too, but take advantage of this time. You've never done the things you're about to do and I know that scares you. It would scare anyone. But you have to really try, promise?"

"Musicky stuff?"

"Shut it you, I'm on a roll."

"Yes, dear."

She laughed loudly before remembering that her parents were asleep just upstairs and she started shushing herself. "I mean it though, you're going to do amazing things I just know it. Madame Marie as much as said so, right?"

"Uh, I didn't really understand most of what she said, actually."

Pushing through my commentary as though I wasn't talking, "Yep - that's what she said. I want you to write about it. Write about all of this, and everything else."

"What if my writing stinks?"

"You keep writing. Especially then. When you think it stinks, that's when you've got to keep at it. That's when you might actually say something interesting. Like you did earlier."

"I will," I said, but I also knew what she was doing, in addition to saying goodbye to me.

She was saying goodbye to how we had always been with one another. Things were changing and we would be apart as they changed and as we figured it out, due to my awesome timing. It was likely going to be weird and take time and I understand now even more why Angie wanted me to write about our day. I think she wanted me to really reflect on not just what happened yesterday but how we got there.

There were loads of bugs hanging around the lights outside of her house so there was an ever-present buzz in the air. Being the goof that I am I very softly started humming at the same pitch. She didn't pick up on it right away but as I leaned down closer to her ear she pulled away, "Ah, you dork, that's you? I thought one was diving at me!" I chased after her briefly but she lithely skipped off the porch and sat down on the steps that led down to the walk.

"Ah, sitting on steps…my nemesis," I groaned as I sat down, still buzzing a little. Angie leaned against me. "So, I'm a dork now?" I asked, knowing full well that I was.

"Yeah, but you're my dork."

I liked the way that sounded. I'm not sure why but I felt compelled to ask this in that moment, but I did it anyway.

"Are things going to change with us?"

She coughed a moment before Yoda made a brief return appearance. "All life is change, hrmm?"

"I guess," I think I was starting to get nervous again, especially if I was answering Yoda directly.

"Hey," she said, wrapping our hands together. "I'd like to think that what's at the real heart of who we've always been with each other will always be there. Things might change but they were always bound to as we got older."

I shifted uncomfortably, not even meaning to and, in response she moved off the steps and crouched down in front of me. "How do you feel right now?"

I had to think about it but honestly, I still felt pretty good. "I feel amazing." She smiled at that, but of course I had to keep going. "But I also feel worried for you, nervous about leaving, and anxious about what's going to happen and stuff."

She nodded a little and paused before she asked, "Do you feel different about me? About us?"

It took me a minute to figure out the right way to say

197

it as honestly, I really didn't feel different. That was the wrong word.

"More," I said. "Not different, just, more."

"More?"

"Yeah. I feel like I always did, I think, but I feel other stuff too that's kinda new, but -" and I stopped myself, but it was too late.

"What?" Her expression looked like she was confused as to where I was going so I thought I should reassure her.

"It's not bad. It's just that," and I'm certain I caught a case of the flop sweats immediately. "Well, some of these new feelings don't feel as new as maybe I thought they might."

She sat back down next to me and smoothed out her skirt with an air of propriety. "You know, I did catch you checking me out a few times."

I don't know why, but this made me feel like a jerk too, so I stood up quickly and started pacing, "Oh my God, really? I'm so sorry, I just -" but before I could even finish whatever dumb thing I was about to say, Angie literally jumped off the step and onto me, pulling us both down onto the grass in her front yard and rolling on top of me and kissing me, saying:

"You idiot! I've been…checking…you…out for years!" Her hair fell on my face and we made out like our lives depended upon it. I have NEVER been kissed like that before and that includes earlier on the beach and again on the boardwalk and then there was the kissing in the rain by the car. There was actually a pretty sizeable amount of kissing in all.

Our hands were suddenly all over one another and I don't know how long we went on like that, right there in her front yard. Time really didn't seem like a very vital consideration in that moment. I don't think anyone saw us, though I don't know that I'd have noticed as I was completely focused on her. Eventually she rolled off of where she'd been laying on top of me and I stretched out my arm, rattling it on the Tracer. We'd rolled all the way down to the sidewalk! We both sat up and leaned against the car.

"Wow," I said, completely breathless and damp and full of dirt and grass stains from the lawn. "I mean, wow!"

"Yeah, I know, right?" She massaged her jaw. "Ow-I think I pulled something."

"Would it help if I kissed it?"

"Worth a try."

I leaned in and gently kissed her left, then right cheeks before kissing her lips. "Better?"

"Yeah."

I hadn't noticed the crickets and other bits of abundant outdoor noise until just then. Her neighborhood has a ton of wooded areas and it always seemed like a bird or a squirrel or a bobcat was scurrying about. A few of the street lamps had flicked off which reminded me of how late it was, but I still didn't want to leave her. I reached up and removed a leaf from her hair. I held it in my fingers a moment before making a show of releasing it into the slight breeze.

I remember totally taking that time to really just look at her, my Angela. It wasn't going to be for the last time, I knew, but it was going to be the last time for a longer time than we'd ever been apart before. With all that had happened, it did feel like I was looking through a different set of eyes, and I wanted to cast them on her as long as I could. I think she knew what I was doing as she shook the grass out of her hair and smoothed it out. Her dark hair was blowing slightly over her left shoulder in the breeze. Her eyes looked away for a moment and then back to me. She'd tossed her hoodie into the middle of her mother's garden, as well as my new bag, which lay partially nestled in a large yucca plant. Her face was rosy and I got distracted when the wind sent the pleat of her skirt in motion. It only revealed her calves but the whole sight of her and everything we'd always been and would be in the future kinda swelled in me and suddenly, I wasn't afraid anymore, for real. I knew then that we'd be fine. Great, even. We'd make it for always, without a single doubt.

It's the most certain I'd felt about anything in my life. No doubt. No worries.

"Take a picture, it'll last longer," she teased.

"I don't know that it would, but may I?" It hadn't occurred to me until she said it, but I wanted a picture of her in that moment.

"Really? You don't really take pictures."

"Well, I think I've grown since the old days."

"Like yesterday?"

"Exactly." I pulled out my phone which had grass all over and cleaned it off with my shirt. I then realized I had no idea what I was doing with the phone. "Um, which button is it?"

Angie pointed to the big button that read "CAMERA" and did her best not to roll her eyes. I lined it up and took a picture of Angie leaning against the Tracer.

I stood up and as I put the phone back in my pocket I felt something else in there. I reached in and pulled out the scallop shell that Angie had given me when we'd first arrived on the beach. It looked just as it had earlier, despite all the wrestling, rolling around, and bumping into things all day, it was still pretty much unblemished.

"It's stronger than it looked, huh?"

I put it back in my pocket as Angie reached out her hands to me to help her up, which I did but not without making several "heavy lifting" grunts and noises that she ignored.

Her eyes were getting heavy I could tell as she asked, "Can you walk me home again?"

"Well, I could do that, but I just kinda did that, so maybe something else is in order." I kneeled down and leaned forward and pat my hand on my back. Before I could say "hop on" she was locked onto my back and her legs wrapped around my waist.

She kissed my ear as she whispered, "let's go the long way around!" I stood up and took a circuitous route to her front door, which was maybe twenty feet away. We ran up the sidewalk some and I crisscrossed the lawn. Her arms were tight around my shoulders. I was about to deposit her on the porch when she whispered in my ear, "Wait!"

I was getting a little tired but we were having fun. "Wait for what?"

She pecked my ear again, which we had both just learned happens to be a particularly sensitive zone for me. "Well, my sweatshirt is way over there. Can we go get it?" I made a groan of protest, but she kissed my ear again and gently nibbled on the lobe which, well, I'm not telling you how that affected me. I took a breath and turned around. It was only about twelve steps to the rhododendron which was currently hosting Angie's sweatshirt. I plucked it out of the plant or bush - I don't know what it is anyway.

"How did this get all the way over here?"

She whispered into my ear again, "I threw it there. It was in our way."

I remember feeling very much like I could have gone another round in the grass just then. How amazing it felt to hold her and kiss her and touch her. Every kiss and every touch, those were the first times we'd ever done such things and it would take time to move into more. It was all brand new and it felt just like something brand new should feel, but with the added bonus of being so incredibly safe and familiar.

I'm completely and totally in love with her. I probably should have said something along those lines instead of the dopey comment I made next.

I am sure I looked sincere and I'm sure I said it with a deep and meaningful tone, but as I said, "There's nothing in our way now..." there was at least a pause before Angie snorted and cackled out loud at my ridiculousness. I knew even as it came out of my mouth that it was dopey. As she cackled, I muttered, "Sorry, the momentum carried me," as I returned to the porch and she climbed off my back.

She touched my face, gently. "It's fine, momentum will do that." She was still laughing though. My hope of moving forward rested in the fact that multiple piggybacks for her generally equate to a good and fun day. This one was definitely the best. The new bag she'd given me remained rather gracefully positioned in the fronds of Angie's mom's prized yucca plant in the garden off to the left of the front door. I stepped over and picked it out and placed it over my shoulder. I looked inside and pulled out the book: it was black leather with a few of those old school bible bookmark tassels. Knowing Angie, I figured there would be something written in the front of the book so I turned to it and sure enough, there in her flowing 'I should be a penmanship teacher' script was the following:

"Dear Avery, you will of course do amazing things at school. But before you do, please take some time and write about today. Whatever comes I know it will be a perfect day together with you, my dearest friend. Go set the world on fire but do so knowing you are well and truly loved, for always. Go, make you ready!

With all my heart, Angie"

I read it twice more, realizing that she wrote it before our day together had even happened. Before even Madame Marie had suggested I "get out of my own way." Before she'd use that "go make you ready" line from Hamlet at the show. It made me wonder something.

"Did you know?" I slipped the book back in the bag.

"Know what?" Angie was leaning on the front door now.

"Did you know how today would go? That I'd, um, 'see you' finally?"

She reached out for my hands and I gave them to her, loving the way she intertwined our fingers. "No." She brought our hand conglomeration towards her lips and kissed the back of my left hand. "I hoped. And I prayed. And I wore an outfit I knew you'd like and I asked Aunt Jenny to get the corn you love. I told Uncle Bob you wanted to play and I hoped that Shellie would let you sit in with his band. So yeah, there's all that but I never expected you to finish a new song and play it for me after tearing down the Anchor Inn to help another couple fall in love, nor did I expect us to go see Madame Marie. Didn't plan on showing you my tattoo either."

"Ok, that last one is BS, Angie. You totally showed me that on purpose."

"Yeah," she agreed. "Guilty as charged. I got a

Mani/Pedi too, and I don't do that for just anyone. Didn't seem to hurt matters though."

"No, it really didn't." I was really enjoying the way she was holding our hands together and the vibrant feeling like we couldn't get any closer but wanted to. Just as I thought that she squeezed my hands.

"You know that I'm going to miss you, right?" Her eyes, despite their tiredness were full of all that we were both feeling.

I didn't realize it was true until I had thought it earlier, so I said it then: "I don't think I've ever missed anyone before."

There was a moment where I thought she was going to push me on that point, but finally she just closed her eyes and nestled back into the door. "It gets easier."

I hoped so already but I didn't say so. Instead I went with, "I think I'll miss you more."

"Oh, I don't think so."

"We'll talk every day?"

"I know."

"Hey, I'm only a train ride away unless I make friends with a Jersey kid with a car, I mean if that happens I can maybe visit in a month or two, maybe even sooner."

"Christmas, my love."

She was right. I owed it to my mom to see the semester through. She'd gotten me the year without taking loan, but we both knew that if I didn't secure a grant or scholarship before the Spring term that I was out of luck. I needed to try and I knew it.

"You're right. I know."

Angie cocked her eyebrow at me, asking "Are you trying to 'Han Solo' me?" Her eyes were full and so tired as she just leaned over and hugged me as we leaned on her front door. We both seemed to be laughing and tearing up at the same time. It felt like the only place I ever wanted to be. I think, if I could've, I'd have stayed there leaning on that door, holding her in my arms for the rest of all time. But I knew that I couldn't.

"Hey Ange, you know what?" I asked as our heads were resting on one another. I felt like I could still smell the breeze of the ocean in her hair, the sun on her skin.

She kind of made a harrumph from her position leaning into me. "What?"

I'm not certain what brought my mind back to this song as it seemed to come out of nowhere, "I really could sing of your love, you know…for like ever and stuff."

She raised her head and nestled it into my shoulder. "Could you now?"

"Yeah, pretty sure I could."

Angie thought for a second trying to remember the lyrics, "and do you feel like dancing?"

"Foolishness?"

"I know," she sighed, but we both stood up together and I took her hand and we fell right into the proper dancing positions that Nana had taught me. And then after a minute we abandoned those and just held onto one another, although I did give her a respectable spin like we'd done at Prom.

"But when the world has seen the light, they will dance with joy…"

"Like we're dancing now…I could sing of your love, forever," Angie leaned into me as she whispered those last words and then we slowly spun around the dance floor that was her porch. We repeated the chorus to each other for I don't know how long before she pulled me close and held me tighter than she had all day, which was saying something.

"Thank you."

"For what?

"For today. For taking me down the shore and spending time with my family and singing for me and for loving me and for," and she leaned back and tapped my forehead, "for finally kissing me!"

I think I was about to say something else entirely, but I noticed a small red and green object in the holly bush off to the right of the front door. "Is that Santa?" I asked.

He'd clearly fallen into the bushes in some part of our earlier activity. Angie picked him up from the holly. "Well, that seems fitting," she offered.

I remembered what I wanted to say once she had secured Santa under her arm. "Angie, I think I need to thank you."

As she often does, she simply nodded reverently at the prospect, "Of course, you may proceed," and she stood almost to attention with Santa joining in.

"Thank you for putting up with me and teaching me and for being my best friend and for this awesome book and bag…"

"And pen," she interjected.

"Yes, and the pen."

"And you shouldn't call or text me until you meet your suitemates at school. And not until you've used that pen and that notebook to start writing something."

I had kinda planned on giving her a play-by-play of the trip but she wore a face that said that this was important to her, so I let it go. "OK, but I wasn't done thanking you."

"Oh, in that case, please continue."

I brushed her hair away from her face and kissed her again, softly and deeply, at least that's what I was going for. There were a few short quick ones after the long one and then I stepped back and cupped her face in my hands. "Thank you for believing in me. I don't really know how to do it myself, but I've always known you're smarter than me, so it gives me hope."

"You're welcome."

We stood there in the noiselessness a while longer. The quiet moments didn't seem to bother me as much anymore. She took my hands, which had still been caressing her cheek and held them up between us.

"Sweetie, you've got a train in a few hours."

"I know."

"You're going to have a blast and do great musicky stuff and things," she said. "I just know it."

"Anything I do will pale in comparison to what you are going to do."

Angie sorta beamed for a second and smiled, surprised at what I'd said and how she'd reacted. "That was good right there," she said, wagging a finger at me. "Well done, you."

"I mean it Angie, you're amazing and always have been. I'm going to work hard at this for me and I guess for my mom, yeah, because I just have to know if I've really got anything, but honestly, I'm going to bust my ass up there for you. Because you know what?"

"What?"

"I love you. I always have and nothing will change that. I'm just so glad I know it now. The rest seems like it'll be easy."

She tilted her head a bit as she said, "Hmmm…would we call any of this easy?"

I tilted my head the same direction and degree as I replied, "Yeah - the way I feel and knowing how we feel about each other and knowing what I need to do, yeah - easy. I'm still a little scared but I think knowing that you love me and you want me and you believe in me, then the rest of the world is going to have to deal with the 'me' they get as a result."

"And who is that?"

"Well, that's the best 'me' yet so far: the one who loves you."

"The one I love…"

"Yeah, that too."

We hugged much like we'd always hugged when it was time to leave one another, sharing one last kiss before I stepped back off the porch.

"I'll talk to you soon," I called.

"Not before meet your roommates and not until you write in your new book!"

"I better get to work then!" I exclaimed as I turned toward the car. She watched me from the porch before opening the storm door and reaching for the main door knob.

"I love you," she called.

I opened the car door with a flourish, "I love you too."

She smiled and opened the door and took a step inside before calling back to me. "Avery?" I have fallen in love with the way she says my name.

"Yeah?"

She shut the door halfway as she continued, "Thank you for today, really. And for kissing me…"

"Kind of a lot…" I interjected.

"Yeah, thank you for that. Saying goodbye to you would have been way harder to bear if all this hadn't finally happened." She emphasized "finally" quite a bit. A mischievous grin spread across her face. "Thinking about all we have to look forward to is going to be amazeballs!"

"Amazeballs?"

She looked embarrassed for a second.

"Sorry…momentum carried me."

She noticed some remaining grass and stuff on her skirt and brushed it off as she continued, a little quieter than before, "And as food for thought, I think we really just scratched the surface there, sweetie," waving her hands at the yard before turning back towards the door.

"Argh!" I groaned, "We can't leave on that note!" I rested my head on the roof of the car, which was cold and damp so I stopped doing that immediately. Drops of dirty car roof dew water rolled down my forehead before I wiped them off. Seriously gross.

"And yet, leave it on that note we shall," she cooed as she opened the door and stepped inside. "Christmas will come soon enough…" and she blew me a kiss over her shoulder as she closed the door.

I heard the door click shut and saw the light go out on the porch. I got into the car and started it but waited until I saw the light go on in her room. It was only on for a minute before it was extinguished and I knew she had gone to sleep. I felt tired too, so I can't imagine what her body felt like with the amount of walking we'd done and everything we did all day while her system was fighting its own battle. Putting the car in drive and releasing the brake felt hard for a moment until I realized that the sooner I started moving forward, the sooner that road would bring me back to Angie, and that was a road I was ready to walk, drive, or otherwise get moving on.

CHAPTER THIRTEEN

I rolled down the window and with one last glance at her porch where we'd danced and the front yard of course, I drove away from Pin Oak Manor back onto Route 130 towards home on the other side of Windsor. I got stuck at the light outside of Carduner's Liquor Store and what must be the last Roy Rogers in existence, which meant I'd be there for a good 5-10 minutes as it's the longest light in all of human history, but it was cool. I still wasn't quite ready to go home. I wanted to celebrate and tell everyone about our day and about how we were in love and all that, but the road was quiet until I heard a thumping bass sound coming from the car pulling up next to me. It was a bright yellow Mustang convertible, one of the newer ones. There were two guys in front and what I guessed were their girlfriends in the back. The music was seriously loud and my car shook in response. I didn't know the song they were listening to but then the DJ came on in between songs and since they were sharing it at such an unholy level of volume, every word is seared into my memory.

"Hey kids, this is Arturo spinning for you on the overnight here at 97.5 WPST, and our next song is a special request going out to my new friends Pam and Kelly, on the way home from Manasquan…"

I didn't think it possible, but the shrieks from the girls in the back seat of the Mustang actually drowned out Arturo for a moment. I'm surprised it didn't break the windows. In unison, Pam and Kelly screamed "That's us! Turn it up!!!" They were slapping their boyfriends on the head and backs trying to get them to somehow break the laws of nature and make the radio even louder as the opening riff to "Shut up and Dance" by the band Walk the Moon filled the air with its surprising catchiness.

Hey, a good song is a good song regardless of genre and I liked this one. Might not make me friends in the rock clubs but hey, a good song is always just that.

I looked over at the Mustang and the girls were basically out of their seats jumping around dancing. They saw me watching and gave me a "come on" look and then loudly called the chorus out towards me. I reached over and tuned my radio to WPST adding more noise to the scene, which brought a cheer from the girls. Even the guys seemed like they were kinda into it all as they did their best version of the overbite head bop. Clearly, their Nana hadn't taught them how to dance.

It had been a long and emotional but awesome day and both despite and because of all that: I felt like dancing. I figured we had gobs of time until the light changed, so I put the car in park and jumped out of the Tracer just as the keyboard solo dance break part kicks in and I just danced around right there in the middle of Route 130 singing along with my new pals Pam and Kelly, who'd jumped out of the car and were dancing along with me.

211

By the time they got to the verse about taking chances and looking into the future I realized that, as a moment capping off the day I'd just had, it was really kinda fitting. The guys were starting to get annoyed that their ladies were dancing with a stranger in the middle of the road, which I can understand but I finally felt like I was having a moment to celebrate how I felt, which was awesome! We were clapping along and having a great time until we were suddenly interrupted by a long low blast of a truck horn from behind us. Apparently, the Amoroso Bread truck driver did not feel like dancing at all, especially now that the light had turned green and we were blocking both lanes with our mini flash mob.

The guy driving the Mustang revved up his engine and bolted off as soon as the girls had jumped into their seats. The girls waved at me. "You're awesome, dude!" I waved back and then shrugged at the truck driver who pulled his truck around me as he called me several things I'd only ever heard Uncle Ted say. I drove home listening to the last bit of the song at a very high level of volume.

I'd never felt so free! So alive! Angie and I did silly stuff together all the time but I'd never just hopped out of a running car and danced with strangers in the blinking lights of the old Carduner's sign and the fading neon letters adorning the building that used to be The Money Store mortgage place, but the only letters that still fired up spelled out "MON STOR." That always made mom laugh.

Honestly, my little dance party was fun and really capped off the day perfectly. It was too late to call anyone and share my news and honestly, I don't know who'd I'd have called if not Angie at this point. I had no idea where Will was and what he was doing, but Pat was already out at basic training and Brian had left for Stanford. After everything, I actually felt like I was ready to go, ready to leave pretty much everything but Angie behind for now. Ready to be that best version of me.

After "Shut up and Dance" ended, the station predictably moved into commercials, so I turned it off and enjoyed the silence as I finished the drive home. The lights were all off at our place as I pulled into our spot. I was glad someone hadn't taken it as I'd have had to park almost a mile away in a common lot so as not to get towed by the condo people, who are just about awful in every possible way. I will absolutely not miss living among them, not even one bit.

It was sometime after two in the morning and I was suddenly really glad I'd packed up my stuff early. As I entered the house, Mom was sacked out on the old brown leather chair that she loved. She looked like a baby in a rowboat in that thing as it was so huge and she was so thin. Her long blonde hair had fallen over her face and moved with each breath she took. The TV was on showing a replay of the earlier Phillies game. I turned it off, which woke her up immediately, flailing her hair away from her face like it was a closed curtain.

"What, huh? I was watching that…"

"It's late mom. I'm just home."

She blinked a few times and looked at the clock on the wall, the one that looked like every clock in every school classroom I'd ever been in, and then looked at me, "It's after two in the morning! Geez, what are you thinking about?"

I interrupted her. I almost never do that.

"Angie told me everything. I love her and we're together now for real."

Mom took her feet off the yellow ottoman that she

also loves and leaned forward, cracking her neck loudly. "Is that so?"

"It is."

"Well, took you long enough."

"Yeah, I get that. I think we're going to be great."

Mom stood up slowly. She's not that old but she always makes these noises of announcement anytime she lifts something, stands up or sits down. "Of course, you think it's going to be great," she growled at me, way more aggressive that I expected. "It's all new for you today. You always love your 'new' things."

That stung a little. She always had feelings about what we both had and didn't have living here together over the years. Chimes Mews was the name on the sign as you drove into our townhouse court, but we all just called it "Chimes Manor" like all the other developments in Windsor. It seemed like she was picking a fight with me and I'd be lying if I said I hadn't expected one. Mom was never known for her clean breaks. She used to find a reason to be mad at me before I went to visit Nana for a week in the summer. I think it just made it easier to let people go if she was pushing them away, but I was already feeling like I was ready to move past the drama she was bringing. She wanted to get into a fight and I really didn't. Honestly all I wanted to do was go up to my room one last time, look at the picture I'd taken of Angie and fall asleep until I had to start a whole new thing by getting on the train to Boston.

But, as always, I had a tough time not meeting her challenges. "Mom, I love Angie, but she is not a 'new thing' to me. She's been the only thing in my life that's made any kind of sense for the last four years."

Mom widened her eyes at that and crossed her bony arms, her eyes now searching me like she thought I'd stolen from her.

"Just like that?" Her tone was about what I'd expect from her at two in the morning but it was starting to irk me, if I'm being honest.

"No, it's not 'just like that,'" I replied, mimicking her tone. "It's just like, I realized that I've always loved her, and -"

She breezed past me dismissively toward the stairs. "Well, did you love her like this yesterday?" She was so ready to make this a fight after I'd had the best day of my life and I almost obliged her. But then I realized she really wasn't fighting me, not anymore. Something happened there, some kind of threshold got crossed. In that moment, I really and truly didn't care what she thought anymore.

"Mom, I had to get out of my own way to see how amazing she is, and I have now. I love her and as hard as it's going to be to leave her tomorrow to go to Boston, I'm going, and I'm gonna bust loose all over that scene. Whether I make it there or somewhere else or not at all, I'm going to go try, for her, for me, even for you, you pain in the ass!"

She chuckled at that, but she still had one foot on the bottom step and both arms crossed.

"I'm going to come home at Christmas in the hope that I'm one step closer to being the guy that actually deserves Angie. You just wait, Mom!" I had been moving closer to where she stood on the bottom step as I said all this. "You just wait. I love her, Mom, I really do. Think I always did."

Mom stepped off the step she'd been threatening to climb and gave a glance to the wall we shared with the Kerns next door as she lowered her voice, inviting me to do the same. She patted my cheek the way Nana does sometimes.

"You should love Angela. She's an amazing young woman."

"I know, she is. It took me so long to see but I see it now. I don't deserve her…"

As I was speaking the above, mom suddenly grabbed my ear hard, the same one Angie had paid attention to earlier.

"Cut. That. Out!" she said, her voice measured and calm but a tone of voice I'd never heard from her before. It was almost sinister. It really hurt at first but then she twisted my ear further which hurt even worse. She pushed down on my ear driving me onto a knee. "Mom, seriously, this hurts!"

"Don't you dare let yourself get lost on what you 'deserve,' Avery." She never called me by my full name. I was always "Ay" to her. Her grip on my ear loosened and I moved away from her a few steps. She pointed her whole hand at me, not just a finger or two, the whole hand as she almost testified. "You love who you love, you hear? Sometimes the things we reap and the things we sow don't add up, but there's no 'deserve' in it at all. There's no ledger that's kept for us on what we feel we might have coming to us. Did I deserve all this?" she asked, gesturing at our home, the only one I'd really known.

"Deserve? Am I worthy of all this magnificence? We are what our choices are and what we make of them." She stepped back and rested her arm on the stairs, with a groan. "What we are, who we love, the people we become, it's not about 'deserving' anything. It's about being somebody who's good and loved and loves back." Mom never talked like this and there was an emotion to her voice, a softening maybe that I'd never heard before as she went on. "If you laughed today-if you cried today-if you loved today, well then damn, son, that's a good day. String a few of those together and you'll have a life that's worth something."

She seemed exhausted suddenly and she sat down on the bottom step. "I love Angela, and I think she's amazing. I'm proud that I raised a son who's turned into a man that a girl like that wants to be around."

I was stunned. Totally and completely flabbergasted as it was the first time she'd ever said, in any way or on any topic that she was proud of me. She'd not been cold or unaffectionate or cruel, that's not the case at all, mostly. It's just that those particular words had never been put together in the same sentence quite like that ever before. "I am proud" just really hadn't come up before.

I wanted to say something but I felt like I had nothing left. I was exhausted and my ear hurt and I stood up with the initial intention of saying something but in the end, I just sat down next to her and hugged her instead.

"She's probably too good for me though, right?"

Mom backhanded my knee. "Ugh, you don't listen. No one is too good for you, Ay, no one. Be good enough for yourself while you're at it." Her tone had changed and I felt like we'd really passed through something important just then. "But she's pretty damned close."

She eventually patted me awkwardly on the back and creakily rose and headed up the stairs.

"Thanks, Mom" I called after her.

She didn't slow down as she called back, "You screw this up with Angela, I'll tell your Nana on you."

I heard her open the door to her room at the top of the stairs as I called up, "Nana gets at least half credit for pretty much anything I did right today." Mom turned back and returned to the top of the stairs.

"Call her and tell her that tomorrow, please. She'd like that and she'll want to hear about Angela. She adores her."

"I know how she feels."

I heard the door to mom's room close after that. The alarms to get up for the train were already set, the ticket already booked. I walked up to my room and fell onto the bed without turning my light on. The window to the right of my bed always seemed to be lit up, either by the light of the sun as it came up every morning, the street lamps, or the Kern's gigantic halogen porch light. Someone had once breathed too close to Ma Kern's Cadillac last fall, so Dr. Kern had to install a whole motion sensing light system that turned on if you even think about moving. I'm pretty sure they clicked on one night when I turned over in my bed. I was pretty much used to it by now but it made me wonder how I'd learn to sleep in a place where I'd never laid my head.

I remember looking around the room one last time, knowing I'd be sleeping somewhere else the next night. Then I thought about Angie. I plugged in my phone and pulled up the picture I'd taken of her and fell asleep with her on my mind. I'm not going to share the dreams I had with you, but suffice it to say, she was knee-deep in all of them.

The Very Next Day

CHAPTER FOURTEEN

Too soon the alarm went off and Mom drove me to Princeton Junction. There really wasn't much more to it than that. Mom was never much of a morning person, especially not at six am.

"Work hard. Call your Nana. I'll see you at Christmas," mom yawned as she pulled up to the station.

I felt really tired as I climbed the steps to the platform. Body tired, anyway. My brain was still racing a mile a minute. I couldn't wait to sit down and start writing something as I knew I couldn't call Angie until I had written something and met my suitemates.

There was a part of me that hoped she might come see me off but I knew she wouldn't. We'd had our day and now I had to work to get myself to the next one with her.

And so, after standing on the platform at Princeton Junction for 27 minutes, the Northeast Connector arrived and I sat down with my bag, my guitar, and Angie's notebook, and I left New Jersey.

The trip itself had some interesting moments. I kept to

myself mostly as I was sorta nervous about the travel at first, until I realized that nobody really bothered anyone all that much. There was this one man I met early in the trip who asked me to play my guitar to take his mind off his trip, which was to meet his six-year-old son for the first time. Fathers and sons are a thing for some people and I hope I was able to help him feel ready.

There were other interactions along the way, but I spent most of the time thinking about Angie and our day. I wrote about it some and worked on the lyrics to the "Garden" song a little.

I thought about music a lot too.

I worried about school and how every kid there was likely to be smarter and better trained and more prepared for the work than I was. I mean, I learned a ton from those years in the Boychoir school, but that's not really the sort of stuff I want to create anymore. I want to do something else altogether and I worried that it would be like that one year I played guitar for the Jazz Ensemble at Windsor High, and we went to all these competitions up and down the state.

As I thought about it, I'd actually liked the performance side of things playing with the school group and I'd loved seeing the other bands and talking with some of the kids from other schools about music and stuff, but when the judging started it usually took the fun out of it for me. Not that we did poorly - our band was good that year, I guess, but once the judges started scoring and people started winning stuff, the same kids who had been fun to hang with got totally focused on criticism instead of just making music. This one kid I'd talked with who played bass for Moorestown High's band and had been really cool earlier in the day, almost immediately turned into a jerk once our rhythm section scored three points higher than theirs. He found me right after, completely flustered, asking, "Dude, didn't you flub your B7th chord on 'Stompin' at the Savoy?"

That kind of junk just took the fun out of it for me. I think I realized early on that that kind of winning didn't matter when it comes to music. Winning was playing "Everlong" at the Anchor Inn and watching music bring Kelly and Shannon together after two years of "smelling each other" as the waitress had said. Winning wasn't a trophy that sat in the band office. It's music!

I thought about that Moorestown bassist on the trip and, who knows, I might've made a mistake on the B7th, but Lawrence, the director of the ensemble hadn't complained, and he totally would have if I'd flubbed anything. That guy had an ear like Sinatra and he missed nothing. He was very cool to me and didn't even give me grief when I told him I didn't want to play with the group senior year.

He just asked, "What are you planning to do instead?" I told him and he was like, "Yeah, go do your thing, kid." So, I did. People keep telling me that, assuming "thing" and "Thang" are interchangeable.

I spent the year listening to everything I could get my hands on. The public library near Nana's was awesome. I started checking out baskets of CD's and even took home some older vinyl LP's and stuff. Not even just older artists, I mean, I got loads of that stuff too, Howlin' Wolf, who was great but Hubert Sumlin played guitar for him and was amazing. Buddy Guy and Muddy Waters and BB King and all the blues guys, I wore those discs out learning to play them - Freddie and Albert King too, but I looked at Jazz too - stuff that the people I was seeing out in clubs and concerts were into like Miles Davis and Arturo Sandoval. I moved later in Marvin Gaye and then went through a whole '80s period with the Smiths (Johnny Marr rules!) and the Cure and then went back to all the Beatles stuff and then Bruce Springsteen and Nirvana and then the Foo Fighters before I mellowed out and got into Mumford and Sons for a few weeks and a lot of folky stuff. Oh, and The Decemberists are awesome. I've heard they might play in Boston this year and would love to somehow see them. I even read the novels Colin Meloy wrote. I got so into them before Prom that I started writing epic six-part songs about the Revolutionary War Battle of Trenton, which stunk like everything else I was writing, but I was learning and working and hopefully sucking less. I was constantly creating and talking about music to everyone and going to shows, most of them free ones but I was at a show at least two or three nights a week and the more I went the more I felt like I could do something in that world. More people started giving me chances, too, like the June Rich show and another one opening for The Bertalots at "John and Peter's" in New Hope.

I spent time thinking about money as I knew I was going to have to make some, either playing shows or getting a server gig like Mom or even doing bar back work again like I used to do at Jim's in the summers. Oddly enough, Jim, of "Jim's Country Diner" fame put me in touch with a friend who runs a little gastropub in Boston that has live music. Between that and Uncle Bob's friend Haywood, I felt like I might have a chance to play, but I wasn't sure how I was going to make things work. I'd never been on my own and outside of Nana's neighborhood and the clubs I visited in Philly and Manayunk, I've never really spent much time anywhere.

I realized that I was so far out of my comfort zone that I might as well not have one. It was actually liberating to realize that.

I was trying to ignore my phone, but it bleeped at me at like five times in a row with messages from Randall, one of my suitemates telling me that since I was arriving late that "they'd picked up my keys" and the obligatory information packet for me and that I should "come right to the dorm" when I arrived. His name was familiar from all the paperwork they'd sent me, but it was weird nevertheless.

I had no idea where I was supposed to be go once I arrived, so it was on the one hand nice to have one less thing to worry about. But, then I started to wonder how they just "got my keys."

I messaged back and asked him for the address so I could try to figure out how I was going to get there from the train station. He sent it to me and added, "We have pizza and everyone is assembled and waiting for you so we can figure out our AWESOME!" And I had no idea what that means at all. Like, not one bit, and I found his use of ALL CAPS reminiscent of FLORIS!

That made me laugh and miss Angie all over again, but it also reminded me that I told Mom that I'd call Nana. I knew it was right around the time she has Sunday dinner with her ladies group from church. She was heading into Mrs. Duttry's house when I reached her. She'd made her Colcannon, the thought of which made me homesick. She was excited to hear about my day with Angie.

After I'd given her the rundown of the day, I said, "Nana, I have to thank you."

"For what, dear heart?" She said this way louder than was needed. She still was of the impression that you had to be very loud to be heard and understood over a cell phone.

"Well," I started, leaning back in my seat. There was a young mother and her daughter in the seats directly across the aisle from me as I talked. She seemed startled when I pulled out my phone and started talking as I hadn't spoken to anyone or even really lifted my head out of my notebook for hours. "Nana, you taught me how to do so many things that I'm really glad to know right now. Things that really helped me yesterday in particular. Opening the door, walking on the curbside with a girl, walking her to the door, knowing how and even when to dance and, just not to be afraid of being me."

I heard Nana laugh. It's a laugh unfettered by trepidation and so full of pure joy that it never fails to make me feel alright all over. "You did all of those things yesterday?"

I found myself laughing too. "I did Nana, and I realized that I really love Angie.

"Oh, goodie. I adore her, Avery."

"Me too, Nana."

"Well that's good! You should, I would think." I heard other voices in the background on her side as she continued. "Well, dear heart, I've got to let you go now, Mrs. Duttry needs my help with dinner."

I felt suddenly really sad, feeling almost like this was another goodbye I wasn't ready for.

"OK, Nana, thanks again for everything. I'm going to really work hard up here for you and Mom and for Angie."

She laughed heartily again, a laugh that now that I think of it sounds more and more to me like Angie's. "Well, of course you'll work hard dear, you always do and you've always had to. It's a new day for you, but we've known for years that you had some gifts and graces. The question now is, what will you do?" She put all the emphasis on "do" and I understood what she meant, and I could almost see her holding her phone in one hand and directing traffic at the Ladies Dinner while she talked to me.

I didn't know what to say to that. I knew that I had a kind of plan but I couldn't really answer her, so I told her I'd do my best. It was just then that I realized that I'd gotten choked up as a tear rolled down my face, landing on the armrest with an almost audible 'bloop.' The mom across the aisle held out a tissue for me and I wiped my eyes.

"I'm going to find my awesome, Nana," I croaked, pulling it from somewhere, "and I'm going to make you proud."

I heard the ambient noise of what was likely to be a raucous Ladies Dinner at Mrs. Duttry's.

"Oh, I'm already proud of you, Avery. I'm always that. You're a good boy, but you must do something for me right now, alright?"

I sat up in my seat at that, almost at attention, desperate for whatever direction and guidance she could give me. I knew the train would arrive soon and while on the one hand I was completely motivated and driven, on the other I was uncertain and scared. I was thirsty for her direction.

I took a deep breath and said, "What's that, Nana?"

"Well, dear heart, I'd like you to stop blubbering to your Nana and go kick some asses and rock some worlds up there in Beantown, if it's not too inconvenient for you? Maybe put some more work into that "Garden" song you played yesterday? I liked that one!"

I was floored, "Nana, you saw that?"

"Well of course I did! Don't you know that your

Nana is always paying attention? Shellie Bennett's mother is part of our Pilates group and sent me a clip over the email. And Angela's Uncle Bob tagged me in a Twitter. Reuben Frank liked the tweet even! I know I'm old, Avery but there's some really cool ways to connect with people now. You really ought to catch up."

"Nana, have I told you lately that you're the greatest?"

There was now music playing on the other end of Nana's phone. It sounded like the Beach Boys. "Well, not in the last few days, but thank you dear. Go now and 'find your awesome,' was it? I love you."

She hung up then. She always preferred to offer the last word of a conversation and I liked giving it to her. I knew she'd have been directing traffic at Mrs. Duttry's house and getting everything and everyone in their place. She's about as petite as mom is but she commands a room like no one I've ever seen, when she wants to.

I slouched back into my seat as she hung up. The mom across the aisle was looking at me, clearly puzzled, but trying to look like she wasn't actually looking. I figured I'd just talk to her as I hadn't really spoken to anyone on board since we crossed into New York hours ago.

"Thank you for the tissue." I waved it at her like a white flag I suppose. The brakes were squealing and the loudspeaker announced that we were approaching Boston Back Bay Station. My stop.

"You're welcome." She seemed nice enough. She looked a little bit like Michelle Obama but was probably only like ten years older than me and her daughter was probably 3 or something. It seemed for a moment like she was going to leave it at that but then she continued. "Hey, are you alright?"

"Yes, ma'am, I think so. I hope I'll be more than that

soon. But I've got a lot to learn. A lot to do. And every great reason in the world to do it. I just need to figure out how."

She smiled politely again and turned back towards her window.

I got another text from Randall giving me the code for the dormitory door and asking for an updated ETA. I messaged back that the train was pulling into Back Bay.

As the train was completing its arrival, I thought of Angie. I wished I could call her, but she made me promise to wait until I'd met everyone and written. I'd written most of the day, so now I only had the one thing left. I could still smell her perfume on me and it made me miss, want, and need her all at the same moment.

It had been some kind of day between Madame Marie, the Anglesea Lighthouse Gardens, Uncle Bob and Aunt Jenny, Andrew and the singers at the Wildwood Chapel, the Christmas store and the dollhouse and crane machine, the Anchor Inn and Garlic crabs, performing with Shellie and The Cozy Morley's and playing that song for Angie. And the Ferris Wheel and FLORIS!

The beach. The boardwalk. The car. Her lawn. Dancing on Route 130! How were all those moments somehow encompassed in one last day, however good it was?

Before I got off the train, I thought about all of those things and more. I'd never been more in love. I'd never been so ready to thrust myself into the things to come.

It was a long day but a good one, after a great one. I wasn't sure what Randall meant, but I had hopes that my "awesome" would be acceptable to them, whatever that means.

As I picked up my bag and my guitar, I was tired and

hungry, but I understood it was time to take another step away from all I've known. I was so ready to meet these roommates, if for no other reason then I got to call Angie afterwards. As she got up to leave, the young mom who looked like Michelle gave me another tissue, "just in case" and gave me directions on which way to head once I left the station.

Upon our arrival in Boston, I stood at the doors as they opened, and I felt like it was time to see what that best version of me was like, and I was ready to do all the things Angie and I had talked about and all the things Nana had said. I stepped onto the platform with the full intention of changing the world, taking one final step away from home, into the larger world that was waiting for me.

CHAPTER FIFTEEN

By the time I stepped outside the Back Bay station with all my bags and guitar, I'd forgotten the directions that the nice lady had given me. I basically went from cop to cop outside the station where the last officer said, in what I now know is a thick South Boston accent (but sounded like a foreign language to me at first): "Good luck, kid - head that way," as she pointed away from the station. "Turn left on Boylston and you'll be fine. Try not to look muggable though." It was hot still, but after being on a train all day it was nice to be outside. Pretty sure I heard her call me a "doorknob" as I wandered off.

I can't say her suggestions filled me with confidence, but I made it to Prince Hall without being mugged, used the code Randall had sent me and walked into the lobby.

There was music coming from everywhere! I knew I had come to the right place. I was tempted to pull out my instrument and just go looking for someone to play with but I was far more ready to put my stuff down and get to my room, if for no other reason than it would get me closer to being able to call Angie. So, following the signs on the walls I climbed the steps that brought me to the third floor and room 317.

I remember hearing the music fade from the downstairs only to be replaced by that which was going on in the halls and rooms I was passing. When I reached the third floor, I entered the hallway to find it largely quiet, at least in comparison to the first two floors and the lounge. The hallway was empty as I walked down toward 317, the only open door on what felt like a deserted hallway.

I nudged it open with my bag and walked into the common room where I found three guys and a girl sitting and staring at one another awkwardly.

"Thank gahd you're finally here!" squawked a skinny, brown-haired kid who had what I was to learn later an entirely different kind of Boston accent compared to what I'd experienced at the train station. "You're Avery?" he asked, half hugging me before I could put my stuff down.

"Uh, yeah - I think so?" I wasn't used to people I didn't know hugging me on first meeting just yet.

"Whooohooo!" cheered a round-faced girl with red hair. "Randall here says you're awesome?" pointing a thumb at the guy who'd hugged me. The next thing I knew, everyone was in motion.

Randall took my guitar case and put it on the table in the center of the common room where everyone had been sitting. A very tall and strong-looking black guy with long hair braids that ended in multicolored beads rose and shook my hand and took my bag. "I'm Freddy. You'll be bunking with Randall over here," he said in a deep voice that sounded like it didn't have a bottom. His grip was strong and he simply glowed with charisma. I'd have voted for him to be whatever he wanted to be immediately and without reservation.

The suite had two sleeping areas at opposite ends and the common room and a bathroom in the middle. There was a bed in each corner of the room as I entered, following Freddy with my bag. Randall's stuff was already all over the place like he'd been here for a week, which it turned out he had.

"Yeah, my parents are on staff," Randall shared as he sauntered in behind us. Freddy gently put my bag on the bed and I dropped my bag from Angie next to it on the bare mattress next to the night stand, across from the equally dull dresser. "I came in last week and started organizing everything."

Having his parents on the staff clearly came with some privleges.

"Is that all you brought?"

I turned and saw a pale-faced guy with seriously black hair that was carrying so much product to hold it straight up on its end that it might be responsible for global warming. He had kind eyes though. He and the red-haired girl were standing next to each other in the doorway.

I felt awkward immediately, looking at my stuff.

"Yeah," I said, noticing all of the stuff Randall had on his side: huge Bluetooth speakers next to a laptop, a fridge, three bass guitars and a box of pedals and other gear and a case of Mountain Dew.

"I travel light," I replied. It's an easier sell than the truth that there really wasn't much to pack.

The redhead smacked the spiky-haired boy in the back of the head. "Don't be like that, he just got here."

"Ow! What was that for?"

"For being a jerk!" She continued in a perfect

imitation of how he'd just spoken, "Is that all you brought?" She moved to smack him again but he ducked. "Cut that out, bro, we're all new here."

I must have looked as confused as I felt and remember wondering if I should have stayed downstairs. Randall then did what, it turns out, Randall does and took over the room with unavoidable and irresistible redirection.

"Yes, we are all new," he began, "Introductions will continue in the main parlor." He began to whisk everyone back into the common room where five chairs sat around the table, where my guitar case was still laying. Randall reminded me of Uncle Bob but he was short and thin where Bob was neither, but they both talk excitedly about everything.

After everyone had found a seat, Randall leaned forward and clapped his hands together. "So, I suppose you're wondering why I've asked you all here tonight?" His eyes were wide with excitement. The silence was awkward before the redhead leaned over and reached for my hand. "I'm Marnie Kennington." She had soft hands and a grip that was not far off from Freddy's. I remember thinking that I was going to have to watch myself shaking hands with either of them if I wanted to not break a finger. "This dope," gesturing at the pale boy with the spiky hair, "is my twin brother, Alex. He's sometimes well-behaved around other humans, but not always."

Alex mussed up his sister's hair, rose and crossed the floor to shake my hand as well. I guess they'd all met one another. "Don't mind her," he offered in a voice that was just a little quieter than you'd have to use to be heard. I felt myself leaning in to make sure I heard him. "Marnie will be living downstairs in her own suite."

They looked so different to be twins but I found that I liked their banter with one another immediately. Randall made a show of "shooing" them back to their seats. "Enough from the 'Riverside Elite' just now, we've got a lot of ground to cover. "You met Freddy just now," Randall said with a flourish of hands to point at Freddy, who seemed to be perfectly happy to be there.

"Freddy comes to us from the far away and exotic city of Cleveland, Ohio."

"Actually, Randall, I grew up in Shaker Heights." His voice was just magic. Randall wasn't ready for the interruption but Freddy's voice simply was unignorably cool. It made me feel like the world made sense if it produced such a voice. Imagine James Earl Jones and Morgan Freeman had a son and you're halfway there.

Everyone just stared at them both before Randall shook his head as if to clear it and asked, "Got it. I'm sorry Fred. Where is Shaker Heights?"

"It's basically Cleveland," Freddy deadpanned until he saw Randall starting to get grumpy and he started to laugh, a rich and sonorous sound that filled the room with a music all its own. I decided right then that I needed to make him laugh as often as I could. We all joined in, even Randall, eventually.

Things moved on from there with Freddy sharing that he'd been an athlete and a singer at a pretty big school for both arts and sports in the Cleveland area, but that he'd decided to focus on music because of his church and his grandmother.

Everyone went back and forth, except me. I was fascinated listening to them and hearing about their lives. Alex and Marnie were so funny the way they bantered and Randall was infectious with his enthusiasm for everything. Freddy seemed so mellow but it was clear he was studying everyone. He's a kid that misses absolutely nothing, I have learned. I started to feel a little weird sitting among them as they shared because I really didn't have any idea where I'd fit in with them. They were all so different from each other and from any friend I'd had before. I was still a little bit in shock to find myself in a dorm in Boston when I'd been at the Jersey shore the day before.

I'd felt really motivated and energetic after I got off the train. Nana's pep talk and thinking about all Angie had said fired me up earlier, but as I sat in the room with these other kids, I found myself spiraling into self-doubt and thought that I didn't belong and was out of my comfort zone, which I was of course, but I think I shut down, which went unnoticed by pretty much no one.

It was Marnie who called me on it. There was a momentary lull in the chatter and she leaned in on her chair which she'd "borrowed" from an open room across the hall.

"Ok, Jersey boy. You've ridden the conversational wave long enough. What's your story?" Suddenly everyone was looking at me.

There was a moment where I didn't know what to say to them all. It was brief. It lasted until I remembered what I'd done the over the last forty-eight hours.

"It's funny you should ask, actually."

I didn't recount my whole life story or tell them everything about the last four years with her, but I talked to them about the day Angie and I spent in Wildwood. I told them about all of it, including playing the song for her and the chapel and playing with The Cozy Morleys and eventually the Ferris Wheel and her treatment starting. And, of course, the fact that she and I were finally together now and how she asked me to write and that I wasn't allowed to call her until I'd done some writing and met my new suitemates. Then I told them I had to wait until Christmas to see her, and that I was really worried about her and completely in love and motivated to completely bust loose on the music scene and whatever else the city and the school had to offer, as I had made promises I meant to keep.

"Well," I sighed after I'd rambled on for what felt like a long time, "I guess that's me, more or less."

I remember looking at them each: Freddy was smiling widely, leaning back in his chair in reflection. Alex looked as though he was deep in thought as he leaned forward on his knees, processing. I learned later that was kind of his natural state. Randall and Marnie, in what was a real preview of coming attractions couldn't talk fast enough.

Marnie cried out, "Oh, we are so calling Angie right now!"

Randall was right in the middle of the room now with his hands waving, "Ah, ah...not until he plays us that "Garden" song. He has to play something for us so why not that?"

Marnie narrowed her eyes at Randall but nodded in agreement. "Everyone else played something earlier, Avery, so I guess it's only fair," she offered as an explanation.

"You mean this song?" Alex had been fiddling with his phone while the rest of us talked and somehow, to this day I still don't know how he did it, he pulled up the video of me performing the night before with Shellie Bennet and The Cozy Morley's. I heard the end of "Everlong" and the beginning of the "Garden" song before Randall waved him off, "turn that off. He's gotta play live if we're going to know what we've got here!"

"Fair enough," Alex replied, putting his phone away. "So, let's hear it then."

I felt immediately anxious and self-conscious, but then, I remembered the path of that song as it developed and what it had done for me the day before. Also, I realized that while this diverse and interesting band of brothers, and sister, were from all over the map both in terms of their lives and their music, I liked them immediately. They wanted to hear what I had and in a school like this, in a moment like that, it felt like a fair challenge. I pulled out my guitar and I played the "Garden" for them and something really cool happened.

After a verse of the "Garden," Randall went and got an acoustic bass and jumped in while Alex picked up a violin and found a counterpoint to the melody that I'd never even considered possible. Freddy and Marnie chimed in on the second chorus with a harmony that was just hauntingly beautiful. The way they looked at one another then clued me into the fact that there was clearly something there between them from the start. It was really cool and I hope Marnie follows through and gives things a chance with Freddy.

I wish someone had recorded that first time we all played together. I'm shocked Randall wasn't recording, actually, because he seems to always be pulling out his phone or his little handheld camera and filming everything. I think it was a pretty "transcendent moment in art" like Professor Jackson-Clark so often talks about. I'm not really sure what that means, but I do know that as the song ended the sounds of all of us together hung in the air for quite a while. That final, "I promise you, that this is me…" sounded very much like it had been sung by a different me than the night before. I suppose that's pretty accurate.

The quiet that hung over the room ended rather abruptly, as I found most silences did this semester, with Alex pointing his bow at me and pronouncing, "Well, it's musically simple but has some interesting places it could go harmonically, and…" at which point his sister smacked him in the forehead.

"Shut up, dummy, you're missing it…" Marnie laughed as she moved towards me, hand outstretched doing that "give me something" motion with her hand. I moved as if to shake her hand and then went for the high five as I had no idea what was happening.

"Give me your phone, dude, we need to talk to your girl."

"It seems only right that we should introduce ourselves," Freddy agreed.

I really wanted to call Angie but I wasn't sure I wanted the whole room to do it with me, but they were all staring at me expectantly. After we'd played my song together as a group, I suddenly felt willing to play along. It had seemed to happen so naturally that, despite the fact that I'd just met these kids, I felt like I was a part of something. So, I put my guitar back in her case and stood up and pulled my phone out, which Randall snatched out of my hand before Marnie could grab it and they were then chasing one another around for it before I could blink.

Eventually they both sat down on one of the desks set into the far wall of the room, near the windows. "Let's see what we've got here," Randall began, studying my phone. Marnie sucked in her breath and pointed at the home screen.

"Is that Angie?" she asked, clapping her hands rapidly together. I nodded, noticing in turn the appreciative nods of the other guys as they'd come over and were peering over Randall's shoulder at the screen. Both Freddy and Alex looked from Angie's picture to me and back again several times.

At the same time that Marnie added, "She's beautiful!" Randall blurted out, "She's dating you?!" She then swatted Randall on the arm, "Hey," she interrupted, tilting her chin towards me, "Who are you kidding, this boy here is decent! They totally go together. Plus," she sighed, leaning back onto the wall, "if a boy wrote me a song like that, I'd totally melt!"

Freddy and Marnie both caught themselves looking at one another just then and looked away. I was the only one that caught it though, I think.

Randall groaned, flipping through the phone. "Jeez son, is that the only picture you got on here? What do you use this thing for?"

The way he said "for" sounded like "fowah" to me and "here" was "heeya," I'd never heard anyone talk like that. It would take some getting used to.

"Well, music mostly and for calling people, I guess. Oh!" I said, "And I started texting this year too!"

Randall's eye sockets simply could not hold the amount of rolling they wanted to do so he rose from the desk and began to pace the room like a trapped animal. "Let's get you linked up to the Wi-Fi," he finally said after a few trips through the common room tapping things on my phone, "and then we can all connect with your lady friend."

"Wait, all of you?"

"What else, guy? She's clearly got you wrapped up so she's gonna be along for the ride too. And, if I may say, this crew here in this room, we're gonna make one helluva team goin' forward! We've got some really good stuff to work with here…"

Alex looked confused suddenly and I didn't disagree with him. I didn't get what Randall was going for. Randall settled himself and then pointed his finger at Alex. "You! You, are a musical genius. Orchestration, theory, scoring, harmonics. You're already better at it than pretty much anyone at this school, including the faculty. And you can play pretty much any instrument from what I hear. Now, Freddy here,"

Randall moved away from Alex and over to Freddy before Alex could even register what he'd been told. "Freddy is just about the most exciting vocal major they've had come here in over fifteen years! And you're kinda handsome from what I can gather from the way that Marnie can't take her eyes off you."

Alex found his voice again at that, "Hey now…" he pleaded while Marnie blushed redder than anyone I'd ever seen, but she didn't respond.

Randall continued, like an unstoppable force. "Listen, it's cool. Heck, I'm straight and I think he's good-looking as hell. It's just information, but hey, Freddy is about the best he is at what he does. Just like you, Alex."

Randall stopped short of giving Alex and Freddy "jazz hands" to sell what he was saying, but it seemed to placate Alex, who seemed to genuinely appreciate Randall praising his skills.

There was a pause as Alex had ingested the truth/flattery that Randall had delivered. Marnie, however had a grave look on her face and now looked slightly pale.

"Randall, how do you know all this? About them?" She asked pointing back and forth between both Freddy and her brother.

Randall looked sheepish suddenly but didn't flinch as he replied. "My ma might be the Dean of Housing."

Alex stood up from where he'd been leaning against the desk and glared at Randall. "So, you read all of our files after rooms here assigned? Wow, hey…that's a little…" Alex was flustered. "That's really something, Randall."

"No, that's not it. I didn't read them after rooms got assigned…" he said but his voice trailed off at the end. He was wearing a satisfied smile as wide as his mouth could carry it. I later learned that this particular smile was the one that made it simply impossible to remain mad at him. "I would never do something like that!"

Alex relaxed and moved over to the window sill and leaned up against it as Randall continued.

"I read the files of all the incoming freshman and picked the guys I wanted to live and work with."

The silence that followed this announcement was deafening. Marnie's jaw dropped and Alex looked like he might implode. I really didn't know what to make of it all as, just based on the words, it seemed kinda creepy and maybe illegal. Then I heard Freddy's deep and joyous laughter filling the room. It was almost musical and completely infectious as before we knew it we were all laughing uncontrollably.

I knew right then in that moment that I was going to be in for a very different kind of year. I really did feel like I connected with them all from the start. The rest would be easy if I could just get out of my own way, like Madam Marie suggested.

"So, can I call Angie now?" I asked, holding out my hand to Randall, who was still fiddling with my phone. I heard Marnie make an "aww" sound while her brother went "ick."

"Of course not!" Randall snapped, his fingers still flipping out on my phone screen. "I had to update the hell out of this thing, but it should be stocked now, son. Look there," he said pointing at an app icon. "Now you can Facetime with her. You know, talk to her and see her while you're talking." He talked slow there and made some hand gestures that led me to believe he did not find my lack of smartphone skills charming.

Mom didn't have Wi-Fi at home anyway so I just never ended up getting into the Instagram and Snapchat stuff or the facetimes either, as I'd had her old flip-phone until graduation. Angie and I just talked conventionally, but the idea of seeing her, even over the phone was suddenly intoxicating.

"Just click there," Randall said, so I did. It took a few rings, the tone of which sounded weird to me. Next thing I know, there's Angie's face smiling at me on my phone. Her hair looked like she'd just let it down from a braid or pony tail and she'd just quickly fluffed it up, but I loved it. She could have been wearing an avocado mud mask and she'd have looked amazing to me. Seeing her smile at me after everything was equal parts relief and pure joy.

"Oh, my, God! Are you facetiming me?" The sound of her voice and the image of her on the screen was overwhelming.

"Yeah, it's all the rage up here in Collegeville," I stuttered.

"Oh, wow! Who showed you how to do that, sweetie?"

At this point Randall casually removed the phone from my hand and took over. "Oh, that would be me, Miss Angela," he smarmed in his "I couldn't be a nicer young man" voice.

"And who might you be?" I couldn't see her anymore as Randall was now walking her all about the suite but her voice was so full of laughter that it almost felt like she was in the room at times.

"Oh, I'm Randall, Miss Angela. I'm going to be Avery's roomie here in our suite." He smiled like he was trying to impress her, which he clearly was. It was clearly working as well.

"Well, that's swell, Randall!" Angie's laugh filled the room and the others surrounded Randall.

"It IS swell, isn't it, Miss Angela?"

Freddy pretty much exploded into laughter after trying to keep it together and Alex might have chuckled a bit too.

"Come on now, let's show you around and introduce you to everyone," Randall went on, continuing to deny me access to the phone. "You can talk to the boyfriend later as we've got some 'getting to know yous' to get done here. None of the rest of us arrived with a soulmate in tow…"

Randall, for all his manic bravado, in that moment said exactly the right thing and that last line endeared me to him a lot. Despite his seeming willingness to say and do anything at any time, in that moment, for me, despite the fact that we just met, he sized up who Angie was to me, and he simply found a way to casually say the best thing ever, and mean it.

One by one, Randall walked my phone around the room to introduce everyone. Freddy was first, then Alex and Marnie. Then he spent some time talking to her himself. Through it all I kept hearing Angie laugh, a sound I love more and more every time I hear it.

They passed the phone around and seemed to be having fun so I just watched, enthralled. This whole situation: the suite, the school, Angie - it was all so new and unsettled and I would normally have been totally freaking out. In the light of everything that had gone on in the last two days, I found myself feeling like everything was awesome and normal, and it was. I didn't really know these kids at all but if they could make Angie laugh, it was a really good start.

At one point, Freddy started singing to Angie. I found out later it was a hymn called "Be Thou my Vision," and it was seriously moving as Freddy is ridiculously good. His voice and presence could have felt really intimidating, but I was really struck in that moment by how easily Freddy and the others just shared musically so freely. There were no tentative or self-conscious moments. It was like those movies or shows on TV where people just break into song. Again, I really felt like I was in the right place.

Second time in as many days, I thought.

They all chatted with Angie for over an hour before they gave me my phone back. I'd had a chance to eat some Boston pizza, which didn't compare to back home, but staved off starvation.

"Thanks, guys," I muttered and retreated into the corner of the room I was to share with Randall, shutting the door behind me. I had to plug in the phone because it was almost dead, probably rebelling from all the work it was suddenly being asked to do. I sat down on the plasticy bed, which was of course unmade. I hadn't unpacked, but that wouldn't have helped as I hadn't packed sheets. I guess I thought they'd be provided, like in a motel, but they weren't, so I was laying atop what amounted to a rubber cushion that smelled of antiseptic. It was cool to the touch and the room was dark. As I laid down on my side and held the phone, all I could see was Angie's face, red from laughing, eyes pink from tearing up as she did every time she laughed too hard all at once.

She was in her room sitting on her big, puffy, yellow

chair that sat in the corner of her bedroom. It was getting late and I could see that she was both tired and wired like I was. We just looked at each other for a minute before she gave a quick exhale and tilted her head inquisitively.

"So, how was your day?"

I laughed. "Angie, it was really something." I gave her a general rundown of the day. I didn't get into everything that I'd written, though I assured her that I had, in fact, spent the day writing, much of it about her. I gave her an idea of how things went on the train and how I was feeling and she listened attentively, but I knew she was tired. She had another treatment coming up in a few days, so, I told her what I was feeling. Nana always said that sometimes you should just say what you feel, as it's the easiest thing to know.

"I miss you," I said, rolling onto my stomach, the screen resting on my crossed arms. The charger cord wasn't long enough for me to move around a whole lot.

"I miss you too, sweetie, but," and she yawned, "you seem to be in capable, and very interesting company up there."

"You've spent more time with them than I have so far."

"Yeah, they were sweet." She brushed her hair back off her face and snuggled into the chair even deeper. "You like them already and they like you. And you are more excited than you thought now that you're actually there and seeing what it could be like." I started to interrupt her completely spot-on observations, but she didn't give me the chance. "Don't you forget what you promised me, sweetie. You are to do your best and be your own brand of amazing. 'Find your awesome' like your roommate kept saying.

"What does that even mean?"

"Yeah, he's something else," she offered, "but I take it to mean you need to go be you, Avery. Learn what you can and do those things that only you can do and see where it takes you! Be open to that awesome journey." She paused and looked away from the screen for a moment. "And, it means you should love me."

"I will, always."

Angie closed her eyes and leaned her head back into the chair and I saw her pull up a blanket that had been on her lap and tuck it under her chin. "That was hot, sweetie."

"Yeah?"

"Yeah, keep saying stuff like that."

"Like singing of your love, forever?"

"Yeah, that's acceptable too." She yawned again. "Stuff like that."

"You're tired. I can see that now with this Faceytime thing."

She perked at that for a moment, "Yes, I'm glad I can see you too now. Please thank Randall for that. I think he's going to be good for you. I'm going to sleep now, sweetie."

The screen had started to move randomly and I was treated to a tornado-like tour of her room. "I figured," I called out. "Hey Ange?"

"Just a second." The screen kept moving until she stuck her phone in the pocket of her robe while she got into bed, which in its own way made me oddly and excitingly close to her, despite how far apart we were. Eventually, she pulled the phone out of her pocket and the room was dark. The screen just showed her face lit up by the phone itself as she was leaning onto her giant pillows.

"OK, I'm back. Miss me?"

"Always. But before you crash I wanted to thank you for the book and the pen. It made a big difference today, I think."

"I'm glad," she sighed. "I hoped it would be useful."

"I love you," I said, hoping she was still awake. She was notorious for falling asleep on the phone with me. One time she did it when her family was vacationing in Canada and the bill ended up being like $142 because her end never hung up.

"I love you." she said.

"Call you tomorrow?"

"Until then."

I was about to click the red button thing when I thought of one last thing. "Oh, and Angie?"

"Hrmm?"

"You look really pretty tonight."

She grinned and opened her eyes a little, "Yeah?"

"Yeah, you really do."

She reached her fingers toward the screen as though she could touch my face through it. It felt like she could to me, a little anyway.

"You too, sweetie."

"Good night, love."

"Night."

As I clicked off the connection I was unsurprised to hear hushed voices and footsteps coming from the common room. I got off the bed and slid open the pocket door to find Randall standing directly in front of me, and the others in equally ridiculous poses of "hey I was just looking out the window" or "Wow, I'm enjoying this box of unpacked stuff..."

"Everything copacetic?" Randall asked, looking past me into the room.

"Yeah," I replied honestly. "Everything is good now."

Randall folded his hands like a little kid at prayer, "So, does Miss Angela approve of us?"

He was being silly, I know and using a "way too polite for human life" voice, but I realized even then that it mattered to him. I'm not sure how I got it then but I certainly get him now after living with him.

"Yeah, I think she likes you all."

Randall looked like he had a follow-up question but Alex rose from where he'd been sitting and grumbled, "Well, that's swell. I'm off to sleep. Course selection tomorrow…" He tousled his sister's hair as he walked past her into the room he and Freddy would share. "Night, Marn"

Marnie swatted his hand but smirked at him anyway, "Night, bro." I learned later that they always made a point of saying something pleasant to each other when they parted. Always, even if it was just until dinner or something. Even if they'd been arguing for an hour, if they parted, it was always, "see you later" or "be good" and at least once or twice it was "love you." They refused to ever leave one another in anger or negativity.

"Good night boys - see you tomorrow," she called as she left the room. Her eyes again passed over and lingered on Freddy for a moment. Even that first night it was impossible to miss.

"Good night," Freddy called after her. He waved at Randall and me before he entered his room with Alex and pulled their pocket door closed.

CHAPTER SIXTEEN

My guitar case was open on the common room table and the chairs from all the desks were all over the place, so I packed up my stuff and brought it near the door to our room before I started putting the room back in order. Randall watched me for a moment with a look I couldn't read on his face.

After a minute of watching me, he scoffed, "Guy - what are you doing?"

I'd just put the chairs away at each desk and was getting ready to reposition the common table and its chairs. "I'm cleaning up. We can't just leave everything out like this."

"Why not?"

I had a chair in my hands and I put it down next to the table but then I found that I had no answer.

"I honestly don't know," I finally said.

"Then leave it. It'll be there tomorrow and it will still be ours. That's kinda cool, right?" Randall was always excited but I knew he was testing me also. "Plus, Alex smells like a neat-freak. We might be able to pawn

248

cleanup off on him."

"Fair point," I agreed and I brought my guitar into the room and laid it all next to my bed and I started to unpack when I realized that I'd never really unpacked before.

Any travel Mom and I did over the years was usually either to Nana's, maybe a night at the shore, and maybe a weekend at wherever Uncle Ted was living his dream. But we never unpacked - it was always living out of the bag. I didn't have a lot to unpack so it didn't take long. The particle board drawers and open closet were more than ample for my stuff. It was just clothes really and some shoes and a bunch of folders of music and a few pictures. I had the one of me and Angie at Prom and one of me and Mom and Nana at Angie's sweet sixteen from a few years ago. There was another picture of me with Will, Pat, and Brian sitting on the ugly orange couch in Will's house before graduation. I put them all on the mirror that hung above the dresser and wondered where they all were and hoped they were doing well.

Unpacking took minutes but after everything was away, I remembered that I had no sheets or a pillow or blankets, except for the tiny quilt that Nana had made me with her church group. I love it and it has all the Philly Sports teams' logos on it, but it's the size of a hand towel. I spent several minutes looking in closets and drawers for them because like I said, I thought they'd be here but they weren't. I actually started to panic a little and was pulling my longer winter coat out of the closet to fold into a pillow when Randall tossed an unopened package of sheets and a pillow on my bed. "Ma always over packs for me. These are yours, son."

They were cotton and blue and just fine. The way he just plopped them on my bed and didn't make a thing of it saved me a lot of embarrassment.

"Thanks. I guess I forgot to pack mine," I mumbled, but Randall waved my awkwardness away.

"It's cool, guy! An artist needs his sleep. Perchance to dream and all that stuff."

Randall, at that moment was of course still weird and a little creepy and devious and charming and thoughtful all at once, and while I really didn't know him at all then, I realized that he was about the most interesting person I'd ever met. I figured, as long as I can last up here, I'm going to hang out with this guy and see what happens.

I made my bed with the sheets and pillow he'd given me and got ready to sleep. I remember sitting on the edge of the bed, about to share a space with this guy, and trying to process it all, but, as he often does, Randall had something more to say.

"So, you wanna know how you ended up in this awesome room with us?" He said it like "ahh-sum" in a way that sounded like he was having his throat checked at the doctor. I was curious though, and Randall looked like he might implode from excitement if I didn't let him tell the tale.

Until he brought it up again I'd forgotten the earlier revelation that he'd finagled things to arrange his room assignment and suitemates. He'd talked about why he'd sought out Freddy and Alex quite clearly. They had talent. I'd been wondering where I fit in with his master plan so I answered, "Yeah, why not?"

I sat on the edge of my new bed and Randall picked up the uncomfortable-looking wooden chair that sat in the middle of the room and dragged it over to me, closer than I was ready for.

Randall looked around the room. His narrow eyes never seem to miss anything, always prying about. "Ok -

that stuff I said about Freddy and Alex was mostly true, but as I was doing all this stuff, I ran out of time! I hacked into the Housing office computer system in Ma's office and placed Alex and Freddy and I into our particular suite, but we needed a fourth! Otherwise they could have stuck anyone in here and I wasn't having that. I needed more time to think but then I could hear my mom down the hall talking to her summer interns. They were the key to the whole operation!"

Randall was clearly having fun in the retelling of his adventure. He spoke almost conspiratorially to me like we were retired spies. "The interns had to be involved as they'd see me going into her office so I spent time getting to know them all summer. One of them, Maggie, was real cute too so I had 'interest' in her as a cover, so Ma didn't get too suspicious as to why I was hanging around her office so much. Maggie let me know which day they'd be running the room lottery for our class and that my mom had a meeting with the Provost," he scanned the room again for eavesdroppers, "so I made my move. I'd gotten the room and the first three of us locked in when I heard Ma coming. The interns were doing a bang-up job of slowing Ma down and were making as much noise as possible so I knew when she was coming. I was planning to 'take Ma to lunch,' so being in her office would be no biggie, but I had to log out of her computer and get out from behind her desk, for starters. I got it done just in time. Cost me a lunch with Ma at Border Cafe and a few tickets for Maggie and her pals to see Penguin Dream Warriors play at the Paradise, but that was easy enough. That reminds me, I was thinking of asking her to join me for the Thunderegg show at the Orpheum. She's wicked cute…"

He hadn't gotten to me yet, but one thing was

perfectly clear to me already and that was that Randall was a player and he was going to be a kid who got stuff done. That said, he tells a rambling kind of story and often needs to be reminded of what he's talking about.

"So, you were running out of time…" I prompted.

"Oh, yeah, hello! Exactly!" He was back on track now. "I had maybe a minute or two to add a fourth to our suite so, honestly I just prayed a little" he said, crossing himself. "I said, 'please Lord, give me someone awesome!' I clicked on you and that was that."

We looked at one another. Randall's fingers and hands and pretty much the rest of him never stopped moving but his eyes could lock in on you when he was serious. "So, let's be ahhhhsum, son!" He clapped me on the shoulder and dragged the chair back across the room, jumped into bed and I think he was asleep before he even landed.

The noise outside our window didn't bother me. It was a bit of a cacophonous drizzle. It was far better than the Kern's spotlights hitting my face.

As I lay down in my new bed, I felt exhausted, but more alive than ever. I hadn't said a real prayer in years, but I did as I went to sleep that night. I got right out of bed and kneeled up against my borrowed sheets. I prayed that Mom and Nana would be healthy and happy. I prayed that things would go well for Aunt Jenny and Uncle Bob, and Shellie and his band. I prayed for the dad I met on the train who was meeting his son for the first time, I think he got off in Cartaret. I prayed for whoever my dad actually was. If it was that Father Pavla, I wished him well, and prayed that he never found reason to come across my path or my mother's again. I prayed for Angie's parents and her family. And for Will and Brian and Pat, and for Melissa Carpenter and everyone else that I'd left behind.

And then I prayed for Angie. I'm not going to tell you what I prayed for as it's not for you. But I prayed. It felt both strange and wonderful to do. I wasn't sure why I did it, but I did it.

I looked at my picture of Angie and fell asleep with her so much in my mind that it nearly felt like I could hold her. I couldn't just then, but it felt that way. It was good and I could smell her hair, feel her hands, taste her lips as I fell into such a sleep that it put into question whether or not I'd ever actually had a good night sleep in my life

Thus, ended my first night in Boston. It had been a really good day.

The Last Good Day

CHAPTER SEVENTEEN

And so, it was Christmas.

Alex and Marnie gave me a ride from school after finals. They live on Riverside Drive in Manhattan and were kind enough to drop me at Penn Station where I could pick up the train down to Princeton Junction. I'm seeing them next week back in the city for my second scholarship interview and audition, which they've really both helped me get ready for. For twins, they are so different but equally awesome.

So, I've done what I said I would do. I went and had a semester at school and worked hard and now I'm headed home. A lot has changed, though.

Randall has been a very interesting friend. He's taken a great deal of getting used to. I mean, I only ever lived with Mom, and now I'm living with three other guys? As for Randall, there's a lot of awesome, but now that I know him I've realized that he exists primarily as an unstoppable bundle of energy. That and a drive to constantly keep moving. I mean, he NEVER stops moving.

Our dorm room remains a stark contract of styles. His

side is still bursting with production equipment and instruments and appliances (he has a rice cooker but hates rice). My side is still pretty "Spartan" as they say. The only things I've added since move-in are a few bits of clothes and towels, as I'd forgotten to bring those when I moved in as well, and the photos that Angie has sent that Randall's printed out for me.

Angie started drawing during her chemo sessions and she's sent me several of those sketches that are on the wall above my bed now. The amazing part for Angie now is that the people in the Chemo wing liked what she was doing so much that she's now leading art sessions during her chemotherapy where all the patients work on a project together to pass the time. Princeton Hospital even set up a gallery for them to show and even sell their work either for charity or to help with their bills, like her friend Mr. Vidler. He's seventy-six and fighting cancer and had never painted before but turned out to be a prodigy at it. One of his paintings was so good it was purchased by a Princeton University History Prof for two thousand dollars, which paid all his outstanding bills and then some. The program was so popular that Angie was written up in the Philly papers for it. I keep that article in my wallet but every picture she's sent me fills the wall above my bed. Angie told me after her "Chemo-Art" initiative took off that Marnie had given her the idea.

It turns out that once the Boston crew got to know me and Angie, especially after they got a sense of what she was facing, they all went out of their way to find a way to be helpful. Neither of us asked them to do any of it, but they started texting or emailing her and even Facetimed with her a few times when I was in class or rehearsal sessions. They sort of adopted us both it seemed, which I felt awkward about at first, but I'm grateful for now.

Perhaps there was something to those prayers I sent off.

It's almost Christmas so everyone on board the train is more polite than I remember. Far more pleasant than the people who ride the "T" in Boston. Randall and I ride around the city a lot on the T to shows and gigs. It turns out that his real gift lies in getting people together. He helped me score a lot of gigs and spots that I'd never have had access to but for him. If he didn't know someone he knew someone who knew them. It turns out that my old friend Shellie Bennett has a pal, Donna Marie, who's married to the guy who books at "The Wayside" (which is a nicer club in Faneuil Hall). He let me play some open mics and curtain jerkers and I actually made a little money. Gary and June Rich came north after all and played a great show at the Brighton Music Hall and true to his word, they let me open for them. Randall took it on himself to get half the campus, it seemed, to show up for that show and they seemed to dig it. Gary was proud that I was doing my "thang" and said to keep it up. That was a highlight of the year so far to be sure. Randall live streamed it so Angie could watch, which made it even better.

I've written a lot of new stuff this semester and having Freddy and Alex and Marnie and Randall around to bounce ideas off has been amazing. I would be completely lost in music theory and composition classes without Alex. The stuff that is easy and natural to him is so not what I'm good at. He actually credited me with helping him "embrace some innovative ways of thinking about melody," mostly because I forced him to listen to Springsteen's "The River" album from start to finish. I challenged him to find the "orchestral framework" underneath it all, but I was really kind of messing with him. I just wanted him to listen to it, but he took the challenge seriously, furrowing his brow from the opening lines of "The Ties that Bind" and not really reacting at all until side four's "The Price You Pay."

He made me replay that track four times before mumbling something about chord progressions and quickly leaving for the practice rooms. I still don't think he's listened to the final two songs but he came back later that night and was giddy with excitement. He said we'd have to wait until spring to hear it. As private as he is with his own stuff, he's been really motivated to help me with my compositional work. If I get another year there from the scholarship board, I know I'll have to thank Alex a ton, which he'll insist on and love, and Freddy too, at which he'll smile politely and deflect the praise.

Freddy has really helped with my singing, which was always raw, despite my choirboy years. That was a long time ago and before my voice changed so I was really a "blank slate," which was the kindest way he could have put it. He's such a genius though and honestly one of the most amazing guys I've ever known. He reminds me of that turtle in "Finding Nemo" because he just kinda rolls with things. Angie adores him. He Skyped into her chemo session last month and sang for her and the others on the ward, taking requests for over an hour! I was at an advisor meeting, which was unpleasant. Despite my good grades, my advisor, Dr. Josephine wants me to focus more on classical guitar performance and stop "playing around for the clubbers," whatever that means. She even suggested I try focusing on Jazz guitar. She's brilliant but I don't think she gets me.

Anyway, I came back to the suite that day and found Freddy in front of the big computer that Randall installed in the common room singing Sam Cooke's "Wonderful

World" into the webcam. As he finished, he smiled sheepishly and gestured to me like, "your turn now." Like I could ever follow him!

But, I hopped in front of the camera and Angie went on about how much she appreciated Freddy calling in. She looked beautiful as always, but more run down than I'd seen her in a while. November was a particularly rough month, but she was smiling. Freddy had just gone and done that for her on his own. I hadn't asked him to do it. I don't even think I'd mentioned it was a chemo day, though I guess he could have looked at my calendar. More than likely he just made a point to know.

Freddy and I have talked about our grandmothers a lot over the semester. He's really dedicated to his and I've made it clear how I feel about Nana. He thinks we ought to get them together for a playdate this spring, when the weather is warmer. He made me start running with him to help with my "breath control and stamina" and to make myself "look like the guy who's dating that astonishing young woman." He wants me to do a 5K with him in March but I just I don't know. I don't mind the running and it's definitely helped me get into pretty great shape, but we'll see. Among other topics, we talked about my issues with church and religion and some of my challenges there, but he never judged. He listened patiently and invited me to his church "when you feel ready." So, earlier this month we went to an advent service at what he called his "East Coast" church over on Clarendon, an Episcopal Church. I liked it more than I thought I would and the music was awesome. I think I'll go again sometime. I feel more open to it than I have in the past, anyway.

Freddy intuitively understood how worried I was about Angie and her treatment and he just took it on himself to show up. It was selfless and amazing and he makes those sorts of things look easy. I've learned a lot from him about how to extend care to the people I love. I'm not used to being cared for like that but I'm grateful for it, seriously. If I'm only able to study here this one year, it will have been worth it, perhaps most importantly because of the time learning from Freddy.

I'm learning a lot and my grades are great. I've got almost a 4.0 going into finals, which I think I aced. It's astounding how much work I get done now day to day because I know my time here is not for certain: it's finite. My focus is not distracted by high school nonsense or "finding a girl" and stuff. Knowing my heart is well and truly spoken for has allowed me a level of motivation and concentration on working and performing that I've never experienced before. I know what's at stake for me and I know who and what I'm working for and towards.

It's been a remarkable few months and I've been really, dare I say it? Blessed. When I think back to how nervous I'd been over the summer about going to Boston it makes me feel very silly. It's been hard being away from Angie but we've done the best we can and I feel closer to her now than ever. I wonder if the time apart might be good for us in the long run. Our coming together on that last day was intense and mind-blowing, but having to wait and nurture our new relationship from a distance has made it stronger.

At least that's what Marnie thinks. She said on the drive to NYC that, "You both have had serious real-life things to navigate right from the start. With your years of friendship as a foundation and then having to be apart, you'll probably skip over a lot of the stupid stuff that new relationships face." I don't know if she's right, but I know that I feel very secure in our love for each other and while there are things I worry about, our feelings for one another are not among them.

I'm looking forward to Christmas way more than I've ever done, not just because I get to be with Angie, but because I have just the best gift for her.

I scraped together enough from all the club gigs that Randall helped me get to purchase the basic Christmas house and a few rooms full of furniture and stuff that she wasn't able to swing when we went to the Christmas Store on the boardwalk. I called the Winterwood store and it's all taken care of. I even asked for Eddie the Elf to handle the sale. Uncle Bob picked it up for me and is bringing it up tomorrow. I can't wait to see her open it on Christmas and can't wait to build it together, for the future. Bob has been enthusiastically following my gigs on the Instagram and Twitter things Randall set up for me and taught me to use more effectively. If I ever get Bob and Randall in the same room together, it just might explode from energy and enthusiasm.

Angie's chemotherapy series finished two weeks ago and she has an appointment later this week to "see where everything is." Her mother has been really positive and engaged and I know how much she appreciated my friends at school helping out with calls and stuff. I'd gotten the impression that her parents, who always generally liked me, were not initially enthusiastic about the prospect of Angie and I being a couple, especially with her undergoing treatment and with me off at school. There may have been concerns about my prospects for the future, which I can understand. Heck, I share some of the same concerns, but it seems that the way my friends and I tried to show up for her and the dedication they've seen in my approach to their daughter and to my work at school has impressed them, according to Angie. That said, I'm going to put my best feet forward this break with them. Yep, both feet.

I haven't really talked to Mom much. She's been working a lot and she was never much for chatting anyway. Nana and I talk a few times a month and she's kept me up to date on Mom and Uncle Ted, who has now decided to stop being a "Little Monster" and following Lady Gaga around on tour. Instead, he's decided to become a lawyer and has enrolled in classes up at Seton Hall.

I can't wait to see her!

I keep thinking of something Angie said back in Wildwood. She talked about the day as though it might be our last good day together. It seems strange now to have thought of it that way, but I know those were the words she used.

I mean, it was a day and maybe it was the last of a kind of day, and it was a good day. OK, that makes no sense at all. But, no, it wasn't good. Not a good day at all! It was great! It was the day that changed my life forever. Maybe it was, in fact the last good day because the rest of them are going to be great?

I really like the way that sounds. I know every day since has been better than the one before not only because it's brought me closer to being back with Angie, but also because it's brought me one step closer to whatever my future is going to become. As long as Angie and music are involved, I'm going to be happy. And that's not nothing.

I'm pretty sure that Mom will be waiting at the station and I think we are supposed to have dinner with Nana at Jim's. Angie said she had to be somewhere tonight so we might not get to be together until tomorrow. Both of our families are planning to get together for Christmas Eve and on Christmas Day as well. First time we've planned something like this. I'm excited to see how it plays out and really can't wait to see her face when she opens her gift.

I'm a little disappointed that I'll have to wait to see her, but it's almost enough to know we're in the same state breathing the same air. She said that she has a few surprises for me and I can't wait to hear them or see them or whatever them. I know the last months have been hard on her and I worry a little that she's maybe not told me all of how she's feeling with her illness.

I can almost hear Randall telling me to "chill, dude" and he'd be right. Randall, in addition to showing me lots of great live music and helping me get spots to play all over the city, has helped me deal with a lot of my own anxieties. He's very much an "it's all good" kind of guy and he's been a good friend. I asked him once why he does so much for me and he answered, "Because I can. And you need the help." He's not often serious, but he has his own kind of grace. And he makes Angie laugh.

I'm grateful for the roommates I ended up with. Despite my misgivings on such things, it seems to me sometimes like someone other than Randall had a hand in it all working out as it has. Talented as Randall may be, there are moments when it feels like having just the right people enter my life at just the right time and just the right place might be a little beyond him. I think we may be going to Angie's mom's church Christmas Eve, so I guess I can ask there.

"Princeton Junction, next stop."

I'm excited to be home! I'm really looking forward to our first Christmas together. Well, together together, I mean. I've really missed her and I can't believe I'll be able to see her and touch her and be near her for the first time in one hundred and twenty days. Who's counting? Me! I was counting! I'm so ready.

I feel different now than when I left. Better. Stronger maybe, and not just from working out with Freddy. I think I'm the best version of me yet. I hope so, as I've really been working hard, on everything, and I like who I am.

CHAPTER EIGHTEEN

As we pulled up to the station, people started clamoring around for their stuff, but I've got everything I need in the seat beside me. Well, almost everything. I'd never missed people or places before, and I have now. I missed home at times and of course, I missed Angie, but even with the distance between us, I've never really felt like she wasn't with me.

Yeah, that might be nonsense. I haven't been able to see her, hold her, touch her, kiss her, or hold her hand in months. I might just burst! My love has held, as I knew it would. I've got Christmas with Angie and then the scholarship audition coming up and New Year's Eve. That's a lot to look forward to. I think we're going to Wildwood for New Years, if all goes well with Angie's doctor appointment. There's been talk of maybe a return engagement with Shellie and The Cozy Morley's for their show at the Anchor Inn. That should be fun on its own, but I wonder if it might give Angie and I the chance to spend some time alone. The mere thought of that is exhilarating.

I can see through the exit windows that it's snowing a little. As the doors open I can see my mom and she looks thrilled to be out in it. As I walk towards her, a gorgeous girl, resplendent in a long black coat and a dark green hat with a bright red flowing scarf turns around and runs towards me. My bag falls with a thud and my guitar lands on the ground with a melodic clang that reverberates all throughout the platform.

Snow falls. We embrace and I twirl her around in the air, laughing and crying and being everything all at the same time because we can. We finally can!

We kiss and we hold tight to one another.

"You're here!" I whisper. "I didn't expect you today!"

"Of course, I'm here, silly! And so are you." And she squeezes me one last time before grasping my hand as she picks up my guitar and I collect my bag. "I believe I told you it would be the best Christmas ever, sweetie…"

"Oh yeah, I think you may have mentioned that."

"Yes indeed. The bestest!"

"Well, I say that every day, from here on in, is only going to get better, Angie. Know why?"

"Why?"

I put on my best Yoda voice, which was admittedly not great, and said, "Cause be, Love for you I do, more each day, all days."

Angie stopped walking and looked at me with an eyebrow raised.

"Really?"

I sighed. "Sorry, the momentum carried me."

She smirked, "You must have some momentum built up after all these months, sweetie, that was, well, oof."

"Yeah, there's that…"

"Wanna try again?"

Mom had waved a quick hello and then shuffled back to her car in the station lot. I stopped on the sidewalk as the snow continued to cascade about us, not amounting to much on the ground but covering our coats.

"I would like to try again."

Angie flourished her hands as though washing away my previous attempt on some sort of cosmic whiteboard. "You may proceed."

I pulled her close to me, holding her face gently in my hands and letting our foreheads touch. The rest of the world, as it so often did when we were together, even before we were in love, simply fell away.

"This, right here, is the only place I want to be. Right here, in your arms, feeling your heart beat and knowing that we are in the same space together at the same time. Always."

Angie exhaled and looked into my eyes. "Not bad."

"Not bad?"

"No, it was pretty good, actually!" She kissed me. That was more than pretty good.

"OK, but, wow, just 'pretty good?'"

"Oh Avery, those are just words. The love is what really matters. And we have that."

"We really do, right?"

"We do," she beamed, taking my arm as we crossed the street and walked towards Mom's Tracer, which had shepherded us on that day to Wildwood and beyond.

"Besides," she said, leaning against my arm as the snow continued to tumble forth, "It's Christmas my love, and we have all the time in the world."

ABOUT THE AUTHOR

The guy who wrote this book is, not surprisingly, a native of New Jersey. Robert Kugler retired from education in order to become a stay-at-home dad. Following his years as a teacher and school administrator, it is not surprising his first novel focuses on the lives and perspectives of young people.

Spending his formative years in South Jersey, Wildwood in particular, has provided a unique perspective on the real New Jersey Shore, not to mention an inability to live more than forty miles from the ocean.

A graduate of both The College of Wooster and Seton Hall University, Robert is an avid Philadelphia Sports fan and enjoys working part time as a mixologist at George Washington's Mount Vernon.

He currently lives in Northern Virginia with his wife and three children and a Labrador named Maggie. He spends as much time as possible in Wildwood, NJ, as it's simply the best beach on the East Coast.

The songs featured in this novel are available at:
RobertKugler.bandcamp.com

Learn more at RobertKuglerBooks.com
@AlohaKugs on Twitter and Instagram
Please follow Rob on Facebook at Robert Kugler, Author
Please leave a review on Amazon and Goodreads.

Made in the USA
Columbia, SC
09 December 2020